Formidable Magic

IRIS BEAGLEHOLE

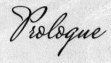

Prologue

Beneath an old yew tree, hidden by foliage, cold, calculating eyes watched as the Thorn witch kissed her vampire lover.

The eyes narrowed and a child-like voice whispered, "You're not going to be a threat for much longer."

The small figure turned and quickly crept behind the tree and through the forest at a supernatural speed.

It wasn't long before she reached her destination: an old drain, inconspicuous to prying eyes. She glanced around to make sure no one else was in sight before descending into the earth and the dark network of tunnels there.

Quickly, she returned to the cavern where only her most loyal of followers were gathered.

"You've returned, mistress," said Despina, getting up from her armchair and dusting off her pale pink cardigan.

Geneviève pulled back her hood, revealing her gleaming

chestnut curls and an unnatural smile. "Indeed I have," she said. "And how are our plans developing?"

"Three more have joined us," said an older woman with blonde hair.

"And the Travellers?" Geneviève asked.

"They're on their way," said Despina.

"Everything is in order," a hulking figure from the corner added.

"Very well," said Geneviève. "We continue advancing towards All Hallows Eve. Focus on the weak and be ruthless. Now go, do not waste any more time."

With a clap of her hands, in an instant the room was cleared without a trace of any of her loyal shifters, witches, or vampires.

Geneviève could finally relax, slumping onto a velvet chaise lounge with a cocktail glass full of human blood. Taking a sip, she savoured the taste.

"Ah, yes, Samhain is going to be interesting..."

One

The weather was turning colder and the fog seemed to thicken over the township, hanging unnaturally still below the clouds.

The last leaves that clung stubbornly to the trees were beginning to let go of their resolve. The oranges and reds of the foliage around the town frosted slowly to brown and the atmosphere took on a soupy quality.

There was a supernatural chill that lay beneath the ordinary frosts of the land that throbbed with a deeper power. An older magic threatened to break free as the spirits that had long lain dormant in the land and its buildings began to stir in restless frustration. Samhain was coming, and it was no ordinary festival.

This year as All Hallows drew near, there was a thickening in the air, an anticipation of chilling potential promising to be a festival the people of Myrtlewood would never forget.

"Is your dad still away?" Sam asked Athena, running their hand along a row of books near their seat. They sat in the library of Myrtlewood Academy, waiting for History and Folklore to begin.

"Yes," Athena replied, looking down at her hands. "He's busy helping Finnigan get set up in the fae realm and doing a bunch of diplomatic stuff with his mother. The treaty is taking a lot more work to implement than anyone realised."

"He'll be back before you know it," said Elise.

Deron giggled at Felix, who was doing his best impression of Ms Twigg – sticking his tongue out pretending he was some kind of lizard – when the door opened and the entire class fell silent.

Ms Twigg stood there looking unimpressed, and Felix quietly melted down into his chair.

Elise and Athena smiled at each other. They still didn't understand quite why Felix was terrified of the very tiny and oddly reptilian teacher. It seemed almost instinctual rather than rational.

"It sounds like you're all having a wonderful time," said Ms. Twigg, entering the classroom. "However I'm sorry to interrupt your merrymaking with actual learning." She gave them a wry smile.

Athena smiled back. She was rather fond of Ms. Twigg, as strange as she might be.

"Now today's class is not only about the history of folklore and mythology. It's also about the present. And I'm delighted to inform you we have an upcoming field trip."

There was a murmur around the class.

Athena looked questioningly at Elise, who simply shrugged.

Beryl, who'd been rather quiet and withdrawn recently, shot her hand up in the air.

"Yes, Miss Flarguan?" Ms. Twigg said.

"Does this concern Samhain?" Beryl asked quietly.

"Very good, Miss Flarguan."

"Sow-wain," said Deron, rolling the word around his mouth that was pronounced so differently from how it was spelt, at least in English. "Is it to do with pigs?" he asked.

Ms Twigg smiled in her chilling way. "There may be some shared etymology. After all, pigs were of great importance for our ancestors here, in this part of the world. Cerridwen herself was often considered to be a sow goddess and she is one of the great dark goddesses associated with this time of the year and of the coming winter."

Deron beamed. He didn't often feel confident with schoolwork and Athena was happy to see him look proud of himself for a change.

"Samhain is unique among the ancient sabbats," Ms Twigg continued. "Now if you could all turn to page one hundred and seventy three in your course book."

Elise raised her hand.

"Yes, Miss Fern?"

"Sorry, pardon me," said Elise. "But you mentioned a field trip. Could you tell us about that before we start reading? Only, I'm curious."

Ms Twigg's smile spread wide across her face. "I'm pleased to see you're all taking such an interest in schoolwork. For some reason you often do as we near the sacred festivals, owing no doubt, to the strange occurrences we've all experienced recently."

Ms Twigg eyed Athena for a moment too long.

Athena gulped, feeling that she was somehow to blame. Of course, the strange goings on in Myrtlewood were attributed to the Thorn family magic being released, which had acted as a kind of magnet for all sorts of magical chaos since she and her mother had moved into the small town.

It wasn't like Athena had planned any of it. Ms Twigg's gaze, however, wasn't blaming as much as it was questioning, as if Athena might hold some kind of secret knowledge that the teacher was after.

"Very well," said Ms Twigg. "If you must know, the field trip that I'm planning for this class involves a trip to a haunted house."

A ring of excitement spread through the small classroom.

"Haunted house," Elise whispered. "Is she for real?"

"Is she having us on?" Felix asked. "Some kind of lizard trick?"

Athena gave him a pointed look.

"Why haunted house, Miss?" Ash asked.

"Well, isn't it obvious?" said Beryl. "Samhain is associated with the other side. You know? When the veil is thin, and the spirits can walk across."

Athena coughed. "What do you mean? I thought the veil was thin around the equinoxes?"

Elise giggled. "Different veil," she whispered.

"Oh," said Athena. "You mean to the dead? The veil to the underworld?"

"Indeed," said Ms Twigg.

"Spook," said Felix, though he sounded more excited than scared, as did the rest of the class.

"So you think it's more likely that we'd see ghosts at this time of year?" Sam asked.

"That tends to be the experience," said Ms Twigg. "However, this is no carnival haunted house. This is research and I will expect you to all write reports on it."

"How do you know the house is haunted?" Ash asked.

A strange expression crossed Ms Twigg's face. "All we have to go on is rumours," she said dismissively. "And it may be that the house is not haunted at all and you'll have to write about that instead. However, each year around this time, I have identified a house known to be haunted in the community and taken a group of students there. Sometimes it's the same house we go to, but we've never been to the Brashville Manor before. It was occupied until quite recently."

"Did the owner die?" Felix asked, sounding far too thrilled about the possibility.

Ms Twigg glared at him and he wilted back into his seat, hunched over. "Lady Brashville passed away recently, yes. Though she wasn't in the house at the time. It's true that emotional resonance can remain behind, and even spirits can return to their former homes and other significant places in their lives, however, you must understand that genuine paranormal activity relating to the dead is very rare. The neighbours of the manor house have reported disturbances, though I wouldn't be surprised if it was just some local hooligans." She looked pointedly at Felix.

"Will it be a night time trip?" Sam asked. "I mean...don't ghosts come out at night?"

"Funny you should ask," said Ms Twigg. "Yes. It will be an overnight visit. So you will all pack sleeping mats and sleeping bags and we will bring a range of technical equipment for monitoring the supernatural."

"A real science experiment!" said Beryl, sounding genuinely excited.

"That's what floats your boat," said Felix. He raised his arms, crossing them behind his head, and leant back until Ms Twigg shot him another stern look. He lowered them down again and sat primly on his chair.

"Now, let us continue with the lesson," said Ms Twigg. "Page one hundred and seventy three. The history of Samhain."

Two

Rosemary put the finishing touches on a tiny pumpkin she'd made out of orange-tinted chocolate in the window display and stood back to admire her handiwork.

It was a great spooky spread of different treats.

"It looks great!" said Papa Jack, emerging from the kitchen to admire the candyfloss ghosts and the spooky haunted house that Rosemary had spent many hours deftly crafting.

"Well, if that doesn't help sales pick up, I don't know what will," said Rosemary. "It's been so slow this month. I thought people were supposed to want lots of sweets for Halloween, but I suppose this isn't America."

Papa Jack chuckled. "People want candy no matter what time of year it is."

"So why aren't they coming in? Is it because I offended everyone during that mayoral race by siding with the werewolves?"

"I don't think so. But everything has a season."

"Maybe somebody's cursed me." Rosemary slumped down at a table feeling the need to sulk, but her mood was quickly picked up again with the first sip of a spiced hot chocolate brought over by Papa Jack.

As she sat slurping the spicy sweet beverage, the door-bell rang and Marjie bustled in looking slightly frazzled and pale.

"What's wrong?" Rosemary asked her dear friend.

"Oh, nothing...nothing." Marjie didn't sound her normal cheery self.

"Take a seat," said Papa Jack, pouring another one of his delicious and warming drinks and bringing it over to Marjie.

"Thank you, dear," she said. "But I can't stay long. Things are fraught at home."

Rosemary gave her a questioning look, but it didn't seem like Marjie wanted to talk about it.

"I just popped in to check on you," said Marjie. "To make sure everything's all right. You looked so glum sitting there. What is it?"

"I don't want to trouble you with my problems," said Rosemary. "It's just the business. It's not doing so well at the moment. It was fine until just a few weeks ago, but since the equinox we've had hardly any customers."

"Oh, it will pick up again," said Marjie. "You make the best chocolates around."

Rosemary smiled. "Thanks, and you're right. I shouldn't worry. I've still got funds to draw on from my inheritance and the money Granny put in the trust for us. I just don't want to waste it. You know what business is like. Bad investments can lead to losing everything."

"Don't I know it?!" said Marjie. "The number of crazy schemes I've cooked up over the years! Most of them failed. Herb almost threw me out on the street. I'm sure of it. Especially after that toilet paper business."

Rosemary gave her friend a sympathetic smile.

Marjie smiled back, though there was sadness in her eyes. "It took a long time for me to find my true calling and create my tea shop. You're lucky you always really knew what you wanted to do, didn't you? You wanted to work with chocolate. You always loved food. It's a perfect match."

Rosemary's smile faltered a little. There was something definitely strange about Marjie at the moment.

The door to the chocolate shop opened and Athena came in dragging her school bag behind her. She slumped down next to Rosemary and took liberties with her hot chocolate, making Rosemary mock-frown at her daughter. "Get your own."

Athena gave her a cheeky smile. "Yours is right here. Besides, you didn't even make this, I can tell."

"I'll bring you another one," said Papa Jack.

"Don't worry about it," Rosemary called out after him. "I've probably had enough chocolate. So has the rest of Myrtlewood, apparently."

"Business still not good?" said Athena. "You know, we should really get you set up better online. You can do internet orders."

"Well, Papa Jack is better at that. I hate admin."

"Remember all those people from around the country were really keen on your chocolate at the Summer Festival."

"You're probably right," said Rosemary. "That's how Liam's business has managed to stay afloat all these years, isn't it? Even when the town totally rejected him, he still had online orders."

"At least when he wasn't off galivanting at the werewolf commune." Athena found Liam's holiday up north fascinating and hilarious, particularly when she'd learned the werewolf colony up near Scotland was complete with drumming circles.

"I like your display," Athena said, gesturing to the window behind them.

"It's great, isn't it? said Papa Jack, coming over with another hot chocolate despite Rosemary's protestations.

"Perfect for Samhain!" said Athena. "We've been learning about it at school and ghosts are totally appropriate. It's not just an American thing after all, Halloween. All Hallows has been celebrated here for thousands of years."

"That's right," said Marjie absentmindedly. "Yes, yes, it has."

"We're going to go and visit a real haunted house." Athena's eyes lit up.

"You are?" Rosemary asked. "Sounds dangerous!"

"Oh no, I think the ghosts are friendly. Besides, we have experience with ghosts."

Rosemary gave her daughter a stern look. They weren't really supposed to talk about Granny Thorn's ghost that had intermittently haunted them in a mostly friendly and sometimes infuriating way. Granny had a way of getting on Rosemary's nerves by being cryptic and little bit flippant when it came to whatever trouble they happened to be in at the time.

"Sounds fun!" said Papa Jack. "A real haunted house? It's the perfect season for it."

Athena beamed. "That's exactly what Ms Twigg said."

"It makes me a little bit uncomfortable," said Rosemary. "All this sort of... celebration of death."

Marjie shuddered and got up from the table. "Right, I better be off, then," she said brusquely and left.

"Does she seemed a bit off to you?" Rosemary asked.

Athena shrugged. "Isn't Marjie always a little bit odd?"

"I mean, in a different way from usual. She came in looking – I don't know, kind of troubled and flustered."

"I don't know," said Athena. "But you're right, I'd have expected her to go into a jaunty tirade about how wonderful the season is and all about the Samhain traditions. Maybe her business isn't going well either?"

"The tea shop seems to be just as busy as usual," said Rosemary. "It's just me that's cursed."

"Not that again, Mum. Nobody's cursed you."

"How do you know?" Rosemary asked. "It wouldn't be that hard for one of my many enemies to put nasty enchantments around the shop so that people get put off when they come near. Maybe that's what was bothering Marjie..."

"You're being ridiculous," said Athena. "Don't worry, business will pick up again. And if not, we can just become estate agents."

Rosemary flinched. "How could you suggest such a thing?!"

Athena smirked and then yawned. "Can we go home? I'm tired."

"Yes, off you go," said Papa Jack. "I'll close up." He shooed them out of the shop.

Three

"Look at all this!" said Rosemary. "Cute little pumpkins and bats everywhere!"

It was a quiet Sunday morning in Myrtlewood. She and Athena had decided to go to Marjie's teashop for a spot of weekend brunch.

Not only was the tea shop decorated for All Hallows, with Marjie's customary streamers, there were hundreds of balloons in orange and black, and little paper bats dotted around the ceiling that had a habit of occasionally flapping about from some kind of magic. Hundreds of little pumpkins and more traditional carved turnips were being set up all around the main centre of the village of Myrtlewood by none other than Ferg. He was standing outside the tea shop, taking his mayorly duties to the extremes of micro-management as he instructed his helpers with serious precision.

As Rosemary and Athena took their seats they overheard an

American accent outside. "This town must really love Halloween!"

Ferg shook his head.

"Tourists?" Athena whispered, trying not to stare at the couple wearing backpacks. "How did they get in here?"

Rosemary shrugged. "Myrtlewood is usually hard for mundane people to find unless it's around the Summer Solstice, but I suppose people slip through—like my parents!"

Athena laughed. "Don't accidentally summon them."

"I'll stop thinking about them right now and focus on this delicious baking." Rosemary bit into her buttery scone and sighed as the tangy taste of Marjie's quince jelly tantalised her tastebuds. "This is perfect." She smiled at Athena, who was tucking into her bacon and egg pie.

A blonde woman in a bright blue turban appeared outside the tea shop, tapping Ferg on the arm.

He tried studiously to ignore her.

"But I simply must set up my stall for All Hallows! People will want psychic readings for Allantide!"

"You do not have a permit, Madam," said Ferg, and returned to supervising the turnips.

The woman, who Rosemary recognised at the local gossip, Crystal Cassandra, crossed her arms and stormed off.

Athena smirked. "At least *you're* in a better mood today, Mum. You've been a bit glum lately. It's like you don't know what to do with yourself."

"Thanks for reminding me," said Rosemary. "I'm supposed to be the one cheering you up."

Athena narrowed her eyes. "What are you implying?"

15

"That you're a teenager," said Rosemary. "No offence or anything."

"None taken," said Athena with a grin. She took a sip of her favourite strawberry and cream tea.

Rosemary topped up her own cup with Lady Grey tea from the pot.

"What about Marjie though?" said Athena, glancing towards the kitchen.

"She does seem strange this morning, doesn't she? She's so quiet, not her usual self."

"And the other day at your shop..." Athena reminded her.

Rosemary nodded. "I usually rely on her for good cheer. But she seems kind of pale and worried."

Marjie was wiping down the counter for the third time in a row, despite the fact that no additional customers had come in.

"Maybe we should do something nice for her," Rosemary suggested. "You know she's always been there for us."

"I don't know what we would have done without her," said Athena.

"I could call around this afternoon to her cottage. Maybe bring her some treats," Rosemary suggested.

"You sure she wants company?" Athena asked.

"Well, Herb's not much good at conversation, is he? Maybe if I pop by after the shop's closed when she doesn't have anything else to do she will open up to me about whatever it is that's going on."

Athena shrugged.

The door to the tea shop opened with a tinkle of bells. Tamsyn came in with little Elowan and Mei in tow. Both girls ran to hug Athena, who beamed at them, and then they greeted Rosemary almost as enthusiastically, though Athena was clearly the favourite.

Rosemary raised her eyebrows and Tamsyn smiled.

"How's it all going?" Rosemary asked.

"Mei's been perfectly well behaved," said Tamsyn. "She's such a sweetheart."

"It's nice of you to look after her while Neve and Nesta are out of town."

"You tell that to Meng," said Tamsyn. "She's not too keen on us staying at their place. But I think she would have been even more put-out if she'd had to move to ours temporarily."

"She's a tough one to please, isn't she?" said Rosemary. "I hope Neve and Nesta are enjoying their little holiday."

"They seem to be," said Tamsyn. "Whenever I send them a message about Mei they just respond with heart emojis. And while they've had an occasional phone call, they seem to be mostly busy having a blissful time. I wonder whether they want to come back at all."

"I'm sure they can't wait to get back to Myrtlewood," said Athena.

Rosemary grimaced. "Well, maybe not. They might decide they're better off without us and all our drama." She laughed but then felt cold. She wouldn't enjoy losing her good friends to some more quiet and peaceful locality.

"Not to worry. They're expected back soon," said Tamsyn. "And everything's going well with the baby."

"That's a delight to hear," said Rosemary. "Neve was so

worried at first. It's not often you get immaculate Beltane conception, after all."

Athena gave her an awkward look.

"What?" said Rosemary.

"You just have to phrase everything like that, don't you?"

Rosemary sighed. "Talk about a tough audience."

Tamsyn said goodbye and guided the little girls up to the counter to order.

"It feels different around here though, doesn't it? It's not just the decorations," said Athena as they watched Ferg with a ladder outside the window, using a ceremonial magic wand to guide the pumpkins into place stealthily, looking both ways to ensure no tourists caught sight of the magic.

"What do you mean?" said Rosemary.

"I don't know. It's spooky. I keep getting a feeling...kind of like the whole town's being haunted or something."

Rosemary felt a shiver of prickles up her arms. "Hopefully it's just your imagination." Her eyebrows pressed together in a frown.

Athena frowned back. "Don't be dismissive. You know, I'm intuitive when it comes to this kind of thing."

Just then, Marjie bustled over with a tight-lipped smile and a fresh tray of tea. As she replaced the teapots on the table, Rosemary reached up and patted her gently on the arm.

"What is it dear?" said Marjie.

"Is there anything I can do to help?"

"Help?"

"We're worried about you," Rosemary explained. "You don't

seem yourself lately. I thought I might come round later and we can have a chat."

"Oh, nonsense," said Marjie. "I'm perfectly fine. Don't trouble yourself. It's just a busy time of year is all."

Rosemary and Athena looked at each other. The shop wasn't particularly busy and neither was Myrtlewood as a whole.

They turned back to Marjie who began to speak rather rapidly. "Erm, I've got a whole boatload of craft projects that I need to catch up on...that I've been neglecting in the warmer seasons. You know, plenty of knitting to get on with."

"Okay," said Rosemary uncomfortably.

"Hey, Marjie," said Athena. "What do you think's going to happen this Halloween? I mean, Samhain. All the other festivals so far since we've been in Myrtlewood have been intense and I was just wondering..."

"Don't worry. You'll be perfectly fine. All Hallows tends to be a very quiet time for the magical world. We collect ourselves, emotionally, and celebrate those who have gone to the other side. Your granny might even make an appearance." She grinned and there was a little sparkle in her eyes that was more genuine than the other smiles she had given them that morning.

"It would be nice to see her," said Rosemary. "It's been a while since she's popped in."

Marjie gave her an odd look. Athena nudged her mother with her elbow.

"I mean...you know...since she was around," said Rosemary.

They weren't really supposed to talk about Granny's ghost visiting them, after all. But it had been quite some time since they'd had a proper visit from the spectre of Granny Thorn.

"Like I said, All Hallows is a family affair," said Marjie. "And as we tuck up for the colder weather, preparing for winter, it's a good time to get on with your crafts. I imagine you've got lots of painting to do, Athena. And Rosemary..." She looked at Rosemary. "Do you have any hobbies?"

"I like food," said Rosemary. "And I've been thinking about learning how to crochet."

"Fabulous!" said Marjie. "An excellent hobby for this time of year. I'll drop you over some supplies if you like."

Rosemary shrugged. "That would be nice. Though, I was supposed to be offering to help you. Besides, I don't really know where to start."

"You'll pick it up in no time," said Marjie, and she toddled off.

"She seemed almost normal," said Athena. "Maybe she's missing Granny. They were such good friends. And you know this is the time when the *other* veil gets thin."

"The *other* veil?" said Rosemary. "How many bloody veils are there?"

"I don't want to know," said Athena. "We've got the fae realm and we've got some sort of celestial godly realm for all those big guys hanging out up there...and now apparently there's also the realm of the dead – the other world or something."

"The spirit world," said Rosemary. "That's what Granny calls it. Speaking of spirits, I could do with a gin and tonic."

"It's not even midday and, anyway, it's hardly the season," said Athena.

"You're right, but I bet Sherry will have some mulled wine

brewing. Maybe we can go to the pub later on. It's been a while since we've popped in there."

Athena smiled. "I'm actually supposed to be meeting Elise later."

"That's nice," said Rosemary. "It's good to see you two are back together and getting along so well."

"It is good," said Athena. "But that's all I'm going to say about it."

Rosemary grinned. "That's probably the best. It's important to have healthy boundaries."

"Good, so I won't hassle you about Burk as much," said Athena returning the grin.

"Oh yeah, that's right," said Rosemary. "I haven't seen him for a little while. Though we do have a date planned for Wednesday."

"Look at us and our normal-ish healthy-ish relationships," said Athena, and she laughed. Rosemary joined in.

Just then, the lighting in the tea shop flickered and went out. The sky outside was cloudy and so dark that it took Rosemary's eyes a moment to adjust, and by the time they had the lights were back on again.

They looked around suspiciously, but nothing seemed to be out of place.

"Weird," said Athena.

Rosemary shrugged. "Stranger things have happened in Myrtlewood."

Four

E ven though it was too cold for ice cream and Mervyn's had been shut up for the winter, Elise and Athena met outside in their usual spot.

"What do you want to do?" Athena asked, after giving Elise a big hug.

Elise brushed a strand of blue hair back from her face. "We could go to the pub since Marjie's is closing soon. Or we could go for a walk."

"Why don't we go for a walk and then go to the pub and see if Sherry has any non-alcoholic mulled cider brewing."

Elise grinned. "Sounds perfect."

They set off around the Myrtlewood town square, but something caught their eye. It was a little sandwich board sign on the side of the road. *Travelling Fair*, it read.

"Ooh, they're back!" said Elise.

"Who?"

"Come on, let's go." She took Athena's hand and pulled her down the side street that lead to the small field next to the playground.

"They come every year, around this time, for the Allantide market," said Elise. "They always have cool things."

"Travellers?" Athena asked.

"In a sense," said Elise. "These ones are magical. The have a night market and cool performances. They usually stay around town for a few weeks leading up to Samhain. It's awesome."

As the road opened up to the green field, Athena took in half a dozen house trucks.

"They must just be starting to set up," said Elise.

"Come on in!" said a stout but fit looking man wearing nothing but a gold waistcoat and shorts despite the chill in the air. He seemed to be in his thirties, with a deep tan, golden brown hair, and a slightly curled moustache.

He bowed. "I'm Gallium, and may I introduce you to the very beginnings of the best experience of your lives! Take a look around, and make sure you come back later on when we're properly open for business. You'll love it."

Athena and Elise smiled shyly and thanked him.

There wasn't too much to see yet, but Athena enjoyed admiring the house trucks with their brightly coloured adornments and stained glass windows.

Athena smiled. "This is pretty cool."

"Wait till you see what they can do," said Elise. "Oh, and they always host this marvellous carnival on Samhain night after the town ritual. People come in costumes. There's music and dancing."

"That sounds like fun."

As they wandered around Athena did wonder whether she was intruding. The fair wasn't exactly open to the public yet. The people she did see, clad in leather and woven scarves, all seemed friendly. They smiled and greeted them.

Athena and Elise held hands as they wandered around. They noticed a particularly cute green house truck with smoke coming out of the chimney.

At its side, a woman sat, crouched over a small table, her hands surrounding a small glass bowl. She was focusing.

"Maybe we shouldn't be here," Athena whispered.

"It's fine," said Elise. She took a step closer and Athena followed, gasping in surprise.

Light glowed between the woman's hands, and inside the glass ball, a plant grew. First it was just a tiny shoot, then larger leaves emerged, and finally a flower.

The woman sighed in satisfaction and looked up to see Athena's surprised face.

"I suppose you saw that, then?" she said. "But I hear this town is magical."

Elise nodded. "Yes. You don't have to worry about that."

"I'm Ursula," said the woman, getting up from her seat to greet them.

Athena and Elise introduced themselves.

"You have an interesting accent," said Athena.

Ursula smiled. "I'm from New Zealand."

"I didn't even know there were witches all the way over there," said Elise.

Ursula shrugged. "I suppose we're everywhere. I've been travelling around with my—"

"With your dearest ones," said a voice. A young woman appeared in the doorway of the house truck. She was pixie-like with a bright purple haircut. Something about her reminded Athena a little of Elise. She stepped out of the house truck followed by a tall, gorgeous man with tanned skin. His long brown hair was tied back and he wore a waistcoat over a white shirt and worn jeans.

The man introduced himself as Rowan and the woman was Hazel.

"So you're all from New Zealand?" said Elise.

"That's right. The magical community there is somewhat smaller than here," said Hazel.

"Yeah. This place is great," said Rowan. "I knew there would be a lot of magic over here when we connected up with the Travellers." He lowered his gaze. "I don't have much magic, to speak of, but Mum was powerful, and I grew up with a travelling fair in New Zealand. Many of the people in our group were witches who knew about this place. A whole magical village! I've never been anywhere like it."

"None of us have," said Ursula.

"What are you doing so far from home?" Athena asked.

"Seeing the world, I suppose," said Ursula. She reached for Hazel's hand and pulled her close for a moment.

Athena jolted at the realisation that they must be a couple. There was a strange resemblance between them – Hazel with her shorter bright purple hair, and Ursula with her longer natural brown tones – similar to Elise and Athena. It was comforting, when Athena usually felt rather odd and different.

"Anyway, what you did just before was amazing," said Athena.

Hazel grinned. "Ursula is powerful."

"I just have a way with plants, I suppose," said Ursula. "They respond to me...and you..." she said to Athena. "You have a lot of magic."

Hazel peered at Athena. "She does, doesn't she?"

Athena blushed. Everyone seemed to be staring at her for a moment, making her feel slightly uncomfortable.

"Yeah, she's the one with all the power," said Elise awkwardly.

"There are lots of magical people around this town," Rowan said. "It's incredible."

"And neither of you are only human," said Hazel, her eyes wide in surprise.

"How can you tell?" Rowan asked.

"I just can," said Hazel. "If you spend enough time on the margins of this world you pick up a thing or two."

Athena gave Hazel a questioning look, wondering what she meant.

"So you have a market stall?" Elise asked.

Ursula nodded. "Yes, that's kind of what I was working on. We sell plants and jewellery and charms. We make them ourselves. Rowan's been at it for longer. He makes beautiful things." She beamed at the gorgeous man.

Rowan frowned. "But I can't make plants grow. Like I said, I'm hardly magical at all."

"That's not true," said Hazel. "I know you've got some magic in you. It just may be the internal kind."

Athena smiled, intrigued by these people she'd only just met who somehow already seemed like friends. It was a mysterious thing that Athena had noticed, having hardly any friends at all for most of her life, that when she did meet people who would later become good friends, she knew almost instantly. There was a similarity in their energy, a spiritual connection that meant communication flowed easily and she didn't have to be so guarded in what she said or did.

"Anyway, I suppose we should leave you to get set up," said Elise. "Come on, Athena."

"That was strange," Athena said as they made their way back towards town and headed for the pub.

"What was so strange about it?"

"Didn't you feel it? Some kind of connection with them..? We all got on so easily, almost like old friends."

"I suppose," said Elise. "They seemed cool. I mean, they're a bit older than us."

"What do you think? In their twenties?"

Elise nodded. "Yeah. I suppose so. They seemed to like you."

"You don't think they liked you too?"

"I'm nothing special," said Elise.

"That's not true," Athena protested, pulling her girlfriend into a hug. "You are absolutely special. You're amazing."

The tips of Elise's hair glowed pink like a blush.

"What's the matter?" Athena asked.

"I suppose I've been a bit low lately. I keep reading my tarot cards. I don't know why, but the death card keeps coming up."

Athena shivered. "I know it doesn't actually mean death, but it gives me the creeps."

"It means transformation. Change...I don't know why, but I keep reading them over and over. I just feel like I'm looking for an answer to something...only, I'm not even sure what the question is. I just feel uneasy."

"Me too," said Athena. "It's been...kind of spooky around here. Like something's about to happen. Still, it's cool that the Travellers are here with the fair. At least that's something fun and not evil."

Elise smiled weakly.

Athena looked at her. "Something is wrong. Isn't it?"

Elise shook her head. "It's okay. Everything's fine."

Five

L ater that afternoon when Athena was off catching up with Elise, Rosemary couldn't help but stop in at Marjie's cottage.

Marjie hadn't technically accepted her self-invitation to come over and bring treats, but Rosemary felt it was really her duty to at least show a bit more than passing concern and support. Marjie had been so extraordinarily wonderful to her and Athena.

Besides, she figured if Marjie wasn't in the mood for company, she could just drop the small hamper of chocolate treats off on the front porch and leave her in peace.

As Rosemary pulled up outside the white-washed cottage, she noticed the garden seemed more neglected than usual. She wandered down the path towards the door, wondering if perhaps Ferg had been too busy with his other dozens of jobs and hadn't had enough time for gardening recently. Besides, he was technically now the mayor of Myrtlewood, though he was keeping a rather low profile aside from his elaborate decorations for All Hallows.

Rosemary knocked on the door. There was silence for a moment and then the sound of footsteps. To her surprise, Herb open the door.

Normally, Marjie's husband was incredibly quiet and reserved, not really one to respond to social calls. Rosemary almost jumped in surprise that he'd been so bold as to open the door at all.

"Oh, hello, Herb," she said.

Herb nodded. "Rosemary Thorn," he mumbled.

Rosemary took in his appearance. In typical Herb fashion, he was wearing a rather shabby mottled cardigan and brown corduroy trousers. What was unusual was the look in his eyes. He seemed troubled, and Rosemary wasn't sure if he was normally like that and just did a better job of hiding it or if something else was up.

"Through here." He gestured in the general direction of the kitchen.

"Thank you," said Rosemary. "I don't mean to be a bother..." She thought about asking if everything was alright, but after an awkward pause she changed course and followed his gesture through to the kitchen.

Marjie was seated at the table, staring down at what Rosemary suspected was a very cold cup of tea.

"Marjie?" she said gently.

"Oh! Rosemary!" She sounded somewhat flustered. "I didn't realise you were here. How can I help?"

"That's what I want to know, actually," said Rosemary, taking a seat. "I brought you a present."

She popped the hamper of Marjie's favourite treats on the table. The corner of the older woman's mouth twitched, but she didn't smile. Not completely.

"How sweet of you, dear. But you needn't have bothered. I'm fine. Really."

Rosemary decided this was the moment to use the influencing skills she'd learned in her business class. Instead of responding she merely held the silence and gave her friend what she hoped was a compassionate and knowing look.

"Oh...if you must know..." said Marjie. "This time of year is hard for me. Always has been. So many losses..." Marjie got up and began making tea again, almost automatically, as she continued talking. "First, there was my brother."

Rosemary nodded. "You told me about that."

"It was awful," said Marjie. "To go like that...to be taken by a werewolf. That's why I was so hard on poor Liam, even though he can't help what he is, and he seems to be doing a good job of controlling himself."

Rosemary smiled warmly at her friend. It had taken her a long time to get to the point of accepting Liam. The werewolf prejudice had been so nasty and prevalent in the town, and so very personal to Marjie. But she'd come around to realising her fears might not apply to every single person affected by the magical virus.

Instead of speaking, Rosemary literally bit her tongue. This was a time for listening and making soothing and acknowledging noises.

Marjie poured out, in more detail, the story of her brother, then she paused for a moment as she carried a fresh pot of tea to the table.

There was a weight in the air and Rosemary couldn't help but feel that things were being held back. "So this time of year reminds you of your brother?"

"Yes, and others..." said Marjie. "Galdie, of course. This is the first Samhain we'll have without her. She always did a lot to brighten up my mood at this time of year, you see."

"I don't quite understand," said Rosemary, and then began to ramble in earnest despite her better judgement. "But I want to. I mean...I can't quite find the right words. What I'm trying to say is, if this is the time of year for remembering the dead and sort of celebrating with them why does it make you sad in particular?"

Marjie sat down and her eyes clouded over as she warmed her hands on the fresh cup of tea, without bothering to take a sip.

Rosemary patiently took a gulp of her own tea, which was hot and rather strong. She suspected it was a Yorkshire brew.

"I never talk about this," said Marjie. "Only to Galdie, because she was around at the time. And she understood. I was just a girl, maybe around Athena's age." She smiled weakly.

Rosemary nodded.

"And Galdie was older, but she was always so helpful and always so wise, kind and generous with her time. She helped me through that dark time in my youth. And I suppose every year since..."

"Something happened when you were a teenager," said Rosemary.

Marjie nodded.

There was a moment of silence before she spoke again.

"Have you ever had a best friend? Someone that you were inseparable from?"

Rosemary thought back to her youth. She'd had close friends at times but nothing exactly like what Marjie was talking about, though she'd always yearned for the kind of friendship – the kind that was naturally very deep.

She felt as if she was only beginning to find friends like that in Myrtlewood as an adult, and Marjie was among them.

Rosemary said as much in as few words as she could manage.

A tear streamed down Marjie's face and she finally sipped her tea. "Thank you dear. Grace and I were inseparable right from the word go. As young children, we'd run around the meadows together in the summer and we'd sit by the fire in the winter and tell each other tales. She was so dear to me. And then..."

Rosemary felt her heart tightening at Marjie's loss. There was an inevitability about the next words she spoke as more tears pooled in her eyes.

"One Samhain, Grace walked me home after we'd been to the festivities and then...she disappeared. At the time some people thought she'd run away, but I knew better. There was no way she would have run away. Especially not without telling me. We told each other everything. I blamed myself. I shouldn't have let her walk me home. I should have walked *her* home instead. I should have stayed with her."

There was so much more pain in Marjie's voice that Rosemary couldn't help but reach across the table to hold her friend's hand. "What do you think happened? Could it have been the fae?"

"No, dear," said Marjie sadly. "The veil to the fae realm is only thin at the equinoxes. Unfortunately, it's an entirely different veil that thins at Samhain—"

"The one connected with the underworld," said Rosemary.

Marjie nodded.

"Could she have gone there?"

"No," said Marjie. "That's not a place where people go – not as far as I know. It's the realm of the dead and not the living. No... I know that Grace was murdered. I just feel it in my gut. There was an investigation at the time, but they couldn't find any evidence. Whoever it was, they were very good at covering their tracks. I always suspected it might have been that awful cult."

"The Bloodstones?" Rosemary shivered.

"Yes. Back in those days I didn't know much about them but there were rumours about the lengths they'd go to for power... even human sacrifice. That hasn't been acceptable in magical society for many hundreds of years."

"I'm rather pleased about that," said Rosemary. "I don't fancy living in town that performs any kind of..." She let her words trail away. This wasn't the time for rambling. "I'm so sorry, Marjie."

The older woman looked at Rosemary, her dark eyes weeping in earnest. "It's been so painful. The greatest loss of my life. Even worse than my brother, as awful as that sounds."

"It doesn't sound awful to me. Grace was special to you."

Marjie nodded. "The most special. Galdie understood that. Every year she would spend time with me around Samhain. Sometimes we'd go to a cabin in the woods and just grieve together...all our losses. There was a coven you see...a long time ago."

"A coven?" That was the first Rosemary had heard of it.

"The Myrtlewood Coven...It was very secret at the time. But I suppose it doesn't really exist anymore now that Galdie's gone. She occasionally called it together. But that was in the years before she bound the family powers. The Coven members would go into the woods."

"Were all the members from Myrtlewood?" Rosemary felt a prick of curiosity. Who else did she know who was part of the coven?

"From here and there," said Marjie with a dismissive wave. She took her handkerchief and wiped the tears from her cheeks and eyes. "I'm sorry, I don't mean to be a blubbering mess."

"Nonsense," said Rosemary. "There's no need to apologise at all."

Marjie shook her head. "An old woman like me...after so many years...but the emotion is still so raw when it comes to Grace. She was taken from me. I always felt that she was my soulmate. I never told her that."

"And you only ever talked to Granny about her?" Rosemary asked.

Marjie nodded. "And now you. Herb has been my rock. He's always been here for me, but he's not the most talkative."

Rosemary smiled. "That's for certain."

"I've never been able to open up to him or hardly anyone at all about my loss. Only Galdie. She looked after me and now she's gone."

"Well, I might not be my grandmother. But I'm happy to stand in, as poor a substitute as I might be."

Marjie gave her hand a little squeeze. "Thank you, dear. That means so much, and you have a great deal of your grandmother's good qualities. Not just her magic, but her kindness, empathy, and her courage. So it's not a poor substitute at all."

"Thank you. That means a lot. And I want you to know that I'm here for you, anytime. Really..."

They sat there in silence, sipping their tea for a few minutes, and Rosemary wondered how else she could help her friend.

"Do you think it might be good for you to open up a little bit more?" Rosemary suggested. "I mean, I'm not trying to offer unsolicited advice or anything, but wise people say that it's good to grieve and open up about emotions, not bottle things up. Maybe you could do something."

"Like what? I'm all ears if you think there's something that will help."

"Isn't there a tradition around here – and in other parts of the world – to make special shrines for your loved ones, especially at this time of year? It's a way to celebrate them...what they meant to you, and keep them alive in your heart."

Marjie sobbed and more tears flowed down her face. "It's been so hard. The grief...it does change over time. But it never completely goes away and it comes back in waves. But maybe you're right. Maybe I have bottled it up too much because it's been too painful to deal with, but clearly I'm not really coping at all. Grace deserves to be celebrated."

Rosemary realised she herself had shed a few tears during the conversation. She wiped them away.

As the conversation came to an end she gave Marjie a warm hug. "Feel free to pop by anytime. I'm always here for you, just like you've always been there for me."

"Thank you darling." Marjie kissed Rosemary on the forehead. "You are a real blessing."

Six

Athena shivered as she looked up at the creepy Victorian villa. It was a grand old house, three stories high, with elaborate trim that wove around the sides, and spirals above the front windows and doorframe. The original colour was a mystery, as the paint was so faded and peeling that it had become an unrecognisable grey.

"This is spooky," Felix said and started making "Ooh" noises.

Elise elbowed him.

The class was assembled on the quiet street, carrying their backpacks, mats, and sleeping bags.

"Settle down," said Ms Twigg as Felix continued to make a racket. "You'll scare away the actual paranormal activity if you keep this up." She looked at him very sternly and Felix paled.

"Sorry," he said in a very tiny voice.

Sam giggled, but Athena couldn't bring herself to feel amused at her classmates.

She felt a chill and looked up towards the abandoned building. Many of its windows were boarded up, with cobwebs liberally woven about.

"Are you okay?" Elise asked.

Athena nodded.

"Hey, Miss," said Deron. "You said nobody's ever been to look for ghosts in this house before. Why is that? It looks pretty haunted to me."

"We only just received permission from the family," said Ms Twigg. "It would be rude to go in without permission."

"Of course it would," said Deron curtly. "I was just wondering."

"I don't like this," said Athena. "I'm getting a bad feeling."

"Tell me about it," said Elise. "It's so creepy. But it's only one night. And you know, ghosts aren't so bad. Even if we do see one, I'm sure we'll be fine."

"That's true," said Athena. "I think it's just the season getting to me. Everything feels strangely spookier than normal. I keep worrying that I'm in some kind of scary movie."

Elise smiled at her. "Well, don't do the silly things that people do in the scary movies. You know, like investigate the strange noises and running up the stairs instead of running out the front door."

"Sage advice," said Athena.

Ms Twigg began running through the list of rules. The students were to stick with their assigned buddies. Playing tricks on each other was expressly forbidden and so on. Athena zoned out until she was startled by a sudden movement as a raven lighted on the fence next to them, making her jump.

"This reminds me too much of the Morrigan," said Athena.

"She is associated with Samhain," said Elise. "But I think she's got better things to do. Isn't she supposed to have a tryst somewhere at a river?"

Athena giggled. "Something like that. You're right, it's just a bird."

But the raven eyed her, as if sizing her up.

"I'm bigger than you," Athena whispered.

Elise nudged her. "Come on, it's time to go."

Athena followed the rest of the class as they ambled up the pathway towards the old house, ready to begin their ghostly experiments.

For all Athena's concerns the evening went surprisingly peacefully. Felix continued to be foolish when he wasn't reined in by Ms Twigg's stern glares and the rest of the class also behaved as they usually did.

They had fish and chips for dinner delivered in paper parcels by Sherry. They set up various magical equipment around the house and got to choose their buddies. Of course Athena chose Elise.

Sam buddied with Deron – the two had been spending a lot of time together recently. And Felix was with Ash.

To Athena's relief, the teacher had decided that they'd all camp out in the main hall of the building, a dusty and cobwebby space that was big enough for the entire class to sleep comfortably in. She didn't much feel like being separated from the bigger group.

During the evening, if any of the implements were set off, the students were to only go investigate in the company of their buddies.

"It's not so bad, is it?" said Elise, snuggling into her sleeping bag next to Athena.

"It's actually kind of exciting, I guess," said Athena. "And you know they say it's good to do things that scare you and make you uncomfortable and all that."

"That's the spirit," said Felix. His bright red sleeping bag was only a few metres away, and despite his sometimes annoying behaviour, at least his stupid jokes brightened the mood, making Athena feel less genuinely spooked.

"Lights out," Ms Twigg called. She extinguished all the makeshift lighting she'd set up with a wave of her hand.

Athena wriggled, trying to get comfortable. The floor wasn't quite the same as her nice, cosy bed in Thorn Manor, but it wasn't the worst sleeping situation she'd ever been in, considering some of the awful sinking springs on the beds in various flats and boarding houses they'd lived in, broke and a little bit hopeless. Overall, life was a lot better now and Athena decided to count her blessings rather than be drawn into past struggles or worse – morbid and terrifying thoughts reminiscent of horror movies. She looked around. Everything seemed to be in order, and so, with only a little trepidation, she encouraged herself to relax and gradually drifted off into a restless sleep.

Seven

I t was the scream that awakened Rosemary.

She opened her eyes and looked around. Moonlight streamed in through the windows. She sat up in bed.

Something was strange.

There was a shimmer in the corner of her eye and she looked over to see a young girl glowing in the moonlight.

"Hello," said Rosemary. "Are you lost?"

The girl, Rosemary realised, was probably more of a teenager. She whimpered and reached forward. "It's dark here."

"It's okay," said Rosemary, instinctively reaching towards the poor girl.

As their fingers met the room fell away and Rosemary was in the forest.

It was so dark between the trees. She was scared, running down a path. Running, running. Running for her life.

She had to make it. There was nothing for it.

The cave was up ahead, the forbidden cave...and there was nowhere else for her to go.

It had always terrified her, this place, but now the danger at her heels was much more frightening.

She dived towards the cave and woke, properly tangled in her bedsheets in a room brightly drenched with sunlight. Serpentine and Nugget were curled up on the pillow next to her. Both familiars opened their eyes a crack, glared at her, and then snuggled back down. Clearly it was too early, even for breakfast.

Rosemary clutched her arms, realising her heart was still racing and she was panting.

She got up and looked around.

The dream within a dream had shaken her, not just because it had been a nightmare, but because it had felt *so* real.

She'd experienced other extremely vivid and surreal dreams before, like the ones she'd had leading up to the Summer Festival and the solstice. Those ones had pretty much come true, all except for the raunchy parts which had happened a little later on. It was as if her subconscious mind or maybe her spirit guide or some other invisible force was warning her or giving her clues.

Those dreams hadn't been especially helpful for the solstice, but after Athena had explained the relationship of Neptune to dreams it had all made more sense. Rosemary had stopped being so suspicious about astro-babble after that entire incident had shown Athena had been correct in her speculations, more or less.

She got up and went downstairs to make herself a cup of tea and texted Athena.

Strange dream, talk later.

Maybe there was some clue to be found in the stars again or some other useful advice that her clever daughter could give her. Rosemary was starting to get the feeling that what Athena talked about in recent days was true – something incredibly spooky was indeed afoot.

Eight

Athena woke with a jolt. The dream had been so real. There was a terrified girl reaching out for her, then she was running through the forest...

But of course it must have only been a dream.

She rubbed her bleary eyes and squinted around the room, recalling she was still on a school trip. Elise was already sitting up in bed, looking at her.

"What?" said Athena.

"You missed all the drama. You slept right through it. I couldn't even wake you, so I stayed here, of course."

"What happened?" Athena asked, looking around the room at her other friends.

Felix looked pale and for a change he didn't say anything.

"There were spooky noises," said Sam. "And some of our instruments were going off in the tower room. So we went to investigate."

45

"Felix went in first," said Ash. "And he swears something rushed at him. Some sort of ghostly apparition."

"Strange," said Athena. "I had a weird dream..."

Her friends looked at her.

Athena shook her head, realising that it was an awkward thing to talk about when Felix was clearly so spooked by a real apparition. "It was just a dream...so what happened after Felix got spooked?"

Sam glanced at Felix and shrugged. "He came running out, babbling that something had flown at him and then he hasn't quite been the same since."

Felix shivered and seemed to be muttering to himself, although barely a sound escaped his mouth and nothing was audible.

"Do you think he's possessed?" said Elise, with strange look in her eye.

"Why would he be?" said Sam.

"I don't know. Maybe the ghost rushed into him."

Athena looked at her girlfriend. Something was odd about her. "Are you okay?"

"Of course," said Elise. "Why wouldn't I be?"

"I don't know," said Athena. "I'm probably just a bit spooked by this whole situation."

Sam smiled at her. "Me too. But don't worry. We'll be out of here in no time. And then we can get back to normal and write a report about Felix being an idiot and getting terrified."

Athena laughed, although, as she glanced back at said terrified friend, she wondered whether they should be taking the situation a little more seriously.

It was only after Athena got back to Thorn Manor and told Rosemary about her dream, and they realised she'd had a similar experience at the same time, that Athena really felt spooked.

"Let's just hope it's a freakish coincidence," said Rosemary.

But neither of them were convinced.

Nine

"Mum! He's here!" Athena called out as the doorbell rang.

"I'm coming!" Rosemary rushed down the stairs.

It had taken her too long to get dressed. She hadn't seen Burk for a little while because they'd both been busy with their respective work and he'd been out of town for several days on urgent Vampire Council business for reasons that he was apparently not able to discuss.

Rosemary missed him, but she wasn't about to admit it – not to him, certainly not to Athena, and barely even to herself.

She'd ended up throwing on a black velvet dress after trying several other outfits that hadn't quite worked for her. In her rush, she had almost forgotten lipstick.

By the time she made it to the door she was panting.

Burk stood there, pristine and crisp in his expensive Italian shirt. His jacket was draped over his arm casually, despite the fact that it was relatively cool outside.

"Your chariot awaits," he said.

"Don't tell me you actually brought a chariot," said Rosemary. "I already feel underdressed."

"It's a figure of speech. I'm learning."

Rosemary smiled and kissed him, leaning into the warmth of the intimacy despite the fact that, Burk, as a vampire, was not particularly warm himself, though he was very fast.

He picked her up in his arms, calling a goodbye to Athena, and whisked her to the car.

Rosemary giggled. "Where are we going? Is it a surprise?"

"Not exactly," said Burk. "I'm making dinner for you at the castle."

"Oh yes, just another castle excursion," said Rosemary. "As if everyone has their own castle."

Burk smiled. "I've missed you," he said, reaching over to kiss her again before beginning to drive. "There's something I want to talk to you about."

"What is that?" Rosemary asked.

"It can wait till we get there."

"Ah-ah. I don't like that," said Rosemary anxiously. "It's not fair to say you're going to talk to somebody about something and then not immediately say what it is."

"You won't have to wait long," said Burk.

"I hope it's not be something bad," Rosemary said. "Because if it's something bad, you better tell me now."

"I don't think so, but that might depend on your perspective."

"This is totally not fair," said Rosemary, crossing her arms in a huff. "I demand to know."

"Wait ten minutes," said Burk. And within that they had pulled up outside the castle and made their way inside, narrowly avoiding Burk's vampire family as he whisked her up to the tower where a beautiful meal had been set up.

"This is nice. I could have driven myself here and saved you the trouble," said Rosemary. "And also: out with it."

Burk smiled, looking particularly dashing as he held up a bottle. "Wine?"

Rosemary nodded. "Something tells me I might need it."

She sat down and received the glass from Burk.

"So what is it? Something terrible happened? Is it to do with the Bloodstones?"

"No," said Burk. "This is a family matter."

Rosemary screwed up her face.

"What I mean," said Burk, "is that my family, at this time of year...well, it's traditional for us to have a family reunion on Samhain night."

"Oh, I see." Rosemary felt a weight lift from her shoulders. She was confused why this was such a big deal, but she was glad it wasn't something more ominous.

"So there'll be a lot of vampires about and ghosts and various other things," said Burk.

"Okay, and..?"

"And you're invited." Burk said this in a rather serious tone.

"Well, it would be rude not to invite me, wouldn't it? Unless I've miscalculated and our relationship isn't getting serious."

"What I mean is that...I have to invite you and you have to decline."

"Oh? Well, okay...I mean, I'm not really part of your family anyway."

"Are you offended?"

"No. I don't even like most of my own family all that much. Why would I want to hang out with somebody else's in particular?"

Burk breathed a sigh of relief and Rosemary narrowed her eyes at him. "What is this really about? You're not usually so ruffled."

"Rosemary, my family...Well, the ones you've met, are my closest vampire relatives and I know you quite like them."

"I do," said Rosemary. "Although they also terrify me and I don't really want to focus on them, particularly while we're on a date. I'm glad that we managed to avoid them on the way here. They don't exactly...get you in a romantic mood."

"I'm thankful for that," said Burk. "However my mother can be quite persuasive. She'll insist that you're coming to the reunion and you will respond..."

"Wait a minute," said Rosemary, raising her index finger in the air. "Why are you so desperate for me not to come?"

"My family is dangerous, Rosemary. The close ones are fine. They're well adapted. They've lived in the human world for a long time. But my distant vampire relatives are much more dangerous. They're bloodthirsty, and some of them are cruel."

Rosemary made a face. She didn't much feel like being eviscerated and consumed like a beverage at any event, let alone a family reunion.

"Exactly," said Burk, reading her expression well. "So you understand."

"I think so," said Rosemary. "I don't have any particular reason to doubt you or be suspicious of you..."

She took another sip of wine and narrowed her eyes at him. "Why is your mother so keen for me to come? Doesn't she care if I become the main course?"

Rosemary felt a little hurt that Azalea would care so little for her life.

Burk shrugged. "She sees the best in people. She doesn't really have the same understanding of risks as I do. You know? Living as long as we do, sometimes you forget about..."

"The perils of mortality?"

Burk nodded. "And she very much wants you to come." There was a heavy warning in his voice.

Based on what little she knew of Burk's mother, Rosemary believed Burk when he said Azalea could be rather persuasive.

"It's okay. I'll say I've got something else to go to that night. Which night is it?"

"Samhain."

"Of course, well, I'm sure I'll have plenty of stuff to do then. Besides there's bound to be something attacking us."

Burk frowned. "That's the spirit. Is there something else I need to know about?"

Rosemary sighed. "Nothing in particular. The business is doing abysmally, and I'm sure I'm cursed. And Athena is getting spooky feelings and we're both having the same kinds of night-mares that I really hope aren't predicting the future. Even Marjie is acting weird."

"That's equally fascinating and troubling," he said thoughtfully. "But unusual energies are certainly brewing. Do you really think you could be cursed? And could something similar be affecting Marjie? Maybe Athena is right to be spooked."

Rosemary smiled at his genuine concern. "Your guess is as good as mine, but how about we change the subject back to the present and talk about this exquisite food."

"You haven't tried it."

"But I can tell." Rosemary took a bite of the salmon gravlax. It was indeed delectable. So tasty that she almost groaned.

She took a sip of wine while she savoured the experience.

"This is amazing. You should really be a chef."

Burk smiled. "Back to the potential dark magic," he said with a flourish.

"I guess it's the topic of the day," said Rosemary. "Well, I don't have any evidence, but I do have to say that I made the most adorable chocolate pumpkins for my elaborate window display and still hardly anyone has come into the shop."

Burk shook his head. "Inexplicable! I don't even eat proper food and even I can't resist beautifully crafted chocolate pumpkins."

"Exactly," said Rosemary, waving her palms in the air in frustration, splaying her fingers. "I wish we could figure out what's going on."

"Surely there's magic for that," said Burk.

Rosemary nodded. "I'd better do my research, but in the meantime I'm going to enjoy this absolutely mouth-watering dish and my absolutely mouth-watering date." Her lips twisted into a smile as she looked at Burk's gorgeous face, noting his tantalising expression...and she wondered if they would last at the table until dessert.

Ten

Rosemary was just settling into bed the next evening. She'd been scratching Serpentine behind the ears, when a whisper rang through her mind.

The answer lies in your dreams.

Rosemary squinted at the kitten. "Was that you?"

Serpentine merely closed her green eyes and turned away.

Rosemary sat there, continuing to pat her familiar, waiting for another message, but nothing came through. She was about to give up and go to bed when her phone rang. She frowned. It was a bit late for a call.

"Hello?"

"Rosemary, you'd better get over here," Detective Neve's voice said.

Rosemary felt a chill. "You're back so soon from your holiday...It's so early in the morning! What's going on?"

"I'll explain in person. It's complicated."

Rosemary's heart began pounding. Something bad must have happened. "Where do you want me to go, exactly? The police station?"

"No...Oh sorry. Come to Marjie's cottage now. Don't bring Athena."

Rosemary felt herself shaking as she put the phone down.

She threw on her jacket – unable to contemplate the complexities of putting actual clothing on instead of her pyjamas – and tiptoed to Athena's room. The light was still on, shining from under the door.

Rosemary tapped gently.

"I'm going to bed soon," Athena called out. "Just finishing this painting."

"Err...That's good, love. I'm going to have to pop out for a minute. Or maybe longer."

There was a thud and Athena opened the door. "What is it?"

Rosemary took in the sight of her daughter in her painting clothes, her hands covered in different coloured splotches. In that moment, she was so grateful for Athena's safety. She didn't know how to find the right words. "I don't know exactly. But Neve called. She wants me to go to Marjie's house, urgently."

Athena's expression tightened to one of horror. "Something happened to Marjie?"

"I really hope not. I'll text you when I get there."

"I should come," said Athena.

"No. You stay here. Neve wants me to go alone. But I'll let you know what's going on as soon as I can."

"Fine," said Athena with a gulp. "But it sounds serious."

"Yes. And it's my instinct to protect you. But I couldn't very well just pop out at night without telling you, could I?"

"Thanks, Mum," said Athena. She threw her arms around her mother.

Rosemary leaned into the hug for a moment. Her heart raced. "I'll be back as soon as I can."

She dashed out of the house and sped through the streets without paying much attention to how fast she was actually driving, hoping that Constable Perkins wasn't lurking around, waiting to catch her and reprimand her for something so insignificant on a night where the roads were quiet, eerily so.

Rosemary continued driving slightly too fast until she turned into Marjie's street.

Her heart leapt to her throat as she took in the flashing lights outside the cottage, the police vehicles and the ambulance...

She parked badly on the side of the road and ran towards the house.

Detective Neve was standing out front, her breath making clouds of steam in the cold night air. She wore a big black puffer jacket over her usual white shirt and plain black pants.

Constable Perkins stood off to the side, eyeing Rosemary suspiciously as he talked on his phone.

"What's happened?" Rosemary's voice wavered. "Is Marjie alright?"

Neve took a deep breath. "Marjie...She's very upset. I think she's in shock. She's not really speaking."

"What happened?" Rosemary asked again. It felt as if she'd been saying nothing but this, over and over.

"It's Herb," said Neve.

"No!" said Rosemary. "Is he..."

Detective Neve nodded.

Rosemary felt a deep wave of sadness. She didn't know Herb particularly well. But he was Marjie's rock. He wasn't the chatty type, but she'd gotten used to his stoic, silent presence around Myrtlewood. She was more worried for Marjie than anything.

"Was it a heart attack?" Rosemary asked. In her mind Herb seemed the sort who would die quietly in his sleep, but that didn't explain such a strong police presence. "Was it..."

"Wait—" said Neve as Rosemary started walking towards the house.

She needed to find Marjie. She needed to reassure her that everything was alright.

"Don't!" Neve called out, but Rosemary was already inside.

Marjie sat in the hallway on a chair, a blanket wrapped around her.

Neve clearly did not want her outside in the cold. Rosemary wrapped her arms around her friend. Marjie's eyes were glazed over.

"Get out of the house," said Constable Perkins. "This is a crime scene. We don't want you compromising it – trying to confuse us with your prints."

"A crime scene?" said Rosemary. "What happened?" she asked for what felt like the millionth time.

That was when she noticed the blood.

Not only was it splattered over Marjie's floral nightdress, interrupting the yellows and pinks with its deeper, more menacing hue, but it also was splashed on the floor and speared into footprints.

"Out of the house, Ms Thorn!" said Constable Perkins.

"Yes, Rosemary," Neve added. "You don't want to see."

But Rosemary wasn't listening.

She stood and tiptoed towards the living room.

There was blood – so much blood. And...Herb.

His body lay on the floor. It looked as though he'd been gouged at and stabbed with knives, except that his eyes appeared almost hollowed out and blue markings adorned his cheeks.

Rosemary screamed. A guttural sound emerged.

Never had she come so close to death itself in all its horror.

Bile started to rise in her belly and she let Detective Neve escort her back outside.

Rosemary panted as she quelled her nausea by taking in the crisp night air. "That was awful."

"Tell me about it," said Neve. "Rosemary, I need you to look after Marjie."

Constable Perkins bristled. "Look after her? We should arrest her immediately!"

"What?" Rosemary and Neve both said.

"She was the only one there!" he blustered.

Rosemary glared at him. "Shut up, you insignificant little man." Her nausea was turning quickly to rage that consumed her entire body.

"Uhh...You—" Constable Perkins started, but Rosemary didn't let him speak.

"I am absolutely sick of you, with your vile, small-minded opinions. I will not tolerate it for another moment. Either do your job properly or stand down."

Constable Perkins paled. Clearly, he wasn't used to being

talked to like that. His mouth hung open as he looked between Detective Neve and Rosemary.

The detective simply looked unimpressed. When she didn't stand up for him, Perkins went bright red. Spittle flew from his mouth and Rosemary winced. "I should arrest you for insulting an officer."

"I don't think that's a real charge," said Neve. "And I'm sure, being a professional, you can understand that at a time like this people's emotions are heightened. So I'll advise you to stand down too."

Perkins almost wilted. His shoulders slumped and he looked down at the ground.

"Thank you," said Rosemary.

Neve nodded slightly. "Magical forensics has just come through. They've taken photos and I've done various other tests for magical traces. There's not much we can do now..."

"But we can't leave Marjie in the house," Rosemary finished.

"No, the clean-up crew will be in later, but she shouldn't stay here. That's why I called you."

"I'll take her back to Thorn Manor," said Rosemary. "Did she say what happened?"

"Barely a word," said Detective Neve.

"I suppose that's to be expected."

"I'm surprised she even managed to call me," said Neve. "My phone rang when we were having dinner and all I got was a few words. Took me a moment to work out who was calling. And so I came round, wondering what on earth...And well, I suppose the rest is obvious."

"Do you think Marjie was in the house? Of course she was.

Why am I asking stupid questions? Whoever did this, they came at night. Marjie and Herb were getting ready for bed. Maybe she saw the whole thing or maybe she was in another room and just heard a noise. I bet it wasn't quiet."

"There's no point in speculating now," said Detective Neve. "Save your energy. We'll know more from forensics. And in the meantime, see if you can get a good cup of tea into Marjie. I know you've got room at home and there's no one else I can think of calling. Marjie knows everyone in town and she has a lot of friends, but she's especially close to you and Athena."

Rosemary nodded. "Even though we've only really gotten to know her over the past year, she's family to us. Of course we'll look after her."

"All right then. Let's go."

They crept into the house again and that was when Rosemary noticed the smell. A dark, sickly stench. Perhaps she hadn't noticed it earlier due to shock, or perhaps it was new.

She wanted to ask Neve if that was a normal stench of death or if it was something more sinister, but now hardly seemed the time.

They reached for Marjie, propping her up.

She walked slowly outside, staring into space as they guided her and supported her to Rosemary's car.

"I should get her a change of clothes," said Rosemary as she strapped Marjie into the passenger seat. "Only I don't know if I want to go back in there."

"Already done," said Neve. She handed Rosemary a bag. "I packed this when the magical forensics team was just finishing up."

Rosemary shivered in the cold night air. "Thank you."

"Marjie has been sitting in the hallway like that for at least an hour. I haven't been able to get her to swallow more than a few sips of water. She didn't touch her tea."

"I'll see what I can do," said Rosemary, glancing at her very pale and clearly shaken friend, who stared blankly into space.

It was a quiet and spooky drive home.

Rosemary was so unused to Marjie in silence. She was always full of life and energy, laughter and warmth. Never had she seen her so cold and still, but it was to be expected at a time like this.

Rosemary's mind raced with possibilities.

Who could possibly have it in for the silent, relatively kind man who seemed to have only one interest in his life beyond his wife? Model trains were an obsessive hobby that drove Marjie up the wall at times, but other than that, they seemed so happy and settled as a couple.

Maybe Herb wasn't the target at all, Rosemary wondered as she pulled up towards Thorn Manor. The front door opened as she was getting Marjie out of the car and Athena came out. "Oh no. What's going on, Mum?"

She instinctively went to Marjie's other side and they helped her into the house.

"Is that blood?" Athena asked.

Rosemary nodded. "I'll tell you more when we're inside."

They settled Marjie into a comfortable armchair in the lounge and Athena went to make tea while Rosemary managed to change Marjie's nighty into a fresh one using a spell she'd been saving for just such an occasion – when the magical working was less effort than just changing clothes manually.

She wondered if she should try to get her into the shower beforehand, but decided in the end that it would be too complicated. Just removing the sight of the blood was the priority for now.

Rosemary did get a warm flannel and wiped down Marjie's arms and feet where the blood splatter had reached them too.

All the while her friend stared blankly into space, occasionally muttering a word or two incomprehensively.

"No...no...no," was the most common, which was perhaps the *most* understandable thing anyone could say at a time like this. Some of the other sounds didn't appear to be words at all.

Athena returned to the room with tea and Rosemary added a little of Marjie's special formula, the one she'd created as a magical pick-me-up, the one she'd given Rosemary on her return to Myrtlewood – the day their friendship had first started.

Rosemary had accused the old woman of drugging her. She laughed about that incident now, except today wasn't a time for laughing.

"Here you go." She handed the cup over carefully. "I've dosed you with some of your own magic."

Marjie looked at Rosemary, a gleam of recognition in her eye.

"Take a sip." Rosemary nodded to the teacup.

Marjie did a she was told and then took another bigger gulp.

After a few moments colour returned to her cheeks, but even though Marjie seemed to be feeling slightly better, Rosemary was sure things were about to get a lot worse.

Eleven

Rosemary woke to a knock on her bedroom door.

She groaned, feeling the heavy weight of the events of the night before, which came back to play through her mind.

"Who is it?" she called out.

"Just me," said a cheerful voice.

The door opened and Marjie entered, holding a tray of tea and scones.

Rosemary rubbed her eyes, unnerved. "Marjie. You should be resting."

Marjie smiled at her warmly.

"What's going on?" Rosemary asked, getting up from the bed.

Marjie's smile faded to a look of abject horror. She dropped the tea.

It clattered to the ground, but not before Rosemary had flung out her hand to slow its descent, narrowly saving the teapot and the cups. However, the milk jug was knocked over, spilling over the scones.

"Marjie, sit down," said Rosemary, helping her friend over to the chair she kept by her bed, which happened to almost always be covered in clothes and other items. She shoved everything off it and onto the floor, hoping that the house might help her in returning them to their rightful places.

"I forgot," said Marjie, staring blankly into space.

Rosemary sat on the bed next to her, taking her hand.

"How could I? How could I forget? I got up and I thought 'Oh how nice. I'm staying with the Thorns.' And then I started baking."

"You got up and baked scones," said Rosemary. "I suppose it's instinctual."

Marjie looked at Rosemary, but her gaze didn't quite seem to register what was in front of her.

"It's okay," said Rosemary. "Grief...is strange."

"Grief," Marjie repeated.

"Here, have a scone." Rosemary picked up the plate, discarding the milk-soaked scones, and carried it over to her friend. Then she poured them both some tea.

They sat there for a few moments, idly nibbling and sipping.

If they'd been anywhere else, on any other day, it could have almost been a normal situation. But it was so far from normal that Rosemary had to keep remembering to breathe.

"You know," said Marjie, "Herb and I always watched those murder mysteries. The kind with the friendly detective and all the gardens and the country fairs and villages."

Rosemary nodded along as Marjie spoke.

"You know what the strangest thing about those shows is?" Marjie was talking as if far away.

Rosemary shrugged. "The body count does seem a little elevated for a small village."

Marjie shook her head. "The strangest thing is how the people react...or don't react to the deaths. You know? This is so significant. It just rips the heart right out of you. This...this void of pain and anguish that I don't even know how to describe or how to see through or how to process. I can't even..." Her words faded away.

Rosemary nodded. "You're right. In those shows death just kind of happens all the time and people sort of almost expect it or get desensitised to it. Maybe the viewers don't want to watch a show that's all grief, but it almost goes the other way. There's murder after murder after murder."

Rosemary winced, realising she was rambling, but Marjie didn't seem to be affected, and perhaps the conversation was soothing, so she continued. "It's all highly unlikely, too, like the candlestick in the library style of death. I'm sure it's so much harder than that in real life...and then they all just sort of get on with it."

"But that's the thing," said Marjie. "We all just need to get on with it."

She looked at Rosemary and smiled again, the warmth returning to her face. "I'll be fine, dear. Don't you worry about me. No fussing."

She got up, picked up the tray, and began bustling about as usual.

Rosemary tried to stop her, but she realised that right now

Marjie behaving in a totally normal way was her coping mechanism. She even insisted on going into the shop.

Rosemary and Athena went with her, shooting each other concerned glances as Marjie wiped down the counters and set up as usual.

Every now and then, she would have a moment where it was like time would stand still. She dropped what she was holding, including a number of teacup casualties. But when she came to her senses, she seemed more concerned about the teacups than about the much more pressing issue in her life.

"People deal with grief in strange ways," said Athena. She and Rosemary sat at a table watching Marjie in the kitchen preparing some more magical baking.

Rosemary shook her head. "What are we going to do with her? We can't just babysit her this whole time. Can we?"

"I guess not," said Athena. "You've got your own shop and I've got school."

"We'll work it out," said Rosemary. "We always do."

"Sometimes I wish you'd say useful things and not just glib platitudes," Athena muttered. "It's going to take more than just us to get Marjie through this."

"True," said Rosemary. "But it's not just us. We have friends. At times like these I kind of wish we had a coven to call on. Marjie said that there used to be a powerful Myrtlewood Coven back when Granny Thorn still had all the family magic coursing through her."

"That's an idea!" said Athena.

Rosemary sighed. "I don't think this is the time to start an organisation. Think of all the paperwork and people politics."

"No, I'm not suggesting that. But how about we call all our friends and invite them over tonight. Maybe they'll all be keen to pitch in in some way. We can set up a roster of people to make sure Marjie's okay."

"Now that's an excellent suggestion!" said Rosemary. "You're hired. But maybe after that we can set up a coven because it sounds cool."

Athena laughed and rolled her eyes.

Twelve

The living room of Thorn Manor was full that evening with the fire lit and many close friends gathered around.

Marjie had been in good cheer, sitting there by the hearth in a cosy armchair with a little glass of sherry, but after Papa Jack had mentioned Herb while giving his condolences she became rather pale.

Rosemary suggested she might feel better if she wasn't in the room for the meeting they'd planned and had guided her up to the spare room and tucked her into bed while Athena rounded up the stragglers in the kitchen, ready for the meeting to start.

She was feeling nervous. She'd never really hosted a meeting before and Rosemary had insisted that as it was her idea she should be the one to run it.

Rosemary returned from putting Marjie to bed and smiled warmly at Athena. They both stood on either side of the fireplace. The room hushed.

"Thanks for coming, everyone," said Rosemary. "As you all know, Marjie is having a horribly challenging time and she needs our support. Athena had an idea that people might want to pitch in." Rosemary gestured to her daughter, who took a short, sharp, nervous breath and then started speaking, slightly too fast.

"Yes, thank you for coming. I thought everyone would probably want to help out..."

"Of course we do," said Una. There were murmurs of agreement around the room.

"So first of all," Athena continued, wringing her hands, "we thought we might talk about what Marjie needs and then maybe set up a kind of roster..."

"What a great idea," said Fleur, from the couch. Elise sat next to her and smiled encouragingly, though Athena noticed it didn't quite reach her eyes and wondered if something was wrong. Elise had been distant lately, a little bit off, but Athena didn't have time to worry about that right now.

"This is a great idea," said Neve.

"We'll do what we can to help," Nesta added.

"Okay, great." Athena pulled up a chalkboard that she'd found in one of Thorn Manor's many spare rooms and began to write. "Of course, Marjie needs food to survive...err that's obvious. We all need food to survive. Oh no, I'm rambling like Mum."

A collective giggle echoed around the room, but it was warm and friendly.

Athena took a deep breath and continued. "You know, it's funny. I've battled all kinds of malicious magical forces, but public speaking still makes me nervous."

"Understandable," said Rosemary. "But you're right, Marjie

does need food and supervision most of the time. She still seems to want to be at work. And I don't mind her being here at night. But—"

"But you can't always be expected to babysit her," said Nesta. "That's not fair on you two. You have other things to think about."

"Maybe it's just Marjie-watch," Liam suggested. "If everyone can pick a day of the week or an evening and they can keep an eye on her at the tea shop or here."

"It sounds like a rather rudimentary plan," said Ferg, who was sitting in the corner on a wooden chair. "However, we simply must not discount that Marjoram Reeves could be the one responsible for this heinous crime."

Rosemary glared at him. "What are you saying?"

Ferg stood up. He was wearing a deep aubergine velvet cloak. He'd been dressing – and behaving – a little bit more grandly since he'd been elected as the mayor, and had seemed even more testy than usual. Rosemary wasn't sure if it was the baubles of office rubbing off on him, or whether he'd secretly harboured such grandiosity in silence the whole time. Ferg seemed more and more like the pompous former mayor every day, and despite the fact that the previous version of him had been grating at times, she was actually starting to miss the old Ferg.

Rosemary and Athena had thought twice about whether to invite him tonight but had decided in the end that he and Marjie were good friends and that he'd have an interest in looking out for her.

Rosemary folded her arms, unimpressed at his interruption.

"I'm merely saying that, in my duty as mayor of this fair town,

I have a tremendous responsibility to uphold decorum, proper conduct, and civic goodwill, and to ensure people fill in the appropriate paperwork of course!"

"Yes," said Rosemary, tapping her foot. "And?"

"Marjoram Reeves was the only one at the house when Herbert Reeves died. Surely she's a suspect." He looked at Detective Neve.

She shook her head. "This isn't an appropriate thing to bring up. That would be police business. And besides, we don't have enough information yet to have any clear suspects."

"Thank you for pointing out the clear role and responsibility of law enforcement professionals," said Ferg. "This is exactly my point. This is police business. She could be dangerous."

"Seriously?" said Rosemary. "You saw that woman sitting here just moments ago and how devastated she is. She could not possibly be the murderer."

Ferg began to protest, but Rosemary intervened. "Look, if you're not going to be helpful then please leave."

"But I'm the mayor," said Ferg. "That's my clear role and—"

"Maybe that's a good reason for you to go and perform some actual mayoral duties," Rosemary said and gestured towards the door.

"Very well. I can tell when I'm not wanted. It certainly seems as if my position of high office is getting in the way of ordinary affairs. I may have a conflict of interest. Don't worry. I'll fill out the appropriate form!"

He put on the fedora that he'd come in wearing and strolled out.

Rosemary sighed. "Oh well. At least we know where he stands."

"On a pile of silly rules," Athena grumbled.

The rest of the meeting went fairly smoothly, with people choosing particular days of the week that they would keep an eye on Marjie. A few close friends volunteered to do a night shift here and there because Rosemary and Athena decided that they would rather just manage themselves most of the time unless they were otherwise occupied on an evening. Even so, there was a roster set up for the confident cooks among them, Sherry included, who signed up to deliver meals to make sure that there was not too much work to do around Thorn Manor in case Marjie needed additional support.

"Thanks for coming, everyone," said Athena, feeling relieved that it had all gone relatively well and that they now had a plan.

People began to leave, but Papa Jack approached Rosemary and Athena as they were packing up.

"Now, Rosemary, I just wanted to say, don't worry about paying me on time this week. I know finances are tight."

"Don't be ridiculous," said Rosemary. "I wouldn't hear of it."

"It's okay. I know," said Papa Jack. "I've seen the takings for this week and I know that there is no money."

"Mum wouldn't dream of having you go unpaid," said Athena.

"I don't want to stress you out, or your mother. Especially not when all this is going on." He gestured around the room.

"Thank you," said Rosemary. "That's very sweet and kind of you, but don't worry. Things will pick up, I'm sure, as everyone keeps telling me. I may have to dip into my savings from time to time, but that's just part of running a business, especially in the early days. We've been lucky so far and hopefully we won't have to close the shop over winter. We'll just keep chugging along. Maybe have some kind of Halloween sale or focus on internet orders, like Athena keeps telling me."

"Very well," said Papa Jack. "You're a star, Rosemary Thorn. And so are you Athena." He gave them both warm hugs before he left.

"What was that all about?" Rosemary muttered as the door closed.

"He's worried about you," said Athena.

"He's got his own family to look after, too. Him going without being paid on time isn't going to help them."

"Are finances really that tight?" Athena asked, feeling nervous.

"They're not looking good," Rosemary admitted. "But we've still got plenty of money saved. Plus, there's the money in trust from Granny. I think I'd be able to justify a withdrawal for the sake of the business. I just can't help thinking that something sinister is going on."

"Maybe," said Athena, feeling a shiver of fear down her spine. "You really think the shop might be cursed?"

Rosemary nodded. "There must be some magical way to find out. I could ask Tamsyn."

"That's not a bad idea, although I think she just left."

Rosemary smiled. "The shop can wait. Let's have some soothing chamomile tea with cream and honey before bed."

Thirteen

A thena sat in class, anxiously picking at her chipped forest green nail polish. She was supposed to be paying attention to Mr. Spruce's lecture, but her attention kept being diverted to Elise, who was clearly zoning out.

She nudged Elise again.

"What?" Elise asked.

Athena shook her head and muttered, "I'm supposed to be the one who zones out in class. You're supposed to be the one who nudges me."

"Sorry," Elise whispered back. "I guess I'm a bit tired."

"Maybe we should skip the opening of the carnival and market tonight," Athena suggested.

"Oh no," Elise said. "It'll be fun. I'm sure I'll feel better by then."

It did seem like a strange thing to be going out to something like a carnival, given the situation with Marjie's husband having just been murdered, but Rosemary had insisted that Athena should make the most of the chance to have a little fun.

Liam was looking after Marjie that evening anyway, and Rosemary was happy to go along to the carnival to see what it was like.

"You mean you're going to scope it out?" Athena had joked.

Rosemary shrugged. "Well, these people did just come into town at a particularly spooky time of year. Maybe they have something to do with the situation we find ourselves in." Athena had shaken her head. "Always the paranoid one, Mum."

"Yes, and at least forty-five percent of the time, my suspicions are confirmed."

The school bell rang, but Elise stayed at her desk. They had been meaning to go and get a hot chocolate from Rosemary's shop before going to the carnival, but Athena was still seriously reconsidering whether they should be going out at all.

"Are you okay?" she asked Elise. "You seem a bit off."

"Sorry, I was miles away. I'm sure I'll feel better soon," Elise replied.

They wandered together, into town, and Elise continued to act strangely, looking around at everything – almost as if it was surprising.

"What's going on with you?" Athena asked.

"Nothing. It's just..." She shook her head. "I guess I'm noticing details that I hadn't before."

"You think it's something magical affecting you?" Athena asked. "We could go to the apothecary and see if they have any idea what it might be. They might have a tonic or something."

Elise shook her head. "No, I'm fine. Really, it's probably just the spooky season, you know?"

76

"That's odd," said Athena as they neared the chocolate shop. "It feels different around here, almost as though we're not supposed to be here. Mum insists that she's been cursed and that's why business is so bad. Maybe she's right."

Athena frowned. She often didn't want her mother to be right, especially not when it sounded like she was just being overly suspicious.

Elise usually ordered the orange hot chocolate, but for some reason, after perusing the menu, she selected rose. Rosemary raised an eyebrow as she took the order, confirming Athena's suspicions that something was off.

"Why are you scowling so much?" Elise asked. "Am I really acting that strangely?"

Athena didn't reply and instead shrugged.

She took Elise's hand as they sat down in their usual booth, but Elise flinched. "Sorry. I guess I'm just on edge."

"I am too," Athena admitted. "Maybe I'm the one who shouldn't be out."

Elise closed her eyes for a moment, and Athena wondered whether she was about to doze off on the spot. When she opened them again, something had changed. She seemed to be more her normal self.

"I don't know what came over me," said Elise. "And I don't know why I ordered a rose drink. It's not really my thing, but it's not bad."

She sipped her hot chocolate.

"Something strange is going on," said Athena, "and my instinct is to curl up in bed with my head under the covers. But that's probably not the ideal place to be in the event of something very spooky happening."

"I don't know. Sounds pretty cosy to me," said Elise with a smile.

Athena smiled back, feeling the warmth returning to her mood. At least whatever had been affecting her girlfriend seemed to have faded.

"Are you heading off now?" Rosemary called from the kitchen as Athena stood up from the table.

"Yes, we thought we'd go early," said Athena.

Rosemary smiled. "Alright. Watch out for anything unusual and don't eat anything weird. I'll come along in about half an hour after I've closed up the shop. I could drop Elise off home afterwards if she likes."

"It's okay. Mum's picking me up," said Elise.

Athena said goodbye to her mother and Papa Jack, and then they left, heading towards the park where the house trucks had assembled the other night.

"I wonder why they're not in the middle of town," said Athena.

"I heard they couldn't get a permit from Ferg," said Elise.

"Of course not!" They laughed.

"They didn't fill out the paperwork early enough or something," Elise added. "But they're allowed to join in the Allantide market that we have in the centre of town every year for All Hallows Eve night."

"That sounds really cool," said Athena.

"Of course we have to go," said Elise. "I've already thought of my costume."

Athena grinned. "I'd better get cracking then. I don't have

much time and Marjie is probably not going to be able to help me this time."

"You could just show up as yourself," Elise suggested.

"As a slightly anxious and bookish seventeen-year-old?" Athena laughed.

"No, as an incredibly powerful witch and fae princess."

Athena shook her head. "I don't think I'm quite as powerful as you make out. And besides, you could go as yourself, too. A rainbow nymph. That's an amazing thing to be!"

Elise shrugged. "Seems pretty ordinary to me. Everyone around here is a bit magical." Athena had an uneasy feeling again.

Elise always seemed to be comparing herself with her in terms of magical power when there was really no need to. After all, magic was mostly useful when things went terribly wrong. Although occasionally, magic *was* the thing that made things go terribly wrong in the first place. And Athena's magic had been responsible for that, multiple times.

Flaming torches lit the entrance to the park.

They walked through, noticing that the torches got progressively bigger, leading to a fiery archway.

"This is so cool," said Athena as they wandered through strips of silk hanging from the archway.

It was almost like walking into another world, which Athena had experienced several times before, leaving behind the ordinary and entering a magical place.

They emerged to see fire jugglers and flame breathers, acrobats balancing on unlikely stacks of objects and terrifying clowns.

Some of them seemed to be magically aided, such as the man in the gold vest who appeared to be hovering on a ball of fire, while others defied the laws of nature in the more usual circus ways – balancing on unlikely piles of objects.

The market stall veered off to the right, with all kinds of incredible objects. Athena noticed mushrooms from the fae realm and wondered if the trade everyone had talked about was already beginning to happen from the treaty, or whether these had been smuggled in some other way.

At least Elise seemed to be her normal self, still. Athena allowed herself to relax and they marvelled at the fascinating items in the market, including jewellery that looked as if it was on fire or made of water; headbands that sparkled as if they had constellations of stars inside; soaps, and creams that promised various outcomes, including looking more like a forest pixie.

Athena paused for a long time at a stall of books, tempted to buy at least ten interesting volumes.

Elise pulled her away before she was too overburdened. "You can come back later," she said. "Look, it's our friends from the other night."

Ursula and Hazel sat behind the stall outside their house truck.

"You made it," Ursula said.

"I'm surprised you recognised us," said Athena. "You must have had lots of people come through."

"Some people stand out more than others," said Hazel with a grin.

"Have you really been travelling around the country like this?" Elise asked. "Wouldn't the mundane people get freaked out by all the magic?"

"We're fairly careful," said Hazel. "Sometimes we have ordinary fairs with little sections that only magical beings can access, but Myrtlewood is an entirely magical village, so we're allowed to go all out."

"It's so cool, isn't it?" said Rowan, looking around. "I always knew magic was real, but I never knew it was like this until recently."

"There are so many cool things that I want to buy!" said Elise. "I don't know if my pocket money will stretch that far."

They examined the charms, plants, and jewellery laid out in front of them in the stall.

"These are so awesome," said Athena, pointing to a row of necklaces that looked as if they contained tiny succulents.

"They're my specialty," said Rowan. "But Ursula and Hazel enchant them with their special magic."

"Have you got anything for good luck?" Athena asked, feeling a prickle of uneasiness again. "Or maybe protection?"

Hazel stood up and ran her hand along the row of beautiful miniature pendants. "This one," she said, pointing to a tiny purple succulent in a glass orb. "I'll enhance the magic for you if you like." She grinned.

"We'll get out of your way then," said Ursula. She pulled Rowan over to the side of the truck.

Hazel put the pendant on the table and concentrated on it. Athena could sense the magic as she worked the chant. She could almost see the words flying around Hazel's head. She glanced over to the side of the truck and caught a glimpse of something. Ursula and Rowan were tucked just inside the door, leaning into each other in a way that was almost certainly romantic.

Elise gasped, clearly noticing the same thing.

Hazel looked up and giggled. "Public displays of affection, hmm?"

Athena shook her head. "Sorry, we just—"

"You thought Ursula and I were together, didn't you?" said Hazel, grinning.

Athena blushed.

"Well, you're right."

"We are?" said Elise.

Rowan coughed and he and Ursula returned to the stall. "Yes, it's a slightly complicated situation."

They stood there, the three of them holding hands.

"You..." Athena began and then shook her head, not wanting to pry.

"It's okay. We're a little bit unconventional here," said Ursula.

"You're all together? Like a triple rather than a couple?" said Athena, trying not to gape at them.

"Not exactly," said Hazel. "We're all friends, and Rowan and I...both have relationships with Ursula. Does that make sense?"

Athena shrugged. "I suppose so." She was curious about how it could work. Of course, she'd heard of polyamory before, but she'd never encountered it aside from online.

"Sorry for prying," said Elise.

"No, it's fine," said Ursula. "We weren't exactly discreet. It feels like we're each-other's people – like soulmates – but Rowan and Hazel don't feel romantically about each other."

"It's nice," said Athena, "that you can all be together like this.
"

"And it all kind of works out. We get along really well," said Hazel. "I mean, sometimes we argue a little bit. But who doesn't?"

"That's a good point," said Athena.

"Here you go," said Hazel, holding up the necklace.

"Thank you," said Athena. She handed over the money.

"Hey," Hazel said, reaching towards Elise. "There's something familiar about you. What...are you?"

Elise's mouth twitched in a smile. "Do you mean in terms of heritage? I'm human and rainbow nymph."

Hazel's eyes brightened. "Ginchy!"

"What?" Elise furrowed her brow.

"Oh, it used to mean 'cool' back in the 1950s." She reached out towards Elise's blue locks. "That's so wonderful. Rainbow nymph – I knew it! My grandmother was like you. I bet your hair colour changes."

"It does," said Elise sheepishly.

Athena looked between the two of them. There was some kind of resemblance, though perhaps it was partly that they both had bright hair of a similar length, Hazel's a lilac shade and Elise's in the usual bright blue.

"You can change your hair too?" Elise asked.

"Not like you," said Hazel. "I have to use magic deliberately, but I've often wondered if the reason the glamour charm comes so easily to me and stays this way is because some of my ancestors were rainbow nymphs. I also wonder whether it helped to keep me alive for so many long decades."

Athena and Elise both frowned in confusion. Hazel only seemed to be a handful of years older than them.

"It's a long story," said Hazel.

"That's for sure." Ursula smiled and patted Hazel's arm reassuringly.

Elise once again had a distant and far-away look on her face.

"We'd better go," said Athena. "Thank you." She waved goodbye and pulled Elise away. "Are you okay?"

"I just started thinking," said Elise. "Do you think that's the kind of thing you would want – to have other relationships?"

"I don't know," said Athena, feeling decidedly awkward. "Please don't say you're getting jealous again."

Elise shrugged.

"Look," said Athena. "All I know is that I want to be with you. And *this* is for you." She held up the pendant.

Elise smiled. "Thank you."

But before she could put it on, there was a coughing sound.

The man with the gold waistcoat – Gallium – appeared behind them.

Elise's eyes glowed red, and her hair became black.

Athena shivered. "Elise? Are you okay?"

Elise turned, held up her hands like claws, and screamed.

Gallium was blasted ten feet back and fell on his back.

A large group of Travellers crowded around him, but he picked himself up, seemingly unscathed.

"Elise!" Athena cried, grabbing her arm.

Elise's hair faded to pale blue, and her face was almost white. Her eyes were closed as she keeled over in a faint.

Athena caught her.

"What was that?" Rosemary asked, coming over.

"Thank the gods you're here," said Athena, never more glad to see her mother.

"I heard something," said Rosemary. "What happened?"

Athena tried to explain, while holding Elise up. Rosemary

helped, and together they escorted Elise to the car as various people from the carnival market came over to investigate the disturbance.

"And the guy, is he alright?" Rosemary asked.

"He seemed fine. He just kind of walked off. I didn't have a chance to check in with him because I had to hold Elise up...but the whole thing was totally abnormal. I've never seen anything like it," said Athena. "She just kind of snapped. I didn't even know she could do that – just kind of hurl people around with her hands."

"I don't like the sound of that," said Rosemary. "Let's just take her home for now."

"Fleur is supposed to be coming at eight," said Athena.

"She can pick up Elise from our place. I'll text her. We'd better just keep an eye on her for now."

Athena's shoulders slumped in exhaustion and relief. She was glad to be able to check on Elise, but the relief was short-lived as a creeping terror took over.

Something awful was happening to her girlfriend, and Athena had no idea what it was or how to stop it.

Fourteen

E lise was settled on the couch in Thorn Manor, looking pale, and Rosemary couldn't help but worry. She responded to their questions with simple, single-word answers only.

Athena sat next to her, attempting to coax her into drinking a cup of tea.

Rosemary paced around the room, wondering what else she could do. She'd called Fleur, who was leaving her dinner party early to pick up Elise.

Rosemary thought of all the different possibilities that magic might offer them. She'd been flipping through spell books recently, trying to figure out what was wrong with the shop.

Maybe they also held some sort of clue as to what was going on with Elise. Although some of the spells she had come across weren't very pleasant-sounding, and Rosemary didn't know if Elise's fae DNA would make attempting such a thing too risky. It would be inappropriate for her to try something without Fleur's permission anyway. She'd tried to get a message through to Una and Ashwyn but there was no response.

The doorbell rang, and Rosemary rushed to answer it, hoping and expecting it to be Fleur. To her surprise, and somewhat to her horror, Azalea stood there on the doorstep, wearing a typical Morticia Addams-style dress that clinched on her tiny waist.

"Oh," Rosemary said.

Azalea smiled in a way that was probably meant to be friendly but looked somewhat maniacal. "Rosemary, I thought I might have a word."

"This isn't really a good time," said Rosemary.

"Very well. I'll wait," said Azalea.

She stood there, and Rosemary didn't know what to say. "What I mean is, maybe we can talk at a different time, you know, on a different day, as opposed to now because we have a situation to deal with."

"Anything I can help with?" Azalea asked, raising an eyebrow.

Rosemary shook her head. The last thing they needed was a terrifying ancient vampire attempting to be helpful. "I don't think so."

"Well, you mortals are funny about time, which I suppose makes sense seeing as your lives are so fleeting. This won't take long, at any rate." Azalea held up a silver pocket watch that she'd produced from somewhere, although Rosemary wasn't sure where since Azalea didn't seem to have any pockets in that slinky dress.

"Three minutes," said Azalea.

"Excuse me?" said Rosemary.

"Can I trouble you for three minutes of your time now? Or would you prefer for me to wait on the doorstep?"

Rosemary shook her head. "Fine," she said, since Azalea didn't seem to get the hint.

"Excellent. It's important for me to get this settled."

"What do you mean?" Rosemary asked.

"Well, with you mortals, I'm never sure how long you're going to be around for, so I thought I might as well get this out of the way."

"Get what out of the way?" Rosemary felt both insulted and mildly terrified.

"The Burk family reunion on Samhain," said Azalea. "You'll be attending?"

"Oh, no," said Rosemary.

"No?" Azalea asked, her smile turning into a different expression that Rosemary couldn't quite read, although her fangs did seem to be protruding from the corners of her mouth.

Rosemary gulped as all the previous reasons she'd come up with for refusing the invitation vanished from her mind. She scrambled frantically to think of something to say. "What I mean is...I have something else on that night. And I would love to attend the Burk family reunion, but I absolutely can't because the other thing is... my own family reunion." It was the first excuse that came to mind.

"I see," said Azalea, taken aback. "Oh, very well, then."

She looked troubled, although Rosemary couldn't quite understand why this was such a big deal. Burk had warned her that Azalea wanted her to come to the reunion and that she definitely should, under no circumstances, accept the invitation.

Rosemary's curiosity got the best of her. "Why is it that you want me to go so much?"

Azalea looked baffled. "You're part of the family, darling. To not include you would be *wrong*."

The word "wrong" took quite some emphasis when Azalea spoke it.

"Well, I'm honoured," said Rosemary. "And thank you for including me. It's very magnanimous of you."

Azalea looked puzzled for a moment. "I'm afraid our time is up, but was there something else..."

The house was silent, and Fleur hadn't arrived yet. So Rosemary took the bait. "Alright, what is it?"

"I wanted to know if you'd heard the rumours about the Bloodstone Society," Azalea said.

"What rumours?" Rosemary asked, interested.

"My contacts tell me they're meddling in dark forces. Dora is worried. She keeps pacing the house, muttering to herself about Geneviève."

"What do you mean by 'dark forces'?" said Rosemary.

"Unearthly forces."

Rosemary raised an eyebrow. "You'll have to be a little more specific."

"Well, it's hard to put it into words exactly, even for one with such a refined vocabulary as myself. You understand the nature of the season, do you not?"

"The season?" said Rosemary. "You mean, Halloween and all that?"

Azalea nodded.

"They're doing something spooky, aren't they?" said Rosemary.

"That's right," said Azalea. "My understanding is they're meddling in the kingdom of the dead, which is something that is simply not done!"

Rosemary thought that was a little bit rich coming from a vampire – a kind of magical creature that technically was dead. She decided against raising the point. "That sounds decidedly creepy," she said.

"So you haven't heard of anything?" asked Azalea.

"No," said Rosemary. "Although terrible things have been happening around Myrtlewood. You must have heard."

She filled her in on the details.

"Fascinating!" said Azalea, her eyes practically glowing. "And from a mortal perspective, it has this crispness about it – this freshness! Your impending mortality really makes you more present in this world."

"Err – thanks for that," said Rosemary.

Fleur's car was coming up the driveway.

"You're busy, that's right," said Azalea. "I'll be off." She clapped her hands and disappeared in a puff of black smoke.

"I wish I knew how she did that," Rosemary muttered to herself.

Fifteen

Rosemary watched the street from the window of the chocolate shop. She had set up a camera outside, but she kept checking to ensure that it was working.

"What are you doing, Mum?" Athena asked.

"I'm confirming my theory," said Rosemary. "Look at this."

"All I can see is the street outside," said Athena.

"Exactly. Wait a minute." Rosemary rewound some of the footage from the camera. "Look, people come up, and then they just walk away. It's like they're thinking about coming to my shop, and then they cross the road. There's no bad smell. I've already checked."

Athena shook her head. "It's a bit strange out there, but I don't think your shop is cursed."

"Come on," said Rosemary. "After last night, we know that something odd is going on." Fortunately, Elise recovered fairly quickly once Fleur arrived and sang her a special rainbow nymph

91

healing song. She'd seemed to be her normal self again by the time they'd left.

Rosemary and Athena were both still worried about her behaviour the previous night, not to mention the magical strength she seemed to suddenly possess.

"It's happening again!" said Rosemary. She pointed outside as a couple approached the shop and then seemed to change their minds and walk the other way.

"Maybe you're right," said Athena. "What are you going to do about it? Hey – are you sure it's not just that people are going away because they're worried about you filming them like some kind of creepy stalker?"

Rosemary gently elbowed her daughter. "I'm not a creepy stalker. I'm just a concerned citizen and business owner."

"Sure, sure," said Athena.

Rosemary went back to the counter. "At least the online orders are going alright," she said. "I've got to pack up a few to send out this afternoon."

"Hey, look, you've got customers," said Athena. The door opened, and in walked Hazel, Ursula, and Rowan from the carnival market.

"Oh, hello there, fair customers," said Rosemary.

Athena glared at her mother.

"What? I'm out of practice."

Athena shook her head and introduced her new friends to her mother.

"This place is amazing," said Hazel, bouncing around and looking at the Halloween display in the window and the truffles in the cabinet. "A magical chocolate shop!"

"Delicious!" said Ursula. "And it smells so divine."

"It was weird outside, though," said Rowan. "Even I could feel that."

Rosemary shook her head. "I can't sense it, myself. That's a problem. What did you feel?"

"It's just a creepy sensation," said Hazel. "Like we shouldn't be going in here. But we pushed through it."

Rosemary smiled as Hazel pored over the menu, expressing a desire to eat and drink every single thing available. They ended up ordering hot chocolates and selecting a range of truffles from the cabinets.

Rosemary took the drinks over to the table. She realised that Athena was sitting in the booth with them. "How do you know each other?" she asked Athena.

"These are the people I told you about – from the fair."

"Is Elise okay?" Ursula asked. "We were really worried last night."

"I think she'll be fine," said Rosemary. "But strange things are happening around here." She narrowed her eyes.

"You think it could be something to do with our lot?" Rowan asked.

Rosemary shrugged. "You've been in town for a few days. What are your thoughts?"

"It's so cool here," said Ursula.

"Seriously cool," said Hazel. "We might stick around for a bit. You know, after Samhain the carnival takes a break over winter, anyway. And what better place than a magical village to spend the winter? Maybe we could even find a real house to stay in. Have a proper bath!"

"House truck life is cool and all," said Ursula. "But it's got its limitations."

Athena laughed. "You can come to our house for a bath. We've got a really nice one."

Rosemary frowned, unsure whether they should be inviting people they hardly knew, who talked funny, into their house, especially given the circumstances. But to say so would be quite rude, especially when they were the only customers she'd had almost all day.

She went back to the kitchen to put on a new batch of pumpkin ganache for the big order she'd just received from Glastonbury, but she kept an eye on the Travellers.

They seemed to be getting along well with Athena, and Rosemary didn't have anything in particular against them. She just wasn't sure whether it was wise to trust new people at this point.

After they'd left, Athena came into the kitchen. "Mum, what's going on? You seem off."

"I'm just not sure we should trust them," she said.

"Why on earth not? You know I've got a very good instinct for people ninety-nine percent of the time. I think they're fine. They're friends."

"I'm not sure about how easily you make friends these days," said Rosemary. "And inviting them over to the house?"

"It's just for a bath."

Rosemary wrinkled her nose. "That is a strange thing to invite people over for, I must say."

Athena looked shocked. "How would you feel if you'd been living in a house truck for months?"

"Fair point," said Rosemary. "But what if they're connected to this whole situation we're in with Herb? What if they were the ones who made Elise do that thing?"

"I don't think so," said Athena, shaking her head. "I have a good feeling about them. And you should see Ursula's magic. It's amazing. She can make things grow."

"What kind of things?" asked Rosemary.

"Plants, just instantly," said Athena.

"I've done something like that."

"Sure," Athena rolled her eyes. "When you were harnessing the energy of spring. This is getting into winter and what she does...well, it's different. Anyway, It's not a competition."

"Fair enough," said Rosemary. "But I do think we should be cautious, not just with new people, but in general."

"You're probably right," said Athena. "But I'm still going to trust my instincts."

Sixteen

"Strange that it's only been a few days," said Athena as she walked into Rosemary's room, adjusting the sleeves on her black dress.

It was the morning of Herb's funeral.

Rosemary looked out the window. The sky was crisp and clear outside. "Feels like a lot longer doesn't it?"

Marjie had been quiet for days, barely eating. She had stopped going into her shop, which had stayed closed. Instead of watching her there, the roster had pivoted and friends had taken turns to look after her at Thorn Manor so that Rosemary and Athena could carry on functioning.

They helped Marjie to dress and escorted her to the town hall where the service was to be held.

Myrtlewood felt rather sombre as they walked Marjie silently along the street.

"Without the tea shop being open, it doesn't feel quite right, does it?" said Athena.

Rosemary shook her head. "It's hard to imagine anything ever going back to normal."

The town hall was packed. The whole town had shown up, including all their friends and other unexpected attendees. Crystal Cassandra sat in the second row, weeping dramatically, and even Gallium was there. Marjie greeted him as if he was an old family friend. "Herb would have been so happy you could make it."

Rosemary and Athena sat in the front row on either side of Marjie, who had grown very pale as the service neared.

Ferg stood at the front of the room, prepared to officiate the ceremony, although he was wearing official mayoral robes in purple and gold that made him look rather like he was trying to be an archbishop of something, and it was a little distracting.

Ferg began to speak in a droning voice. "We gather here, on this sad day, to pay tribute to our friend, Herbert..." Rosemary tuned him out, paying close attention to Marjie, who'd begun to tremble.

Several people stood up to speak, all commenting on Herb in the same way. Rosemary found it odd. At previous funerals she'd attended of former co-workers and family friends, she'd learned a lot of surprising details about them, but everyone seemed to have exactly the same experience of Herb. They all said he was quiet, loved his trains, and was a supportive husband.

Rosemary was almost suspicious, but then again, she reassured herself that she'd been rather suspicious of everything lately.

She brushed her concerns away and gave Marjie's arm a little squeeze.

Just then, the older woman pushed herself up from her seat. "I must speak," she said.

Herb's friend from the model train club fell silent as Marjie continued to stand.

Rosemary helped her towards the podium.

All was silent for a moment, then Marjie spoke in a faraway voice. "I must confess," she said. "I was the one who did it. I killed my husband. I killed Herb."

Rosemary felt as if ice had frozen through her veins.

She looked at Athena, whose eyes were wide in shock.

Rosemary shook her head. "No. You don't mean that." She looked out to the audience. "She's going through a hard time, she doesn't mean it."

"I do mean it," said Marjie. "I killed him."

"I thought as much," said Ferg, with a resigned sigh. "I suppose we'll have to cut the service short."

"No," said Rosemary. "We'll deal with it later. At least let Marjie stay at her own husband's funeral."

Ferg shrugged. "Very well. The police can question her afterwards."

Rosemary was in disbelief. There wasn't much more to say at the service, apparently. And so they followed the casket in procession down the streets of Myrtlewood and across to the old town cemetery on the hill nearby.

The previous silence quickly became murmurings of gossip behind them.

"You can't possibly mean that, Marjie," said Athena. "Just tell me what happened." But Marjie had fallen silent again.

As they entered the cemetery, Rosemary got a strong sense that they shouldn't be there, but surely that was just the creepiness of all the old gravestones. She looked across the grounds to see an enormous old gnarled yew tree which certainly added to the spookiness.

Marjie remained silent and Rosemary and Athena shot each other worried glances.

Marjie burst into tears as Herb's coffin was lowered into the earth.

Rosemary rubbed her back. She was clearly grieving. None of this made any sense. Why on earth would she kill her husband?

After the burial, they accompanied Marjie back into town – to the police station as Marjie requested.

"It was my fault. I killed him," she said over and over.

"Must be a trick," said Rosemary as Detective Neve led Marjie away to be questioned. "Somebody's put a spell on her to confess. She can't have really done it."

Athena shrugged. "It's so strange. Maybe you're right. Something spooky is happening around Myrtlewood."

"Marjie is not a murderer," said Rosemary. "She can't possibly be."

"I agree with you," said Athena. "We'll just have to figure out how to prove that."

They stood outside the police station, looking at the deserted streets. Rosemary pulled her daughter into a big long hug before they made their way back to Thorn Manor.

They opened the door to find music playing – a sort of 1920s dancing number.

"Hello!" Rosemary called out. "You didn't leave that on, did you?" she asked Athena.

"It wasn't me."

They wandered in towards the parlour where the old gramophone was playing.

"Poltergeist?" Athena suggested.

"Maybe Thorn Manor is just trying to cheer itself up," said Rosemary.

"That's the spirit," said a familiar voice.

That was when Rosemary noticed the faint form next to the gramophone. "Granny?"

"A hah! You *can* see me. I knew it!" Granny Thorn said, moving closer.

"Not as clearly as when you've been in the mirror," said Athena.

"Or in the reflection in the door," said Rosemary.

"But we can sort of see you."

"Oh, good. This is a brilliant time of year!" Granny Thorn crowed.

Rosemary felt frustration and relief and excitement all at once. "Granny, you must know – something awful has happened."

"Oh, yes," said Granny, unperturbed. "Do go on with your mortal gossip."

"It's not gossip," said Athena. "Herb's been murdered."

"And Marjie has confessed," Rosemary added.

Granny chuckled. "I was wondering when she was going to get sick of that man with his ridiculous trains. Enough to drive anyone to a little light homicide, don't you think?"

Rosemary gave her grandmother an unimpressed look.

"Granny Thorn," said Athena, "I know that in the spirit world, they don't care about that sort of thing like they do here. But please have a little sensitivity. We just went to the funeral. And Marjie is not herself."

"She got up there in front of everyone and started telling us how she killed her husband," said Rosemary.

"Hah! Foolish of her," said Granny. "I would have buried the body, and nobody would have ever found it."

Rosemary raised her eyebrow. "What did happen to your husband?"

Granny Thorn laughed. "Husband? Don't be ridiculous. Anyway, I'm here on important business. There's the family reunion coming up?"

"Oh no, not you too."

"'tis the season," said Granny Thorn exuberantly. "So stop moping about and get planning. We need thousands of candles at our plot. I want more than the Flarguans. At least double."

Rosemary couldn't help it – her mouth twitched in a smile before she reined it in.

"It sounds like some kind of competition," said Athena.

"You bet your britches!" said Granny. "On All Hallows' Eve, we reunite with our families, present and past, and those Flarguans always try to get the jump on me. I won't have it."

"I'm pretty sure Beryl's parents are locked up," said Athena. "I doubt they'll be much of a threat this year."

"Even still," said Granny Thorn, "this is important."

"I understand it's important to you," said Rosemary, "and I'll see what I can do, but we really do have more pressing matters to figure out. I think I'm being cursed, for one, and Marjie probably was too."

"Oh, nonsense," said Granny Thorn. "Everyone always thinks they're cursed, and it always ends up being something else."

"Okay, Granny," said Rosemary. "If you're so sure, maybe you can prove me wrong and do some investigating. Can't you tell that kind of thing from the spirit world?"

"I could take a little look, I suppose," said Granny. "But only if you get straight to ordering the thousands of candles."

"Oh, very well," Rosemary said, folding her arms. "It's nice to see you, by the way. I wish I could give you a hug."

"Come All Hallows' Eve you shall!" said Granny. With that, she disappeared, leaving the room slightly hazy and sparkly for a moment.

The gramophone switched off.

"That was unexpected," said Athena. "Though maybe it shouldn't be at this time of year. She really wants us to organise some sort of reunion."

"It's just like Burk's family," said Rosemary. "It's an obsession! Who wants to spend time with their extended family anyway?" Rosemary shook her head.

Athena shrugged. "Some people might like their families."

"Maybe I'll like my dead family more than some of my living

relatives. Why doesn't she ask Elamina to do this? She'd be into all the pomp and ceremony, surely."

"Yes, but Granny doesn't like Elamina, remember? We should invite her anyway," Athena said.

"Why is that?"

"I don't know, it just seems rude not to," Athena replied. "How about you leave the organising to me?"

"Alright," Rosemary said, putting on the kettle for tea. "But if you make me have a stilted conversation with my cousins, you're fired."

Athena smiled. "I make no such promises."

Seventeen

ater that very same day, Rosemary returned to the police station, leaving Athena busy ordering candles for Granny's planned reunion, which they no doubt would be expected to attend.

Neve had phoned her after questioning Marjie, to let her know she could come down to visit, but that Marjie was going to be held there until further notice.

It was upsetting news.

Rosemary was sure, beyond a doubt, that Marjie was innocent. The police station wasn't the most comfortable or inviting atmosphere for somebody clearly deep in grief and shock, and who probably had her mind meddled with by some sort of sinister magic, at least as far as Rosemary's suspicions went.

Constable Perkins begrudgingly led Rosemary to an examination room where Marjie slumped listlessly on a wooden chair. Her floral dress was unnervingly bright in the dull room.

"Marjie," Rosemary said softly. "I'm here. It's me."

Marjie looked up at her. "Oh, there you are, dear," she said. "Sorry. I've made such a mess of things."

"Oh, no," said Rosemary. "It's okay."

She crouched down and hugged her friend and then took a seat on the opposite side of the table, clasping Marjie's hands in hers.

"I'm sure you're innocent," Rosemary said.

Marjie shook her head. "That's the thing. I'm not innocent at all."

"Well, then I'm sure you..." Rosemary knew she was clutching at straws.

Marjie's cheeks hollowed as her jaw dropped. She looked grim.

"Tell me what happened," said Rosemary. "Just tell me everything you remember."

"You know, it's funny," Marjie said. "It was your suggestion that started the whole thing."

"What are you talking about?"

"Oh, no, dear. Don't get me wrong. I'm not blaming you," Marjie said. "It was just...you recall our conversation the other day. Remember when I told you about Grace?"

Rosemary nodded.

"Well, after that, I was thinking about it. And I realised you were right. So I started to gather some things together to make a little shrine, you know, to celebrate my friend's life. And then Herb came home. I started to tell him about Grace and talk to him about my grief. He became quieter than usual...if you can believe that."

"Hard to imagine," said Rosemary.

"Anyway, I was lighting a candle in the little shrine that I'd made that night. Grace's picture was there in the living room, and Herb came in again. He just stood there. And then he started talking...and then all of a sudden he confessed."

"What do you mean?" said Rosemary.

"It was him, you see," Marjie said. "He was the one who killed Grace."

Tingles ran all across Rosemary's skin. "Oh my sweet Bridget. I can't believe it."

"Neither could I. Can you imagine?" said Marjie. "Living with that man for decades. And we'd never talked about Grace. I never talked to anyone except Galdie...But he must have known we were friends. He grew up in Myrtlewood just like me. He was a little older than us, sure. And we didn't get together till later on in our lives. But I just assumed...Anyway, he told me that he was the one who did it. That it was all his fault."

"And?"

"And I saw red."

"Tell me what exactly happened," said Rosemary, starting to understand that maybe Marjie had killed her husband, and maybe she didn't blame her for it at all!

"I don't know," said Marjie, shaking her head. "He just keeled over and there was blood everywhere. But it happened right after. I just...I felt this explosion of rage."

"So you didn't do it on purpose?" asked Rosemary.

"Of course not," said Marjie. "But still...I meant it in that moment. I thought it, and then it happened."

"So, you think it was your magic?" said Rosemary.

"What else could it have been? I've never felt so angry in my life."

"But you didn't say anything before?" Rosemary furrowed her brow.

"I suppose I was in shock about the whole thing. And everything was a blur. One moment, I'd be happy, and the next, I'd remember he died. But it took me a while to piece everything together, like a broken mirror...all these shards of my life."

"That's how trauma works, I think," said Rosemary. "Our minds can become a little unglued. It can be hard to piece things together, especially in any kind of meaningful order."

"Sometimes," said Marjie, looking down at the table, "it would strike me in the night that I'd killed him. And then, at the funeral...I don't know. It's like I kept forgetting and then remembering, and everything else would take over. You know, I'd want everything to go back to normal. And everything would seem normal. And then it wouldn't...it was as if I was underwater."

"It sounds like grief..." said Rosemary.

Marjie nodded. "But who was it for? Herb or Grace?"

"I'd imagine both," said Rosemary gently. "It was a lot for you to find out and to go through all in one night." She squeezed Marjie's hands.

"You still want to be my friend after all that?"

"Of course," said Rosemary. "I'm here for you, no matter what."

She was starting to understand Granny's flippant attitude to murder in a way that made her uncomfortable.

"But even if your magic killed him," said Rosemary, "it's hardly your fault."

Marjie shook her head. "I know you're trying to reassure me, but I know what I've done, and I'm willing to face the consequences."

"You didn't really mean to."

"Didn't I?" Marjie gave her a solemn look.

Rosemary had tears in her eyes before leaving the examination room. But as she did, Detective Neve was standing outside, waiting for her.

"Cup of tea?" she offered.

"Please," said Rosemary. She followed Neve through to the small staff kitchen.

They sipped Irish breakfast tea out of blue police mugs and filled each other in on what they both had heard from questioning Marjie.

"What do you think, then?" asked Rosemary. "It's hardly her fault."

Neve shook her head. "There's a classification: IMR, involuntary magical response. Sometimes these cases get let off if we can prove there's no malicious intent. The problem is that in this case, there clearly was."

"And Marjie had a reason for that," said Rosemary. "Her friend..."

"Yeah, that's part of the problem," said Neve. "That shows she had a motive – that it *was* malicious."

"But you can understand why," said Rosemary, taken aback.

Neve stiffened. "We might understand why very well. But you can't just go around killing someone, even if you've got a really good reason for it. Can you?"

Rosemary shook her head and sighed. "I suppose not. I was so sure that it wasn't her, that she was being set up somehow."

"You thought somebody was framing her?" Neve asked.

"Well, something like that. I was sure someone must be messing with her mind, making her confess, enchanting her somehow. But maybe that's just me making up excuses for my friend."

"It's understandable," said Neve. "We all love Marjie, and she's the last person we'd expect to commit murder."

"That's for sure," Rosemary said. "So, what happens now?"

"We'll hold her here, fill out some paperwork, and then we'll wait for decisions from the higher-ups. Somebody will probably come and examine her. Magical killings like this are relatively uncommon. Usually, people are either very clearly intentionally trying to murder somebody else, or it's a total accident. Whereas this is all kinds of shades of grey. It wouldn't hurt if she had a lawyer."

"Of course, I hadn't even thought of that," said Rosemary. "Maybe I should ask Burk. I don't really know any other lawyers."

"I think Burk's a solicitor by specialisation, you'll find," said Neve. "She might need a different kind of lawyer...someone little bit more combative. Still, it can't hurt to ask. He might know of somebody who could help."

Rosemary nodded. "She really has to stay here?"

"Until further notice," said Detective Neve. "But I'll do what I can to see if she can be released on bail. She seems unlikely to hurt anyone else. Unless...oh, no this isn't the right time to be making jokes."

Rosemary shook her head. "I'm supposed to be the one

putting my foot in my mouth, not you. Alright, I better get going and update Athena on all this. I just feel so bad for Marjie."

Neve nodded. "We all do. But at least she knows she's got support. She's got friends like you. That means a lot. Without that, things would be a lot worse."

It was cold comfort for Rosemary to hear those words, especially as she left the police station and pondered how things seemed like they *were* going to get a lot worse no matter what she did to try to improve the situation.

She texted Burk as she got in her car, and by the time she arrived back at Thorn Manor, he was standing on the doorstep.

Rosemary practically collapsed into his arms; he held her for a moment, and she took comfort in his strong presence. Burk had always been there for her when he could be and had helped her through some tough situations, but she'd never dealt with anything quite like this.

As soon as they got inside, Burk began making tea. They sat on the window seats. Athena came downstairs and Rosemary updated them both on the situation and what Marjie had said. "She's going to need a lawyer."

"I'm happy to volunteer my time," said Burk. "I'm usually a solicitor, but over the decades, I have been a barrister before, and a judge and a Justice of the Peace and a magistrate." "Yeah, yeah, we get it. You're really old," said Athena with a smirk.

"Old and fancy, I'll have you know," said Burk.

Rosemary could tell they were trying to lighten her mood with their banter, but it wasn't exactly working.

"Thanks for volunteering," said Rosemary. "It's good to know you know how to be a barrister. Although, isn't that about coffee?"

"Mum, we've been over this before. It's spelt differently and pronounced differently, too."

Rosemary nodded. "That's right. Anyway, why do I get the feeling that this is only the tip of the iceberg, and this season has a lot more in store for us?"

Athena folded her arms and shivered. "I told you things were gonna get weird. And I don't mean that in a good way or a spiritual way like Granny says that word means."

Burk spent the night at Thorn Manor. Rosemary couldn't sleep, so he just held her, occasionally stroking her hair in the way she liked.

Her mind kept returning to Marjie and the uncomfortable police cell.

She hadn't seen the actual cell, but she was sure it wasn't comfortable. She'd brought in some of Marjie's things, as well as extra blankets and cushions for her, but she knew it was only going to do so much to improve the situation.

That night, Rosemary had a dream of a girl being chased through the woods. Only, this time she was sure the girl in her nightmares was Grace.

Eighteen

Athena checked her phone for what felt like the hundredth time.

No reply.

She had sent Elise messages and even tried to call her, but nothing.

Fleur had assured her that Elise was fine, just tired, but that didn't stop Athena from worrying all weekend.

It certainly didn't help that Elise – who was normally so good at responding to texts so promptly – hadn't sent her any messages at all.

Athena set her phone aside on the kitchen table, hoping that not looking at it would help.

Just then, the doorbell rang.

Rosemary wasn't home, and Athena hesitated before answering it. But then she remembered her invitation. She checked outside and sure enough, her new friends were on the doorstep. She let them in and greeted them warmly.

"We thought we would take you up on that offer of a bath," said Rowan.

"Bath, bath!" Hazel cried. "Thank the Goddess!"

Athena laughed. "It's not normally something I offer to strange people I meet."

"We're not that strange," said Rowan, but then he looked at Ursula, who looked at Hazel, who was spinning around in excitement at the anticipated bathing. "Okay, maybe we are a little strange. But hopefully it's in a good way."

Athena showed them the big bathroom upstairs and put on some tea.

She chatted away to Ursula and Rowan while Hazel was taking the first bath. Athena was pleased to learn that her new friends shared a lot in common with her in terms of important things, like their taste in music and their open-minded attitude to werewolves and other maligned magical creatures.

Hazel emerged looking blissed out, wearing Rosemary's robe. "I hope you don't mind."

Ursula shook her head. "Hazel, I'm pretty sure that's an inappropriate thing – to wear somebody else's robe!"

"But it's so cosy," Hazel whispered.

Athena laughed. "Mum might find it a little bit odd," she admitted.

"I'll go and change," said Hazel apologetically. She came back in her own clothes moments later and sat at the table.

Rowan was outside admiring the garden. They could see him

from the windows looking at the different plants. Ursula excused herself to take a bath.

"How are things going? How's Elise?" Hazel asked. "I suppose you're sick of people asking about your friend."

Athena shrugged. "Like I told Ursula and Rowan, I don't really know what's going on. You saw what happened the other night. She was really...strange. She doesn't usually use magic like that. Her magic is different, more subtle, and it's beautiful. But that – the other night – it was scary."

"It did give me quite a fright," Hazel admitted. "Do you remember what happened leading up to it?"

"Not exactly...oh, that's right. I bought the charm from you, and I was about to put it on Elise, then she flipped out. Her eyes glowed red. I can't even remember the order that it happened. But all of a sudden, she knocked that guy over with her magic and he flew through the air."

Hazel nodded. "There have been times when I wanted to do that to Gallium, but my magic doesn't work like that."

"Like I said, I don't think Elise's should either."

"I have a theory," said Hazel, nibbling on a biscuit. "But you might not like it."

"What is it?" Athena asked.

"I think something otherworldly is going on," said Hazel, looking down at her hands on the table. "I don't normally talk about it, but for a long time, I was trapped...by an evil mage."

"You were?" Athena asked.

Hazel nodded. "He used some kind of dark otherworldly magic. At least that's my theory. He kind of trapped me, so I was frozen in time."

"That sounds awful."

Hazel nodded. "It was, for a long time...until I met my soul-mate." She smiled.

Athena was still puzzled about how the soulmate thing worked when there were three people involved, but she decided it was better not to ask questions.

"Do you think somebody's doing this to Elise?" she asked. "Maybe a mage, like what happened to you?"

Hazel shook her head. "This is different. Very different, but maybe it's a similar power source. That's all I'm saying. I've come across a lot of different kinds of magic. This just has a feeling of belonging to the underworld."

Athena shivered.

She heard the sound of the door opening and turned to see Rosemary entering the kitchen.

"Mum."

"Oh..." Rosemary said. "Hi."

"I'm gonna go and find Rowan," said Hazel, clearly reading the awkwardness in the air, and quickly skipped out of the room.

"I forgot you invited them over," said Rosemary.

"You mean you wish that I didn't?"

Rosemary nodded. "I don't think it's safe to be inviting people you hardly know right into your house."

"They're fine, Mum. They're trying to help," Athena reassured her. She told Rosemary what Hazel had said.

"I don't like it," said Rosemary. "And we can't believe everything they say just because it sounds like they're trying to help."

"Still," said Athena. "We don't have much else to go on at the moment, do we?"

Rosemary shook her head. "Just promise me they won't stay long."

"Okay," said Athena. "But please, let them get cleaned up first."

Rosemary crossed her arms and sighed. "Fine, but I don't like it," she repeated.

Nineteen

R osemary would usually rely on Marjie for advice on what to do about her obviously cursed shop, but this clearly wasn't the time. She'd been putting off doing anything about it, having bigger problems to deal with, but her suspicions told her whatever was happening to the shop was connected to the other spooky things happening around town, so she called Tamsyn.

"Let's meet up on Sunday at your shop," Tamsyn suggested. "I have a spell in mind that might at least help to reveal what's going on, even if it probably won't fix it."

"That's wonderful," said Rosemary. "Thank you!"

"Hmm...the other thing you might want to do is your own energetic clearing," Tamsyn added.

"What do you mean?"

"Well, if someone has targeted your shop like this, it's probably because of some kind of weakness around money – I know you're loaded now, but you've told me before how much you struggled financially for most of your life."

Rosemary frowned into the phone, aware that Tamsyn couldn't see her. "What are you implying? That I have weak money energy?"

"Hey, don't take it personally," said Tamsyn. "It's just something that will be helpful to reflect on. Scarcity affects people, you know. It stays in your mind and body, just like all the self-help gurus say. If you're struggling with feeling powerless about money, even though you have plenty of it, I'd say it's worth doing some processing of old emotions you might be carrying around with you. Make sure all the parts of your brain know that you're safe now and that it's okay to have enough."

Rosemary sighed. "Your words are striking a nerve, so I know they're true. I'll think on it."

To prepare for the spell, Athena and Rosemary gathered together five bunches of sage, a bag of onyx crystals for protection and depth, along with tiger's eye for revealing the truth, lemon balm for clarity, and fennel seeds for energy, just as Tamsyn had instructed.

They met her outside the shop. It was still early enough for Myrtlewood town to be quiet, which was just as well because Rosemary wasn't sure exactly what kind of magic they'd be revealing and she had a feeling it might be nasty.

Tamsyn had brought her own supplies. They spread the

magical herbs and crystals out in front of the shop in the area that Rosemary had identified as affected.

They didn't bother about the inside because nobody seemed to be troubled once they'd gotten through the doors.

"You're right. It feels awful around here," said Tamsyn. "You know, it was only once you mentioned it to me that I realised I was meaning to pop into the shop a couple of times over the last week to see you and maybe get a few truffles. And then I changed my mind, like I had a bad feeling and then I stopped thinking of it."

"It seems to affect everyone except for me and Athena," said Rosemary. "And maybe Marjie, although who knows what's affecting her, at this point."

"Have you gone to see her again?" Tamsyn asked.

"I'm planning to, right after this," said Rosemary.

"Well, let's hope it doesn't take too long," said Tamsyn. She began to create the sacred space and sprinkle the blessed water over the herbs. They sizzled as she did so, creating a pungent odour in the air.

"It's revealing something!" said Tamsyn. "All right. The chant comes next."

They held hands and closed their eyes, then began to speak the ancient Gaelic words of the chant.

Le cumhacht an dáimh, na daoine seancha,
  Leigheas an gcurseach a lámh amháin,
  Go soiléir ar fud an tsaoil,
  Le teacht ar an bhfírinne agus an solas.

. . .

By the magic of the ancient powers
  Let the curse be lifted now
  May the light of truth shine bright
  And banish darkness with its light

As the words echoed around them, Rosemary felt a tightness in her chest.

"Remember what I told you about scarcity," Tamsyn whispered. "This is a good time to let go of old patterns you have around money. You're safe now."

Rosemary's heart thudded like drum.

It was true, so much of her life had been plagued with scarcity. She wouldn't have dreamed of asking her dear old Granny for money, and she'd lived pay check to pay check as a solo mother, in low-wage jobs, just trying to make it through each day and each month, with a few extra cheap treats of crisps and Jaffa Cakes to get them through emotionally.

All those memories and all that emotion was still with her.

She took a deep breath and slowly exhaled, letting go of the powerlessness, sadness, and fear.

We're safe now...we have plenty of money. I have enough.

She heard a sizzling sound and was tempted to peep, then a burning smell overrode the pungent air, followed by the most nauseating, odious scent she'd ever inhaled. It made her want to hurl. In fact, as the spell came to an end, Rosemary had to cover her mouth.

She heard the others coughing.

"It's disgusting!" said Rosemary, opening her eyes to see

clouds of sickly yellow-brown smoke.

"Mum, look!" said Athena, pointing at the outside of the shop. "It's all covered in slime."

Indeed, a greeny-yellow slime now clung to the outside facade of the chocolate shop, which was congealing around the edges, forming into webs in places.

As the air cleared further, the slimy webs all over the shop became more clearly visible, as did grapefruit-sized fluorescent orange spiders with long spindly legs, their bulbous bodies striped with black.

"Eww!" said Athena. "I don't like this. Can we get out of here?"

They all moved to a safe distance across the street.

The spiders themselves didn't seem to be bothering anyone, but the whole situation was disturbing.

Rosemary immediately called Neve, who showed up on the scene within a few minutes.

"You're right," she said to Rosemary. "The shop must have been cursed. Sorry for doubting you."

"Everyone always does," said Rosemary. "I'm used to it."

"What do you think this is? Some kind of prank?" Tamsyn asked.

"I don't think so," said Detective Neve. "Somebody planned this very carefully and disguised it even more carefully. It's like they were trying to subtly sabotage you."

Rosemary frowned. "That makes me dread what else they might have been planning – whoever is behind this. Putting people off my shop is only going to do so much. If they're going to go to this much effort, you'd think they would have done more things just to muck up my business."

"It's affected your mood, though, hasn't it?" said Athena. "But you're right. I bet anyone going to this much effort has got a lot more planned."

"I'll call the clean-up crew," said Neve.

Rosemary nodded and turned back to Tamsyn. "I don't suppose there's anything you can do to trace this?"

Tamsyn scrunched up her face sceptically. "I don't think so," she said. "I can give it a try, but my magic will need to recharge. And besides, anyone who's gone to this much trouble has thought ahead and created diversions so that they won't be easily traced."

"Thanks anyway," said Rosemary. "And thanks for helping, both of you."

"Anytime you want me to reveal you some slime and magic spiders, I'm here for it," said Athena. "Just don't expect me to go anywhere near them."

Rosemary smiled. "It's a deal. Hey, I was going to go and see Marjie after this. Do you want to come?"

"Yes, actually," said Athena. "I want to check how she is, see if there's anything we can do to reassure her."

Rosemary put her arm across her daughter's shoulder, and they walked the short distance to the police station where Marjie was still being detained.

Constable Perkins sneered at them from behind the front desk. "Come to confess a crime?"

"Oh, sod off," said Rosemary.

Athena elbowed her, and she turned her words into an

unconvincing cough.

"What was that, Miss Thorn?" said Perkins.

"We'd like to see Marjie," said Athena. "Are we allowed to visit?"

"Under strict supervision, of course," said Constable Perkins. "If our number one criminal has accomplices, we should know about it."

Rosemary glared at him.

He smiled and then led them through to an examination room, the same one that Rosemary had visited the last time.

A few moments later, Marjie came through the door. Rosemary and Athena both hugged her. It looked as if Marjie had been weeping, and she seemed a lot paler than usual. They helped her over to a seat, then sat down themselves.

"We're still trying to help get you out of here," said Rosemary.

Marjie shook her head. "It's no use, dear. I've told you I'm guilty."

"You might think that," said Rosemary, "but I'm still sure you're not."

"I remember it plain as day," said Marjie.

"What exactly happened?" Athena asked. "When Herb came in to talk to you. Before you knew...what did he actually say?"

Marjie's eyes became distant, as if she was lost in the memory.

"He said, 'I may not have much time – I love you – I can't hold this any longer – It was my fault. I killed Grace'," Marjie replied.

"He said he may not have much time?" Athena asked. "Doesn't that seem odd?"

Rosemary raised an eyebrow.

"Nooooo!" Marjie exclaimed. "I saw red. So much blood."

"It's okay," Rosemary soothed, patting Marjie on the shoulder as she cried. They waited for a moment and then she began to speak again through her sobs.

"He said – it was his fault about Grace. He can't hold it any longer – he killed Grace."

"And then what happened?" Rosemary asked.

Marjie wiped her eyes with a hankie. "I just screamed. Noooo! I tell you – I saw red and then he keeled over."

"Marjie, what do you think it was that you did?" Athena asked.

"I don't know," said Marjie. "But like I told your mother and Neve, I must admit that in my absolute rage and despair, I willed him dead. Maybe that was enough."

Rosemary shook her head. "No. I'm sure if that was enough, Perkins would have died fifty times over by now, along with a long list of people I despise in my weaker moments."

Athena rolled her eyes. "Okay then, Mum. What do you think happened?"

"I don't know," said Rosemary, "but maybe somebody really was trying to set you up. Or they were trying to hurt you to get to me. Somebody really did put a curse outside my shop, Marjie, like I thought."

Marjie shook her head. "You think somebody was waiting there in my living room – and cursed him just at that moment – to make me think that I did it – and then confess?"

"It sounds a little implausible, doesn't it?" said Athena.

"I don't see why," Rosemary said. "Or maybe they killed him

124

and then implanted a memory that made you think that you did it."

Marjie shook her head. "It's really no use. Neve's tried all these angles before, you see."

"What do you mean?" Marjie asked.

"They've examined the house and nobody else was there that night," Marjie said. "Not that I thought there was."

Rosemary slumped forward, defeated.

"Besides," Marjie added. "The examiner checked my memory. Nothing's been tampered with."

"Well, there go my theories," said Rosemary. "But I still don't think you're at fault. I don't think your magic even works like that, Marjie."

Athena shot her a quizzical look.

"Pardon me for saying this, Rosemary," said Marjie. "But what would you know? This world is still fairly new to you."

"It just doesn't make sense," Rosemary insisted.

"Look, you're a dear friend," said Marjie. "And I appreciate all the support. But at some point, you're going to have to let this go."

Rosemary sighed and wiped the tears that were spurting from her eyes. "I'm not going to lose you," she said, "even if you insist that you did this. We'll fight it. Burk will represent you. People will empathise with the situation with Herb. People understand that it's not really your fault."

"Will it be a trial, then?" Athena asked.

Marjie took a deep breath. "Detective Neve tells me that they're just waiting on the final tests to come back from the labs in Glastonbury, and after that, there'll be a trial."

Rosemary shook her head. "I promise you we'll fight this. Don't give up."

"Thank you for your unwavering support, my dears," said Marjie. "And your kindness. Both of you. I love you so very much."

"Love you too, Marjie," Athena said.

"Visiting time is over," Constable Perkin's voice sounded through the room.

Rosemary and Athena looked at each other. They got up and gave Marjie long and warm hugs before saying goodbye.

As they walked out, Athena turned to her mother. "Are you really sure she didn't do it?"

Rosemary nodded. "I don't know why, but something doesn't add up. I know that she's a good person, and I don't believe she has it in her."

Athena bit her lip in thought. "You know what? Despite all the evidence, my instinct is telling me you're right."

Twenty

Athena winced as Elise took a seat furthest away from her, and even Beryl looked confused and alarmed at her despondent demeanour.

It was Monday and Athena had been looking forward to going to school all weekend, mostly to see Elise. However, she was bitterly disappointed. Although Elise was there in body, her mind and spirit seemed almost entirely elsewhere.

The teachers were wary too, concerned to the point where several of them asked Athena if she knew what was wrong.

At lunchtime, Elise was nowhere to be found.

Sam, Felix, Ash, and Deron all wanted to know anything about the situation Athena could tell them.

She went over it several times – how Elise's behaviour had been strange leading up to the fair, but that night, the events were inexplicable.

"Do you think she might be cursed, like your mum's shop?" Sam asked.

Athena had filled them in on those details too. She shrugged. "Maybe...I mean, it could all be orchestrated, couldn't it? This thing with Marjie has really taken a toll on us, especially Mum... and then the shop...and now this. I mean, if somebody did want to plan an attack on us – and we all know who that might be – going after our closest support people would be one hell of a way of doing it. We've probably only survived as long as we have because of our good friends and Myrtlewood."

"They haven't gone after your Mum's boyfriend though," said Ash.

"I'm not sure if even the Bloodstone Society would be brave enough to go after one of the more powerful vampire families in this hemisphere," said Felix. "That sounds like a foolish thing to do, even to me!"

"It does, doesn't it?" Deron replied. "But imagine the adventure!"

The boys grinned at each other.

Athena shook her head. "Anyway, I want to find out what's going on with Elise. I've looked into some spells, but most of them are really complicated...and all of them involve affecting her in some way. I don't think she would fancy having magic dust blown in her face. Besides, I don't want to be thrown across the room if I try...or worse."

Sam grinned.

"What are you smiling about?" asked Ash.

"You fancy witches with all your fancy books," said Sam. "You overcomplicate things. Maybe what you really need is some folk magic."

"Do you have anything in mind?" Athena asked.

"How about a charmed apple?" Sam suggested.

"What?" Ash asked.

"You know, a charmed apple..."

Felix shook his head.

"Nope, never heard of it," said Deron.

"Come on. Surely," said Sam. "Oh, alright, then. A charmed apple is literally what it sounds like. You just get an apple and you enchant it so that it reveals the nature of the person who's eaten it."

"Do you mean like a mood ring?" said Felix. "We've already got Elise's hair here for that."

Ash sighed. "Speaking of Elise's hair, did you notice that it's turned almost grey-blue?"

"Yes. We noticed that," said Sam flatly.

"It was black the other night," said Athena.

"You didn't tell us that," said Felix. There was an accusatory note in his voice. Athena knew he was protective of Elise. They'd been friends for a long time.

"Sorry," said Athena. "I'm sure I've missed some of the details. It was a pretty weird night."

"Why didn't you invite us to come with you to the fair?" Felix asked, narrowing his eyes.

Ash elbowed him. "Felix, it was a date. We don't get to go on other people's dates."

Felix rolled his eyes. "But if we had been there..."

Athena shrugged. "I'm not sure it would have made much difference, to be honest."

"That's true," said Sam. "But like I was saying, I think a charmed apple might do the trick."

"So it will reveal if she's been cursed?" Athena asked. "And it's perfectly safe?"

"Yes," Sam replied. "The darker red it goes, the worse the curse. It's a fairly blunt instrument, but at least you have an idea of what you're getting yourself into."

"So, it will definitely go red?" Ash asked.

"If she's been cursed, it will," said Sam. "But it can also reveal other things, like if it's just a virus, or some other magical reason...depending on the colour. There's a rhyme that goes with it to remind everyone what each colour means – Red is a curse, seek aid and be well..."

"It's definitely worth a try," said Athena. "So you'll bring the apple, we give it to Elise and...hope she bites into it?"

"That's the idea," said Sam.

"Alright then," said Athena, looking around at her friends, who all nodded.

"We're counting on you," Felix said to Sam, who blushed slightly.

"I'll...see what I can do."

Twenty-One

I t was early. Rosemary groaned. There was a noise. It was far too early for a noise.

She gradually realised that the noise was her phone.

"This better be good," she grumbled, reaching for the cursed item on the nightstand as it vibrated. "Hello?"

"Rosemary," said a familiar voice.

"Neve? What is it?" Rosemary asked, suddenly wide awake and chilled with anxiety. "Has something happened?"

"You might say that," said Neve. "The test results came back."

"What test results? Is the baby okay?"

"The baby's fine," said Neve. "Thanks for asking. Surprisingly, it's all going perfectly normal."

"What test results? Is that a health problem? Are you okay?"

"Rosemary," said Neve. "I'm trying to explain."

"Oh sorry," said Rosemary. "Carry on."

"You remember we took some special tests because of Herb's death, and the circumstances?"

Rosemary sighed. "Of course. Marjie said you were waiting on the results for those before you went to trial."

"Well, here's the thing," said Neve. "The results came back with some unexpected findings."

"What do you mean?" asked Rosemary. "Can they prove it was Marjie?"

"Not exactly," said Neve. "In fact, this might be a chance to prove it wasn't."

"Really?" asked Rosemary, scrambling out of bed.

"Well, according to the magical lab, the reason that it took so long to identify the power involved is that it's very old magic."

"Oh," said Rosemary. "Sounds ominous."

"Yes," said Neve.

"You don't think it's likely that Marjie could have drawn on some old kind of magic by accident?"

"Perkins seems to think so, but I'm not convinced. It seems very unlikely that she'd do something like that accidentally," said Neve. "This is complex stuff, the kind of thing you read about in the history books."

"So you're saying we can prove she didn't do it?" said Rosemary.

"Well..." Neve hesitated. "Others might read something different, and maybe they'll think it's premeditated, which is even worse!"

"Oh, no," said Rosemary. "We can't have that."

"Exactly," said Neve. "You must understand that I don't trust Perkins with this."

"Good call," said Rosemary. "Can I help?"

"I don't want to trouble you," said Neve. "But I was thinking we could go round to Marjie's house and see if we could find any other clues. You know?"

Rosemary frowned, not particularly wanting to go back to the site of that horrible incident. "I thought they scanned the house."

"They did a general scan," said Neve. "But they were looking for traces of magic. Maybe there's something else we can find that will point us in the direction of whoever's responsible. It might not even be magical, just some other kind of evidence."

"Looking for clues!" said Rosemary, trying to dress herself, frantically and one-handed, while she continued to talk on the phone. She might not relish the idea of returning to Marjie's cottage, but the thought of being useful was like a lightning boost of energy. "I'm in!"

"Okay," said Neve. "How about I meet you outside Marjie's house at 9:30. I've got a couple of things to clear up here first."

"Good call," said Rosemary. "I'll send Athena off to school and come to meet you."

"Great. Oh, your shop is all clear, by the way. You can open up today."

"Thanks so much," said Rosemary. "I'll let Papa Jack know. It's his turn to open. I don't much like working Mondays."

"I like your style, Rosemary Thorn," said Neve. "I'll see you soon."

Rosemary hung up the phone, her heart full of hope for the first time in weeks.

It was old magic, not some sort of accidental murder. Surely Marjie was innocent.

The cogs in Rosemary's mind carried on churning as she continued to dress and washed her face. Given what Athena had told her about Elise and what they knew about the shop, she wouldn't be surprised if the same people were behind it all. She just hoped that the rumours about the Bloodstone Society growing in power and meddling in dark magic weren't as ominous as they sounded.

She made her way downstairs, dressed in whatever clean clothes she could find.

"Mum! What are you wearing?"

Rosemary looked down at her outfit. "What? You don't think orange and pink stripes go together?"

"No," said Athena. "Especially not when it's orange-and-black stripes and pink-and-white stripes at the same time. It's really not a good look for you."

"Well, I have more important things to think about this morning," said Rosemary. "My coat will cover most of this."

Over tea and toast, she filled Athena in on her phone call with Neve.

"That's promising," said Athena when Rosemary mentioned the old magic in the test results. "When she said 'old magic', does that mean that it happened a long time ago?"

"I don't know," said Rosemary. "I got the impression that she meant old magic as in drawing on the ancient magic, like the sort of thing Elamina talks about?"

Athena raised an eyebrow. "You're not going to start getting suspicious of our cousins again, are you?"

"Maybe not," said Rosemary. "I just can't think why Elamina would meddle in something like this. I mean, I'm sure she'd love to embarrass and undermine me, but this seems beneath her. Besides, I think she's got plenty of other stuff to deal with, given she's now got a new post with the Arch Magistrate's lot, taking her parents' seat in the Witching Parliament. What interest would she have in Myrtlewood?"

"That's a good point," said Athena. "And I'm glad you're no longer super paranoid. It shows you've grown as a person."

"Thank you," said Rosemary, although her mouth puckered up as if she'd eaten a lemon. "That's some backhanded compliment."

Athena smiled. "I wouldn't want you to get too big for your boots," she said, taking a bite of toast. "I wish I could come with you to Marjie's house."

"It might be a bit gross and morbid. And maybe dangerous," said Rosemary.

Athena shrugged. "Sounds like my kind of thing. As long as there's not goo and spiders."

"Who knows?" Rosemary shrugged. "They should probably check for that, although it would be a surprise if they didn't pick all that up with their magical scan earlier. But anyway, you've got Elise to think about."

"That's right!" said Athena. "Today we're going to find out if she's cursed."

Rosemary sighed. "Great. That also sounds morbid and dangerous. So we'll both have our hands full. But make sure you call me if anything weird happens. And are you sure you don't want me to escort you to school?"

"Don't be silly, Mum. I'm going to be fine. I'm a powerful fae princess witch, remember?" Rosemary chuckled and finished off her tea. "Alright, take care, and I'll see you later."

Marjie's house was looking worse for wear. Rosemary parked on the side of the road, waiting for Neve to arrive. She didn't want to go in alone. It was too creepy.

Cracks in the whitewash were evident, and there was mildew that Rosemary was sure was not as pronounced just a week or two ago.

She spotted the detective's car pulling up behind her and got out to greet Neve.

"Hey, ready?" said Neve.

"As I'll ever be," said Rosemary.

They made their way down the path to the backdoor entrance of Marjie's cottage.

Neve fished a key out of her pocket. As she reached up to unlock the door, Rosemary almost wanted to stop her.

What if it was too dangerous? They had no idea what kind of things might be lurking in there. The door swung open.

It felt almost like the house was still inhabited.

Marjie should have been there, offering pots of tea all around.

They walked in slowly and quietly, tentatively watching for signs of danger.

The whole place was spotless.

"I guess your clean-up crew does a good job," said Rosemary. "No blood splatter in sight."

They looked around the main areas and nothing seemed to be out of place.

"I'll check the bedroom," said Neve.

Rosemary wandered up to the mantelpiece, recognising the little shrine Marjie had told her about. There was the photo. The girl looked familiar, with long brown hair and pale skin.

"Grace," she said and heard a sound outside.

Rosemary looked out the window, but there was nothing out of the ordinary. *Perhaps it's just a mouse or a fox or a rabbit, making that sound,* she reassured herself.

Rosemary looked back at the shrine. She took the photo of Grace and slipped it into her pocket.

There were candles and crystals and incense set there. She could imagine Marjie there, lighting the candles and thinking of her friend...and then Herb approaching from behind and confessing to the crime.

All of the anguish and rage that Marjie felt in that moment.

And Herb, what would he have felt? Rosemary didn't even want to think about it. Then again, Herb was always a strange character. So quiet.

He'd never said a thing about Grace.

He'd been hiding it all these years.

Something told her that even in death, Herb still had something to hide.

While Neve continued to rummage through the bedroom, Rosemary decided to go to the one space that Marjie never went: Herb's train shed.

If Herb was hiding anything from Marjie, surely that was where he would keep it.

Rosemary couldn't help the feeling of being watched as she made her way cautiously out to the shed, but she pushed through her fear.

There was an equally likely – or perhaps more likely – chance that it was just her imagination wigging her out, than actually being watched by any kind of sinister being.

To her surprise, the door to the shed was ajar.

Perhaps the police left it that way...or maybe they never even bothered to investigate out here and Herb might have left it unlocked that evening before he died...

It was a scary thought. And it felt emotionally uncomfortable, walking into a space that clearly belonged to him when he was no longer of this world.

The way that the shed was set out made sense intuitively to Rosemary.

There was a big table in the middle covered with different model trains, their tracks, and little pathways for them to go under and over, complete with fake grass and a village that looked slightly like Myrtlewood.

It was intricate and quite beautiful in its way. Rosemary wished she was seeing it in better circumstances. She liked miniature things, but this was a rather haunting scene.

There were shelves on both sides of the shed and a little desk at the other end in front of the window.

The shelves contained all kinds of boxes that Rosemary began rummaging through, finding spare parts for the model trains, batteries, and tiny little trees, old bills and brochures from various model train conventions.

It was all so simple and mundane.

It made her wonder what really happened the night Grace disappeared. Herb's confession to Marjie had been vague and it was hard to imagine this gentle, stoic character as a violent murderer. Had he deliberately gone after Grace and killed her? Or had it been an accident? Was he under some kind of compulsion, just as Rosemary had suspected that Marjie was. It seemed out of character, or was she just trying to make excuses?

Rosemary approached the table, taking a closer look at the trains and the village.

A maroon red carriage sat in the centre, but there was something odd about it.

Upon closer inspection, Rosemary was sure she could see paper inside it, unlike the other trains with their perfect seats and passengers...

She picked it up, finding it easy to open, as the top of the carriage came away in her hands. It was a note addressed to Marjie.

Rosemary sat down at the desk and began to read Herb's small and neat handwriting.

My dearest Marjoram,

If you've found this, it means that I'm gone – because you never come in here – and I can't tell you this until after I've gone. The only reason I'm daring to write this at all is because I know the magic binding me is old, older even than the written word. They warned me not to write it down in case someone reads it, but I can't bear to leave you without any explanation. I owe you this much, and so much more.

I've been holding this secret for so long, holding myself back from speaking, remaining silent, even though it almost killed me at times to do so...

As Rosemary read on she began to cry. It was a heartfelt confession. Herb clearly loved Marjie very much, and yet he was confessing to killing her childhood best friend.

The reason became clear as she continued reading.

Herb's mother had been dying, and the only way he knew of to help her was to take a blood oath to a certain secret society that was only too familiar to Rosemary. He didn't name it, but she was sure from the way he described it in his letter that it was the Bloodstone Society.

After taking the oath, his first task had been the very worst thing he could imagine: the worst thing he'd done in his entire life. He had to lure or chase a girl to the forbidden cave where she would be sacrificed.

Herb had only been seventeen years old, and the girl had already been pre-selected. He had no choice in the matter. The blood oath compelled him to do it, otherwise his life and all his family's lives were forfeit.

He didn't know Grace well; they'd been at school together but in different years.

It was a demon's bargain, and he'd hoped that the gods and goddesses would take pity on her, and that the girl would survive.

Years later, when he met Marjie, he hadn't realised at first that she'd been the best friend of Grace.

He'd figured it out over the years. He'd always loved Marjie. He'd always tried to protect her, but he'd also been a card-carrying, blood-oath-swearing member of the Bloodstone Society all that time.

He confessed that many of the model train conventions he'd gone to were actually Bloodstone Society gatherings.

He'd done some terrible things, or at least participated in them, although he'd always kept very quiet and pretended to be rather stupid, so that they didn't ask too much of him. And that had paid off. He'd been able to avoid the worst of their requests with strategic incompetence.

Rosemary could imagine him standing there in a hood when the Bloodstone Society was attacking Thorn Manor, not long after she was first in Myrtlewood. Perhaps he was even up on that hill at the Summer Solstice Festival, one of the robed men who got away...and there it was, staring her square in the face.

"I couldn't tell you because the blood oath forbade me," it said in the note.

That was what killed Herb! Old magic in more ways than one. A blood pact, Rosemary understood, was a kind of magic that dated back many thousands of years, and Herb had taken the oath when he was a mere teenager, decades earlier.

No wonder there was no trace of the culprit in the house.

Herb, himself, was the one who had chosen to take that oath, even if it didn't feel like a choice at the time.

Not only that, but as the note revealed, there were thousands of others like him, bound to the Bloodstone Society through a demon's bargain.

It was no surprise to Rosemary that the same society who had murdered her own grandmother also preyed on the young, especially teenagers, before their brains had fully developed, getting them to tie themselves into their dangerous magical cult for life.

"How awful," Rosemary muttered. There was a sound behind her and she jumped.

"Only me," said Neve, coming in. "Did you find anything?"

"Yes," said Rosemary. "What about you?"

"There's nothing to speak of in the house. The cupboards are full of Marjie's old business adventures, like the recycled toilet paper scheme and the pot painting shop supplies. What's that?" Neve asked, pointing to the note.

"A full confession from the murderer," said Rosemary.

"What?" Neve's jaw dropped as she read the note. "So, it was Herb who killed...Herb."

"But not in the way you'd expect," said Rosemary.

"Let's not get into that right now," said Neve. "It's making my brain hurt."

"This should be enough to let Marjie off the charges, I hope," said Rosemary.

"It certainly should be," said Neve. "I'll file the paperwork *before* I let Perkins know."

"Can I come?" said Rosemary. "When you tell him? I want to see his expression! It would make my day."

Neve rolled her eyes and chuckled. "You really are incorrigible sometimes."

"Hey, life is all about enjoying the small pleasures, like the suffering of one's enemies."

They made their way back out to their cars.

Neve sighed. "It's strange, you know. This is good news, in theory."

"But it doesn't feel that way, does it?" said Rosemary. "I mean, good that Marjie is off the hook...but what about all those others? The Bloodstones have been conscripting an army this whole time, secretly...Young people who have no other options – or think that they don't – sign up for the promise of power or salvation and then they're trapped for life..." Rosemary had another thought. "Oh no!"

"What is it?" said Neve.

"Athena thinks that Elise is cursed. She's got strange powers."

"You don't think?"

"I don't know," said Rosemary. "But I better call Athena."

"Alright," said Neve. "I'll take the letter in to the station."

"Wait a minute," said Rosemary. "Before you do that, let me take some photos."

"You don't trust me?" said Neve.

"It's not you," said Rosemary. "It just that it seems like too much of a vulnerability. Marjie's life – her fate – could lie in this one fragile piece of paper."

"Fair enough," said Neve. "I'll do the same."

Rosemary sat in her car and called Athena. There was no answer, but Athena texted back:

. . .

In class but don't worry, everything is fine.

I'm worried, Rosemary replied, and then proceeded to type out a message explaining the key points of what she'd just learned.

We've got this, Athena replied.

Twenty-Two

Athena cupped the smooth green-and-red apple in the palms of her hands.

As promised, Sam had prepared the charmed apple. They'd handed it to Athena before school.

It seemed like a perfectly ordinary apple in almost every way, apart from how unusually light it felt.

It was morning break by the time she had the chance to offer it to Elise.

"You're not eating," said Athena, approaching Elise, who was sitting alone in the courtyard.

"I forgot to bring my food," said Elise, her tone flat.

Athena was sure that was a lie. Fleur always made sure Elise's lunchbox was full.

"Here," said Athena. "This is for you."

She held up the apple, feeling a little bit like the wicked stepmother in Snow White. "You should eat something."

For a moment she was worried that Elise would get suspicious or just not take any interest in the apple at all. But, to Athena's relief, Elise absentmindedly held the apple up to her mouth and bit into it with a crunch.

Elise stood up, chewing thoughtfully. "Tastes funny," she said and wandered away, dropping the apple into the rubbish bin.

Athena followed after Elise so as to make sure she didn't see anything suspicious. Sam – who'd been keeping an eye on them – was rifling through the trash.

Elise was not particularly good conversation, and after a moment Athena gave up and returned to the friend group who were sitting in their usual spot.

Her friends' expressions were all grim.

"Is it red?" Athena asked Sam. "Come on, tell me how bad is it?"

She had expected the apple bite to have turned a shocking blood red and was alarmed when Sam held it up in their palm.

"Blue!" said Athena. "What does blue mean?"

"Sam's trying to remember," said Felix.

"Remember?" Athena said. "Can't you just look it up online?"

Sam shook their head. "It's not like that. This is serious folk magic."

"So of course there's a nursery rhyme," said Deron.

"I think I've got it," said Sam, and began to recite:

A charmed apple, the truth shall reveal,
Beware, a secret it shall unseal.

This fruit, a window to the soul,
Its magic, knowledge shall unfold.

Red, a curse, beware its spell,
Green is from illness, rest and be well.
Yellow, a plague of emotions to rise,
Blue is possession, seek aid, be wise.

"Possession...Yes, of course," said Sam.

"Elise is possessed?" said Athena, "Oh my Goddess. That's not what I thought at all."

"You thought she was cursed," said Ash.

"Or that she'd taken some kind of blood oath..." said Athena. "That's not related to possession, is it?"

"A blood oath? Sounds cool!" said Felix.

"It is very decidedly not cool," said Athena. "If anyone ever asks you, do not take a blood oath! Not even if they offer you something amazing."

She explained what Rosemary had told her.

"That sounds awful," said Ash. "All those teenagers trapped into some kind of cult they can't break away from."

"Yeah, that's right," said Athena. "Although, now that I think of it, I do know somebody who left the Bloodstone Society." She quickly texted Rosemary.

Her response came a moment later: *I had exactly the same thought...Great minds!*

Athena turned back to her friends. "So, Elise is possessed?"

"Well, you learn something new every day," said Felix darkly.

"Possessed by what?" Deron asked. "It is a ghostly time of year..."

"I thought you were possessed," said Sam. "Isn't that what Elise said, when we were at the ghost house? That Felix might be possessed..."

"Do you think that could have been when it started?" said Ash in a hushed whisper.

Athena thought back to that day. "That might be the case... That was when Elise first started acting strange, and then she's been kind of in-and-out of being herself ever since. In one minute, she'll be staring off into space, the next minute, she'd be back to being her normal, cheerful self again."

"Could it be part of the blood oath?" said Deron. "You know, like maybe that was the sacrifice she had to make to get power."

"Why would she want power, though?" asked Ash.

Felix laughed. "I can't believe you're asking that question. It shows how different we are!" He folded his arms. "Of course Elise wants power. Her girlfriend's probably the most powerful fae witch in the world. Imagine comparing yourself to that all the time."

Athena sighed. "She has been doing her tarot readings a lot lately. And talking about how she'll never be as powerful as me... maybe it's all part of it. But I don't think she'd ever do that. Take a blood oath."

Sam shook their head. "I don't think so either. I'm pretty sure whatever is affecting Elise is not something that she's chosen."

Twenty-Three

"You can pick her up this afternoon; the paperwork's all through."

Rosemary felt the tension leave her shoulders at the news from Neve's phone call. "Thank you so much."

Rosemary arrived at the police station ten minutes later to find Perkins looking disgruntled. "She's still a suspect, you know," he said. "A threat to society."

"*You* are." Rosemary scowled at him.

A few moments later, Marjie emerged into the waiting room where Rosemary was sitting impatiently.

Marjie looked tired, pale, and somewhat bewildered.

"Oh, Marjie," said Rosemary, giving her friend a big hug. "I'm so sorry you had to go through all this."

"It wasn't me," said Marjie, baffled.

"No, I knew it wasn't."

149

Marjie smiled weakly. "You always believed in me...even when I didn't believe in myself. I just don't know how..."

"We'll talk about it when we get home," said Rosemary.

They arrived back at Thorn Manor to find Athena making tea in the kitchen.

"It's a bit early for school to be out, isn't it?" Rosemary asked.

"I wasn't feeling too good. Something went down with Elise."

Athena explained the situation with the charmed apple.

"Possessed? That sounds bad," said Rosemary.

Marjie shook her head and tutted. "Trouble is brewing."

"You can say that again," said Rosemary.

They sat on the window seats, sipping tea in silence.

"I'm so sorry about your friend," said Athena after a while.

"Grace," said Marjie. "You know what? It's actually good to talk about her. But tell me. Do you know what really happened? What happened to Herb?"

Rosemary shook her head. "Neve didn't explain the full story to you?"

"She didn't say much at all," said Marjie. "I'm ready to hear it, though. As much anger as I've felt at Herb recently, it's almost made worse by the grief. We shared a life together, you see. So many little things keep reminding me of him. When they brought me breakfast in that awful cell, I'd think of the way he'd always burn the edges of the toast and cut them off before he brought breakfast to the table. I'd do a crossword to keep entertained and I'd almost see the kind of notes he'd leave me in the margins if he'd worked out the word. It's been so awful – I just hating him so much, but also, he was my companion and losing him is like a part of me is missing too. I need to know what happened, Rosemary."

Rosemary nodded. "I'll never completely understand it. But I do have this letter." She pulled out her phone. "Are you ready for this?"

"As I'll ever be," said Marjie.

Rosemary read the letter out loud, pausing every now and then to check her friend's expressions as they changed from curiosity to anguish.

"Keep going, dear." Marjie was looking so distraught that Rosemary almost didn't want to continue, but she was urged on by the older woman. "I need to know the truth."

After Rosemary had finished reading it out, they sat in silence again.

"He loved me," said Marjie.

Athena nodded.

Marjie sobbed. "I always knew that, you know, and I always felt he was holding something back. I used to heckle him about it when we were younger, just like I heckled him about his trains. That maybe they were the only coping mechanism he had, the only escape..." Her fist was gripped so tightly around her teacup that her knuckles were white. "I can't believe he did that," said Marjie, unleashing a torrent of curse words, the likes of which Rosemary had never heard before.

"It's understandable to be angry," said Athena, looking impressed.

"Of course, I'm angry!" said Marjie. "I'm angry at him for

everything, for what he did to Grace, for what he did to himself, and the lie that he lived – that he made me live with him – for so long. How dare he?"

Athena shook her head. "The whole situation is horrible. And you have a right to be angry."

Rosemary agreed.

Marjie burst into tears.

"You have a right to do that, too," said Rosemary. "And don't you dare apologise."

Margie wiped her eyes. "It's just all a bit much."

"It is," said Athena. "It totally is. We would understand if you want to keep cursing Herb's name over and over. We can even make a dummy of him if you want to punch something."

Marjie's face crinkled into a smile. "So sweet, my dear." She sighed. "Enough of him. I'll think about him later, and the whole sorry mess. It's a tragedy, isn't it? That boy could sign his life away...but I have a lot of processing to do about all that later."

"Very well," said Rosemary. "What do you want to talk about? Or would you rather have a rest?"

"Oh no, I've been resting enough," said Marjie. "I've been bored out of my mind in that Goddess-awful place. I want to talk about Grace. Herb wasn't the only one bottling something up for all those years. I was too. It was too painful. And now that I can talk, I just want to tell you all about her."

"She was special," said Athena. "I can understand that."

"The most special," said Marjie. "The day I met Grace Brashville—"

Athena gasped, putting her hand to her mouth.

"What?" Rosemary asked.

Marjie looked at her.

"That's the name of the house," said Athena. "The Haunted House."

Marjie shook her head. "What are you talking about, dear?"

"For our school trip, we went to the house and Felix was sure he saw a ghost. And then I dreamed – Mum and I both did—"

"We dreamed of a girl running through a forest," said Rosemary.

Marjie's expression was stunned. "Grace?"

"I think so," said Rosemary. "I saw the picture at your house: a photo of Grace that you put on your shrine, and she looked familiar. I couldn't place her at first. But I had my suspicions, and now it seems so obvious. She must have been the girl we saw in the dream – she looked a little different. She was kind of glowing, and her hair wasn't as dark. But actually..."

Rosemary reached into her pocket. "Where did I put it? It must be in my jacket. I'll go get it."

"The photo?" said Athena.

"Wait a moment," said Marjie. "You think that Grace is haunting the house, haunting your dreams? That means she's a restless spirit!"

A shiver ran down Rosemary's spine. "That does not sound good."

"It is not," Marjie confirmed.

"Do you think we could talk to her?" Athena suggested.

"Granny's got an old Ouija board around here somewhere," said Rosemary.

"Oh no," said Marjie. "Absolutely not. It's dangerous, far too dangerous. A séance might be okay for a settled spirit, when it's gone beyond the veil of this world, but a restless spirit is certainly too dangerous. You've heard about poltergeists, haven't you?"

"Sort of," said Athena.

Rosemary shook her head.

"Just trust me," said Marjie. "You do not want to go around messing with that kind of thing."

"I'm willing to take your word for it," said Rosemary. "Poltergeists do not sound like something that I want to go anywhere near."

"Well, if a séance won't help, what do we do?" said Athena. "In the movies, they always call a priest, but it seems inappropriate in Myrtlewood."

Marjie tsked. "A priest is not going to do you any good. No. A very experienced medium maybe. But most of them are frauds like that batty Crystal Cassandra. She drives me up the wall. It's hard to find a good medium. And even if we could, the chances of them wanting to deal with a spirit that's restless like this is fairly unlikely."

"Is there anything that would work?" Rosemary asked.

"Ideally, we'd find someone who could navigate between realms," said Marjie. "To calm the spirit and guide her home. I have heard of such a being, probably more of a legend than anything. My old Pa knew of one called a Dreamweaver. I don't know if we've seen one in the world for a long time. Although there are rumours that one has returned to the world."

"That sounds interesting," said Athena. "But also, not very practical. We don't even know if they exist."

Do you really think somebody could guide her home from this realm?" said Rosemary.

Marjie nodded. "That would be ideal. Instead of fighting her we could find a way to soothe her. Gently lead her back to the spirit realm?"

"What about a ghost like Granny Thorn?" Athena suggested.

"Maybe," said Marjie ponderously.

Rosemary put on the kettle for more tea and went to fetch her jacket.

"This was the one I was wearing when we went to your house to investigate. I hope you don't mind us rifling through your things. That's how we found the letter."

"Don't mind it at all," said Marjie. "You probably saved my life in some ways, or at least the quality of it. I didn't like my chances of being locked up for years in a cell in Bermuda or Glastonbury, or wherever they'd put me."

"Of course not," said Athena, patting Marjie on the arm.

Rosemary reached into her jacket pocket and found a photograph. She pulled it out and held it up for them to see.

"What am I looking at?" said Athena.

Marjie screamed.

"It's a photograph," said Rosemary, turning it over to look.

She felt her heart pause in her chest for a moment too long.

The picture that had been clearly visible of a young girl was now almost entirely black, except for a face twisted in terror.

She looked around at Athena and Marjie, dropping the photograph to the ground, afraid that it might contain some sort of bad magic.

"This is not good," said Athena.

Marjie shook her head.

Rosemary took a deep breath and tried to calm her racing

heart that had gone from paused to beating far too fast in the space of a moment.

She knew her expression was just as terrified as Marjie's and Athena's were.

Athena might not yet realise or want to admit it, but Rosemary was sure that Elise must be connected to this restless spirit – she could even be working for the Bloodstones – and that opened up a whole new world of risk.

Whatever had happened to the photo was an ominous sign of what was coming next.

Twenty-Four

"**A**ny luck?" Sam asked the next day at school as they sat in the courtyard eating lunch.

Athena shook her head. She had scoured the books and the Thorn Manor library, but all of the records of possessions she could find seemed to have happened a long time ago. Many of them were ancient. "It turns out possession isn't as common as horror movies suggested."

Elise was there in the classroom that morning, at least physically present. Athena wondered why she was even coming to school – was she still partly thinking as herself? Was she still fading in and out? Had Grace had taken over?

Athena had explained to their other friends about the theory that Grace must be the one possessing Athena, and they talked over and over about that night and the house.

It seemed odd that a spirit would possess a body, restless as she supposedly was, only to carry on life as a slightly zombified version of ordinary activities.

"Unless she's collecting information for someone," said Ash, opening her lunch box.

Athena grimaced. "Don't say that."

"What do you think's going on?" Felix asked later that day as they watched Elise sitting in the corner of the courtyard by herself, staring into space.

Athena shook her head. "Maybe there's some kind of internal battle and she's just kind of gone into automatic robot mode – not completely here. Either that, or the restless spirit is attending Myrtlewood Academy."

"I hope she's finding it interesting," said Sam.

"Or she doesn't really realise what's going on completely," said Ash. "Didn't Grace go to Myrtlewood High back when she was younger? Maybe both personalities are kind of in there in some kind of confused state, whether they're struggling for control or not. It might not be an entirely deliberate situation."

"You mean Grace might not fully be awake in there?" said Deron.

Ash shrugged. "I mean, Elise doesn't seem to be fully awake. Does she?"

"Like a dream," said Athena. "I don't really understand it."

"You'd think Felix would have been possessed," Deron had said over and over again until Felix had punched him in the arm.

"Felix was spooked," said Sam. "But maybe it was a distraction, and Grace rushed right past him and somehow landed inside Elise's mind. What did she say happened?"

"I don't remember exactly," said Athena. "She said you guys

went off when you heard the disturbance, and she stayed with me. Maybe she was dozing slightly. You know, half asleep."

"That might have made her vulnerable," said Sam. "Half asleep and half awake. That's when your mind is kind of liminal. You know, in between spaces."

Athena took a bite of her sandwich and pondered this for a moment.

"But I was the one who dreamed of her...of Grace," said Athena.

"True, and so did your mother," said Ash, "but I suspect even a powerful restless spirit would have struggled to possess one of the Thorn witches."

Athena sighed. "Elise is always going on about how powerful I am. And maybe that is what protected me, although there were other people there..."

"Yeah, that's true. And we couldn't wake you," said Deron. "Maybe the spirit was trying to possess you. In fact, maybe the whole thing was set up!"

"What do you mean?" said Athena.

"Well, you think the Bloodstone Society is after you again," said Deron. "Maybe they were trying to instigate the whole thing. Isn't it suspicious that all of a sudden this haunted house that's been abandoned for years is suddenly available for ghost hunting school trips?"

"I suppose that is a bit convenient," said Athena. "And the connection to Marjie...and the Bloodstone Society. They were the ones who took Grace, maybe they're in control of her still," said Athena, her mind spinning in paranoid circles that reminded her too much of her mother.

159

"Suppose they were trying to get to you," said Ash, "but your magical defences kicked in, so you couldn't wake up – you and your mother and your family magic. Maybe that dream was her trying to possess you and failing. Your magical genes protected you, and the restless spirit gave up and went for Elise, who was right next to you."

"That makes me feel even worse," said Athena. "But it does seem like a strange coincidence, especially when you think about the situation with Herb, and with the magic shop. You haven't..." She looked around at her friends. "You haven't seen anyone suspicious? Nobody's tried to approach you guys and get you to sign a blood oath or anything? Mum wanted me to ask."

Her friends all shook their heads.

Athena continued. "Mum's fixated on this idea that the Bloodstones are out recruiting an army of young people because she thinks we're obviously too stupid to resist, since our brains aren't technically fully developed yet. It's kind of insulting, actually."

Sam patted her reassuringly on the arm.

"Well, teenagers aren't always known to make the best decisions..." said Ash.

"But it seems like the best decision at the time," said Felix. "That's what's important!"

Athena shook her head. "Adults make dumb decisions too, and besides, I doubt anyone would talk about it if they had taken a blood oath. I mean, wouldn't that kill them?"

She looked around.

The friends all stared at each other for a while and then

returned their attention to their respective lunches, except Felix, who had wolfed his down in a minute flat, as usual.

"No. You'd have to be desperate to do something like that," said Sam. "And none of us are...at least as far as I know."

The bell rang for class. Athena kept an eye on Elise all through the alchemy lesson. She seemed to be following the instructions, though it was unclear which personality was in charge, especially since Elise had hardly any expression on her face the entire time.

"We've got to do something," Athena whispered to Sam.

Sam nodded. "But what?"

"Maybe I'll try and talk to her after school."

"We'll come with you," said Sam. "You might need backup."

As soon as the final bell rang, Athena grabbed her bag and followed Elise. She was already getting out of the class. She noticed their other friends lagging behind them.

"Hey, Elise," Athena called out, but Elise was walking fast. She'd already made it through the school gate by the time Athena caught up with her.

"Hey, wait up."

Elise turned, her expression vacant.

"Look, I know there's something going on," said Athena. "Just listen, Elise. You're being possessed. If you're in there, talk to me. Tell me you can hear me."

As Athena watched, Elise's eyes turned black.

The darkness spread to her hair, from the roots right down to the tips, which tinged bright red. Her face became impossibly pale. "No!" she screamed, her voice taking on that unearthly resonance again.

She held up her hand, and Athena felt herself being blown back through the sheer force of the magic.

Sam and Deron caught Athena before she could hit the ground.

Elise stood there for a moment.

Felix's eyes were wide in wonder. "She's turned evil! Amazing!"

Athena glared at him.

"Please, Elise!" Athena called out as she scrambled up to go after her girlfriend. But it was too late.

Elise dashed away with preternatural speed.

"She went that way," said Sam, pointing towards the town square. "I guess we go after her."

They followed in the direction that Elise had gone in.

"I hope she's not going on a rampage," said Sam.

"Though it could be kind of cool," said Felix.

"Stop that," said Athena. "Nothing about this is cool. Nothing at all."

"Sorry," he said sheepishly. "Maybe it's too soon."

Athena elbowed him as they ran.

The town square was eerily quiet.

"Where do you think she could have gone?" Athena asked. Her eyes fell on the sign for the Travellers' fair. "This way."

It was a stab in the dark, but Elise had first flipped out when they were at the fair. Maybe it was somewhere she'd return to.

They ran quickly towards the eccentric collection of tents and house trucks.

The market was just getting set up for the evening, and many of the stallholders had frozen in place. Not properly, as if by magic – they'd just stopped to stare at the girl with black hair, her eyes now glowing bright red. She stood with her head slightly bowed in the centre of the stalls, close to where they'd been several nights before.

"Elise," said Athena tentatively, stepping closer. She decided to change tact. "Grace?"

Elise raised her head slightly.

"Grace, are you in charge now?"

Grace nodded.

Athena felt a lead weight in her gut. "Grace, we're friends. We're friends of Marjie's. We're here to help. We know something terrible happened to you, and we just want to help you."

A single red tear slowly sank down Elise's cheek.

"It was awful – what happened to you," said Athena. "Just tell us how we can help."

Elise-Grace didn't move, so Athena took another step closer. "Grace," she said, stepping forward again. "Grace, we're here to help."

Something shifted, and Grace's eyes glowed brighter.

Athena took that as a good sign. As she moved closer, Grace, in Elise's body, tipped her head back and opened her mouth wide, screaming so loud it surely would have echoed over half the town.

She held up her hands and blasted Athena backward, along with the other friends and several of the stalls.

Then, like lightning, she was gone.

Athena lay on the ground, panting. "Wow. That really did not go well."

"I don't know," said Sam. "At least we know that Grace was

the one in charge. She sort of responded to you. Did you see that tear?"

"Of course I saw the blood-red tear," said Athena. "I'm not blind."

Felix shook his head. His expression was thoroughly impressed. "You have to admit, it is kind of awesome."

Athena wanted to punch him in that moment, but Sam held her back.

"Look, Felix is as worried and upset as the rest of us are," Sam said. "He's known Elise for a long time, and she's usually the one to keep him in line. We all just have different ways of coping."

Athena took a deep breath. "You're right," she said.

"But do try to rein it in, Felix," Ash added.

Felix shrugged. "I'm not good with the feels, okay?"

"What do we do now?" said Deron.

Athena heard the sound of steps approaching and looked behind her to see Hazel.

"Did you see all that?" Athena asked.

Hazel nodded and then introduced herself to Athena's friends, something Athena had totally forgotten to do in the shock of the moment.

"Possession, huh?" said Hazel, as they sat around outside the house truck sipping the tea that Ursula had brewed. "Here's the problem: possession is way rarer than you'd expect, and restless spirits are powerful."

"You can say that again," said Felix.

"She does seem to be jacked up on magic, doesn't she?" said Rowan, leaning against the truck.

Felix looked at him and then adopted a similar pose, clearly thinking Rowan was cool.

"I don't understand," Athena said, shaking her head. "I feel like this should be simple, and there should be a plan and a way to help, and I just don't know what to do." Tears sprang from her eyes, and Sam consoled her.

"It's okay," they said.

"Yeah, we'll figure this out," said Deron.

"There must be somebody who knows about this stuff," said Ash.

"Actually, Gallium does," said Hazel. "He was talking about it the other night. Or at least he tells a good tale around the campfire. I think he's encountered several genuine possessions and a few others that were hoaxes."

"He does know a lot about old magic like that," said Rowan.

"Who's Gallium?" Sam asked.

"We met him the other night," Athena explained. "Err, he's the one who got in the crossfire of Elise flipping out the other day. He might not really want to talk to us."

"I'm sure he'll be keen," said Rowan. "Only he's not here at the moment. He'll be back later tonight. Or you could come by tomorrow."

"I guess I'll have to try," Athena said. "He might be the only lead we have."

Twenty-Five

osemary looked up at the towering castle. She slouched over her steering wheel and whimpered a little in the privacy of her own car.

She didn't particularly want to visit Azalea, but with Burk out of town, it seemed like she had no other option but to face her boyfriend's rather terrifying – if friendly – mother alone.

She'd called Burk, of course, and he'd explained that Azalea was the one who'd gotten him out of his pact with the Bloodstone Society.

He didn't know exactly how it had happened and he'd offered to follow up with his mother. However, Rosemary decided that it would be easier to have a proper conversation with her in order to work out the mechanics of whatever had gone down.

She had only ever visited the castle with Burk there, and it seemed scary to be going in alone, because as amicable as Charles and Azalea had both been, they were most certainly deadly and unpredictable.

The sun had only just set. Rosemary decided it was slightly less frightening to approach while the sky wasn't too dark.

She dragged herself out of the car and made her way to the front door. It opened before she had a chance to knock.

No one was there, so Rosemary took a tentative step into the house.

She heard strange grunting noises and worried that someone was being attacked, but as she approached cautiously, she realised it was simply a fencing match in the large lounge room. Azalea and Charles, she in a black fencing outfit and him in white and gold. They moved so quickly that it was sometimes a blur. Rosemary got the impression that she was intruding on personal time, so she slipped back out of the castle and waited a moment, pondering whether to knock again or simply come back some other time.

"Rosemary!" Azalea stood there, somehow now clad in a flamboyant, slithery black gown which sparkled at the edges.

"Hi," said Rosemary, clenching her hands nervously. "You...look n—"

"Darling!" said Azalea. "Burk told me you might come." She smiled her creepy smile, and Rosemary tried to mirror while remembering the sorts of things that she shouldn't say, such as using the word "nice" as a compliment.

"You look stunning," she said tentatively.

"Thank you," Azalea replied. "Now, come in! We have human-suitable beverages for you and everything."

"Err...Thanks," said Rosemary, her smile turning into a

grimace at the awkward word choice. Azalea led her through to a rather ornate parlour with a roaring fire and plush brocade seating. Oil paintings hung from the walls, along with various other trophies and all manner of weapons.

Rosemary took a closer look at some of the portraits. They seemed to be of various Burk family members throughout the ages. Azalea in a curly wig and lavender dress, as if she was in the court of some French king – which she probably was; Charles in Edwardian dress looking terribly dapper. She smiled at one where Burk looked just a little bit like a pirate.

"He worked for George the Second, you know," Azalea said.

She disappeared and returned promptly with a tray of tea.

"Are those bloomers?" Rosemary asked.

Azalea laughed. "Ah! You're so refreshing. Now come sit. Tell me, how can I help you? All my son would say is that you had some questions. And please tell me, can I convince you to come to the reunion after all?"

Rosemary shook her head. "I'm afraid not. I've got my own family ties – like I said."

"Oh, the burdens of family," Azalea replied with a nostalgic smile. "I do prefer to be tied up in other ways. As Charles knows well."

Rosemary almost spat out her tea. "Too much information."

Azalea almost giggled. "Charming."

"Now, the thing that I need to ask you about...well, there might be a few things, actually." Rosemary went into more detail on the various situations that had been unfolding around Myrtlewood, updating Azalea from the last conversation they'd had.

"Fascinating!" said Azalea, who was on the edge of her seat as if watching a thrilling performance. "There's such immediacy in your mortal perception. I can see why Perseus adores—"

Suddenly, there was a crashing sound, and a rather stout man with bright ginger hair lumbered into the room.

"Fresh meat!" he cried in a croaky voice.

"Uncle Elbert!" Azalea scolded as the clearly ancient vampire bared his teeth and lunged towards them.

Rosemary screamed and held her arms up, wondering whether her magic sunlight could dust a vampire so ancient. She also wondered how much of a faux pas it would be.

Azalea held Elbert back with her palm, looking unimpressed. "We simply cannot have this kind of interruption! Rosemary is not food. She's family."

Elbert growled again.

A creaking sound caught Rosemary's attention and a bald-headed creature slithered into the room. He almost didn't have limbs, moving like a snake, clad in black rags, his skin mottled and peeling, almost translucent.

He was clearly ancient beyond words.

"A feast!" he cried and also lunged towards Rosemary.

"Enough!" Azalea shouted. Rosemary felt herself being whipped up into Azalea's arms as if she was nothing more than a cushion. They moved with such speed that Rosemary had to hold her breath in case she lost her lunch.

Burk had carried her before, fairly fast, but it was nothing like this. She wasn't sure if it was because Azalea was older and stronger and therefore quicker, or perhaps Burk was just being cautious, so as not to make her motion sick.

Either way, she appreciated being swept out of danger at such pace.

Gradually, things stopping moving, and Rosemary reached out to try and get her bearings, her hand landing on something soft.

She was sitting on a bed.

It was Burk's room, and Azalea sat next to her after firmly closing the door.

"Why are we in here?" Rosemary asked, slightly confused. "And who were they?"

"Family?" said Azalea, tutting. "Perhaps Perseus was right about the reunion after all. It could be dangerous for you. Oh, well. It's hard to remember the level of your human fragility, being immortal for so long."

It took a moment for Rosemary to recover. "Are we safe?"

"Of course. Perseus has had special anti-vampire protections put in place for this room before he ever invited you over. I just activated them," Azalea said.

"Sweet of him," said Rosemary.

Azalea winced at the word 'sweet.'

Rosemary shrugged. "I mean – thoughtful."

Azalea smiled. "Now, tell me, what was it you wanted to ask me about?"

"Okay," said Rosemary. "Going back to the Bloodstone Society – and I told you about Herb?" Azalea nodded. "Turns out that he'd taken some kind of blood oath."

Azalea sighed, as if slightly disappointed. "That pesky little club! Honestly, they have no boundaries."

Rosemary wasn't used to the Bloodstone Society being

170

described as pesky or little, but she quite enjoyed the idea. "Anyway, you're the only one that I know of who has ever gotten anyone out of a blood oath...There must be thousands of people trapped by them. At least that's what it sounded like from Herb's letter."

Azalea nodded. "I did, didn't I. Now what happened with that? It was a long time ago..."

Azalea went so quiet and still as a statue that Rosemary wondered if she had gone to sleep with her eyes open.

"Was it a spell?" Rosemary prompted? "Did you have any help?"

Azalea shook her head. "Unfortunately not. I've just dredged up the memory. You're probably not going to like this. I merely went and tracked down that little cretin that Dora hates."

"Geneviève?"

"That's the one! I locked her in a room, and then I negotiated with her for seven days until we came to an agreement."

"An agreement?" said Rosemary.

"Yes, basically just bribery. I gave her a lot of money and some rare gemstones and magical artefacts, and she agreed to free my sons."

"Both of them?" Rosemary asked.

Azalea sighed melodramatically. "Yes, both of them. It was a tragedy really. I went to such lengths to have my sons freed. Only, one of them went straight back and joined the cult again." There was a deep sadness in her eyes, which quickly disappeared. "Never mind! Now we have you in the family." She beamed.

Rosemary gulped, feeling particularly awkward about how

she'd managed to kill Burk's brother before she really knew anything about him at all.

She couldn't quite understand the family's flippant reaction to the whole situation, but then again, there were probably a lot of things about vampires and the Burk clan in particular that Rosemary would never completely understand.

"Well, I guess that is a bit disappointing," Rosemary said. "I mean, bribery is not going to work on a mass scale, is it? They're not going to give up all that power for all the money and artefacts in the world...and I wouldn't know how to track Geneviève down and lock her in a room, anyway."

"You must promise me one thing," said Azalea.

"What is it?"

"Don't tell Dora about that. She would hate that I negotiated with her enemy."

There was a clicking sound and Dora entered.

Rosemary frowned. "I thought there were anti-vampire protections on the room."

"Hah!" said Dora. "That's not going to work on me. And I did overhear everything." She glared at Azalea, who rolled her eyes.

"Very well, *Maman*," she said. "You win this round."

"I suspected as much anyway," said Dora. "When you got the boys out of their club...I suppose it was worthwhile."

She still looked unimpressed.

"Why did you come up here?" Rosemary asked, feeling slightly on edge. Dora was one of the most terrifying of the Burk family, despite looking like a young child of twelve or so. Today, her hair was arranged into two pigtail plaits and she wore round spectacles. Rosemary wondered why the ancient being dressed like a little girl, but assumed that like Charles and his penchant for pastels, that many of the decisions these vampires made were down to one thing: boredom.

"I want to get her," said Dora. "*Geneviève.*"

"Well, I guess we're partners then," said Rosemary. "For better or worse. We're on the same side; we might as well help each other out."

"Sure," said Dora. "If we must be."

"Do you know anything about the blood oaths?" Rosemary asked.

"Possibly nothing that you haven't already discovered," said Dora. "But they might be the key to taking down the Bloodstones."

Rosemary raised an eyebrow. "What do you mean?"

Dora took a step further into the room. "My theory is that the blood oaths were weakened when you and your daughter came into town and banished Geneviève. She's the one who holds everything together, like a lynchpin. I was watching them scramble around. They couldn't get their act together or keep their lesser members in line very easily – or so my sources told me."

"What are you suggesting then?" said Rosemary.

"When the Bloodstone powers were weakened, I suspect the bonds were too. They're all kind of tied up in each other like a web. And I don't think they've properly grown back yet. But they probably will do in time."

"So there might be a chance to break the bond," said Rosemary.

173

"I suspect so," said Dora. "All of those blood oaths are at the foundation of the Bloodstone Society. They give Geneviève her power, and that's always given her the upper hand."

"So what do you want to do?"

"I want to take her down," said Dora determinedly.

Twenty-Six

Athena hesitated outside the carnival.

Night had fallen and things really had picked up since she'd been there a few hours before. There were more visitors and the market was all set up.

She'd told her friends she'd come back another time to talk to Gallium, but then headed home to find that Rosemary wasn't there.

The empty house was cold comfort and she couldn't stop thinking about Elise. Athena had made herself an early dinner and then wandered back into town.

She wasn't sure exactly what she was afraid of. She'd just had a bad feeling all the way as she walked through Myrtlewood, as if she was being watched.

Surely the market was safer with all those people around, including her new friends, but what if it wasn't?

She took a deep breath and walked in.

It was drawing close to Samhain, and more people had arrived in Myrtlewood for the season.

As she looked around, Athena wondered how many of the people were in town for their very own magical family reunions or some other celebrations around town. She'd heard of several costume parties, which sounded like a lot of fun. Although, it now did not seem like she and Elise would attend the Samhain night carnival together in fancy dress.

She sighed and carried on through until she spotted Hazel and Rowan. They were talking to some customers: three girls with wavy green hair. Rosemary would have stared awkwardly at the scene, but Athena just assumed they were some kind of forest nymphs. If they'd stood very still in the woods, she would hardly have noticed them at all.

Hazel caught her eye and wandered out from behind the stall.

"Athena!" she said, giving her a big hug. "How you holding up?"

"I'm okay," said Athena. "I just came back like you suggested."

"Oh yes, Gallium is over here," said Hazel, leading her along the row of stalls and tents.

"This one," said Hazel, gesturing toward a tawny canvas structure, striped with green and dark red.

"Gallium!" Hazel called. "Are you in there? He might be out fire juggling."

"Looking for me?" said a voice.

They turned to see Gallium standing there, wearing a gold waistcoat. "I was just about to start getting ready for the performance." He looked Athena in the eye. "Can I help with something?"

"Yes, thank you," said Athena. "I wanted to talk to you about something..." She looked around in case of eavesdroppers. "Do you know anything about possession?"

"As a matter of fact, I do," said Gallium, folding his arms.

"Oh good," said Athena.

"Come right this way." He ushered her into his tent.

Hazel waved goodbye, and Athena smiled. "Thank you," she called out.

Gallium took a seat and gestured to Athena to do the same.

The inside of the tent was cosy, covered in rugs.

A lit candle illuminated a wooden table with a silk scarf lying across it.

"Do you do tarot readings or something?" Athena asked. "This seems like the right kind of setting for it."

"Is that what you're after?" Gallium asked.

"No," said Athena. "I think my friend is possessed." She tried to explain the situation with Elise.

"You're talking about the girl from the other night," said Gallium, his voice taking on a more serious tone.

"Yes," said Athena. "There was a girl who died a long time ago. A restless spirit. We're pretty sure that she's possessing Elise. Do you know what can be done about it?"

"As a matter of fact, I do," said Gallium. Athena's heart leapt with hope. "But it's complicated." He clasped his hands together and raised his index fingers to his chin. "You know that magic works in a give and take fashion."

"Of course..." said Athena. "This is why we don't do harmful things because it might return to us, like the threefold law and all that."

Gallium raised an eyebrow and pressed his lips into a thin line. "That's not exactly what I was talking about." A shimmer ran across skin in the low light. "I mean the natural give and take of the universe."

Athena shook her head. "I'm sorry, I'm confused. How is that different?"

"Well, sometimes, a sacrifice has to be made in order to save somebody you care about...if they need it," Gallium explained.

"I suppose..." She would give up all her possessions to save Elise in the blink of an eye.

"Do you mean money?" Athena asked. "Because I can pay—"

"Not exactly," Gallium replied, a gleam in his eye. "What I would need is a special kind of promise."

Athena felt a chill, uneasy at the way the hairs on the back of her neck stood up. "What kind of promise?"

"Have you ever heard of a magical oath?" Gallium asked.

Athena's heart raced. "You mean a blood oath, don't you?" She stood up and pushed the table away, knocking it to the ground. "You! You're one of them."

Gallium laughed. "Athena Thorn," he said. "I've been keeping an eye on you."

Athena screamed and tried to run out of the tent, but found she couldn't move.

She stared at Gallium as her mind raced.

The Travellers must be associated with the Bloodstone Society. Did that mean...? Were her friends not really friends at all? Were they all part of this plot against her?

"From the moment you stepped in here," Gallium said, his

178

mouth twisting into a half-smile, "no sound has escaped this tent. And neither will you," his voice crooned.

Athena shook her head. "No."

"Did you even tell your mother where you were going this evening?"

Athena took a sharp inhale of breath.

She had meant to text Rosemary, but it slipped her mind.

"Perfect," said Gallium quietly. "Then I have you here all to myself."

"No!" Athena shrieked and then calmed herself as best she could. She couldn't afford to react in the way he'd expect her to. She had to do something different.

She decided to bide her time and see what other information she could get out of him while she worked out how to get out of the situation.

Her magic was strong, and she could probably blast the whole tent away. But she wasn't sure whether that could backfire – whether the cocoon of energy he'd placed around the tent could have a ricochet effect and injure her. Or whether a huge surge of power could be bottled up and explode like a bomb, killing innocent people in the process. Her mind raced as she spoke.

"Things...strange things have been happening since you've been in town," said Athena. "And before that, too..."

Gallium smiled. He thought he was very clever, clearly.

Athena decided her best bet was to give him an opportunity to show her exactly how clever he was.

"I might have been in town a few days early," said Gallium. "You know...setting up for my colleagues to arrive."

"Was it you who cursed the shop?" said Athena.

Gallium chuckled. "I may have helped with that. But it wasn't my idea."

"What *was* your idea, then?" said Athena, sounding slightly disappointed.

Gallium smarted. "I've had a lot to do with this entire plan," he said defensively. "I told the leaders all about the ancient yew tree and how to harness the old Samhain magic. It's my specialty, you see. Every year, we come to Myrtlewood for the season, and every year, I've learned a little bit more about this place. I've studied it. My family has always had an affinity for underworld magic. My great-great-grandfather was thought to have brought back his wife when she passed.

Athena cringed. "Eww."

"It was romantic," said Gallium sternly.

"And that's what you're trying to do, isn't it?" said Athena. "There have been rumours about dark magic. Are you making zombies? That would be very fitting for Halloween."

Gallium spat at the ground. "How dare you use that word and sully the season of Samhain! This is not an American costume party," he said bitterly. "This is sacred. This is powerful."

"Okay, sure," said Athena, getting a good feel for Gallium's sensitive spots. "So, what exactly did you do?"

"I'm not going to give you any more information," said Gallium, biting his bottom lip.

"Why not? Are you scared that I'm actually going to get out of here rather easily?"

Athena crossed her arms.

Gallium scowled. "Of course not, little girl. You're just a

puppet. I'm going to trap you here until you sign a blood oath, and then we can do whatever we want with you." He grinned.

"How long have you been involved with the Bloodstone Society?" asked Athena.

"Enough with your questions!" said Gallium.

He pulled out a knife.

Athena didn't flinch.

"Now, what is your weakness?" he asked.

She glared at him.

"Your friend, Elise," he continued. "Yes…What if I were to summon her here?"

Gallium reached into the chest behind him and pulled out a Ouija board. "I could bring her here right now and trap her. I do have an uncanny power over the dead."

"No," said Athena, trying to keep her voice even. She wasn't sure whether she should call his bluff or divert him to another topic because he had clearly found one of her biggest weaknesses.

It was my fault for telling him about Elise.

Athena tried to calculate how much magic she could possibly use in a confined space while protecting both herself and the people outside.

The problem wasn't that she didn't have enough power, but that she had far too much and this silly little man obviously had no idea of it. It struck Athena that the Bloodstone Society must know very little about her magic. When she and Rosemary had first arrived in Myrtlewood, her power hadn't even shown up yet, and the last time they'd attacked at the Summer Solstice, her magic hadn't been effective against the sirens. Despite all their spying, this secret society was clueless, and that was to her advantage. Gallium had no idea that he was the most vulnerable person in the tent.

"Whatever you're thinking, it's not going to work," said Gallium. "You're trapped here."

He stood took a step towards her, brandishing the knife. "Maybe we don't even need a Ouija board. Maybe I'll just kill you right now and put us all out of our misery. Imagine how useless your mother will be without you! Imagine the grief!"

He took another step forward and thrust the knife at Athena's throat. She felt a very subtle prickle of the blade as her thoughts went from racing to utter panic.

One false move now, and it could all be over.

She drew in a long, slow breath and looked Gallium in the eye.

"Bluffing," she said.

"Am I? Care to find out?"

Just then, Athena felt herself hurled over by an alarming force.

The entire tent had been blown to smithereens.

She looked around; Gallium was sprawled on his back, and Elise or, perhaps more accurately, Grace stood in front of them. Her eyes were a deep dark red, her hair blacker than midnight.

Grace screamed, and everyone watching cowered from the sound.

"Elise...Grace—" said Athena.

She watched as her possessed girlfriend held her hand out towards Gallium. His clothing caught alight in flames. He screamed, and ran away.

Athena looked around at the shocked faces of stallholders and customers alike.

"Uhh, that was all part of the performance!" said Rowan.

Athena shot him a suspicious glance.

Elise-Grace screamed again.

"You saved me," said Athena, after the noise died down.

Those blood-red eyes stared at her, and a tear streamed down her pale face.

"Come with me," said Athena. "I'll take you to Marjie; we can figure all this out."

"What's going on here?" said the voice of a woman in a black dress striped with gold, who was approaching from behind Elise.

The woman stared at them through kohl-rimmed eyes, and then trembled.

"You're one of them," said Elise in a deep resonant voice. She blasted the woman with her unearthly magic – then the woman disintegrated in flames before their very eyes.

Bystanders screamed and began to run away. Elise turned, spearing one more glance at Athena.

"Don't follow me," she said and took off into the dark night.

Athena looked around at the chaos of the market. Some people were cowering; others were clapping as if it had all been a brilliant performance with amazing special effects.

"We really do have tourists," Athena muttered to herself. Her new supposed-friends were nowhere to be seen, and Athena didn't really want to see them right now, especially not if the Travellers were involved with the Bloodstone Society.

"Athena," cried a familiar voice.

"Mum!" Athena felt herself wrapped in Rosemary's arms. "How did you know to come?"

"I got home, and you weren't there," said Rosemary. "I was worried stiff, especially when you didn't answer your phone."

"It was on silent. I'm sorry," said Athena. "But how did you know to come here?"

"Just a hunch," said Rosemary. "I knew Elise had been here before. I figured you might go after her."

"Good guess," said Athena. "Although that wasn't exactly why I came here."

"Come on, we can talk about it at home," said Rosemary, helping Athena along. "I have a few things to tell you, too."

Twenty-Seven

"It's okay, Nugget," Athena said, scratching her squirrel familiar behind the ears as he tried to steal her toast. "You'll get your breakfast in a minute."

Nugget glared at her and scampered off to pounce on Serpentine, who squealed and took off towards the lounge.

In the week leading up to Samhain, Myrtlewood High was closed, as it usually was for the sabbats.

Athena was worried about Elise, and all her conversations with friends circled around the recent occurrences – where had Elise disappeared to? What happened to Gallium? Who else was associated with the Bloodstone Society?

Athena didn't feel safe being alone. She was sure Gallium would come after her at any moment, so she stuck close to home. She missed her girlfriend, but she didn't expect that Elise – or Grace as she seemed to be more of now – to go to school, even if it had been open, not after the recent explosive events.

Fleur was beside herself. She hadn't seen her daughter for days and kept checking in with Athena to see if there was any news.

Rosemary had dropped off some meals for the Fern family, and apparently so had other townsfolk. But no amount of general kindness or homemade food was going to do much to soothe a mother whose daughter had been possessed and disappeared.

There were several sightings of her around the town.

Constable Perkins even came over to Thorn Manor to ask a series of questions, implying Rosemary and Athena might be to blame and that Elise was some kind of bad seed.

They'd tried to explain the situation to him, to no avail.

Marjie, at least, had perked up and was using her strong networks around the town to gather information about where Elise-Grace might be.

She'd made an enormous map of Myrtlewood, stuck it on the kitchen wall, and pinned red dots to the locations of the sightings to see if they could discern a pattern. There was none, as far as Athena could see, but Marjie was sure that Elise-Grace was spending a lot of time near the old cemetery.

After the events at the carnival market, Athena was sure Elise was going after the Bloodstones, but they hadn't reported any more people combusting into flames. So, perhaps the secret society was living up to its name and they'd all gone to ground or cloaked themselves in some other way.

The evening before Samhain, Neve called around to Thorn Manor, bringing Nesta with her, who was looking rather plump and rosy-cheeked.

"You're glowing," said Rosemary, giving Nesta a big hug. "It seems like ages since we've seen you."

"I haven't been out and about much," said Nesta. "Partly because Neve's worried about everywhere being dangerous, but mostly because I'm quite tired now."

"It's getting close, isn't it?" said Rosemary.

"A few more weeks," said Neve. "Hopefully, the baby will be born a bit before Christmas." "Sagittarius baby, then?" said Athena, taking her turn to give Nesta a hug.

They sat in the living room with tea and cakes that Marjie had whipped up.

"I see you've been back in the teashop," said Neve.

Marjie grinned. "Reduced hours," she said, "but it's so good to be back on my feet, doing things for myself. I just can't quite face going home to the cottage yet."

"Fair enough," said Rosemary. "That place was really creepy. Maybe you could move house?"

"Oh, who knows?" said Marjie. "A lot of my life is wrapped up in that little place. Maybe with a good magical cleansing and a fresh coat of paint, I might want to go back. After all, you managed to live *here* after your granny was murdered...Ohh, that doesn't sound like a great thing to say, does it?"

"Never mind," said Rosemary.

Marjie still wasn't quite herself. She seemed on edge.

Neve shot her an anxious look. "To be frank, this isn't entirely a social call."

"Have you got information?" Marjie asked. "Can you help us find where Grace is?"

Athena frowned.

"Oh, and Elise of course..." Marjie added.

"It's not exactly news," said Neve. "MIB – you know, the

Magical Investigations Bureau team – has done a sweep of the entire village. They found some interesting results."

"What's going on?" said Rosemary. "Did they investigate the carnival? I knew those people were dodgy."

Neve nodded. "They've found connections with the Bloodstone Society – Gallium and the other woman who was attacked have been involved in some operations believed to be related to them."

"What about the other Travellers?" Athena asked.

"Everyone else comes out clear, so far. They might not all be associated. Not as far as we can tell anyway."

"I hope not," said Athena. "I like to think my instincts are right about people. And I like Ursula, Rowan, and Hazel."

"Well, you can't be too careful," said Rosemary. "Stay away from them for now."

"I have been," said Athena. "I wonder if there's some way they can help."

"How?" Neve asked.

"They're powerful," said Athena. "Ursula can make plants grow, even in this season."

"So she can grow crops, big deal," said Rosemary.

"And Hazel, well, there's something otherworldly about her. It doesn't seem bad, though. I think she spent time trapped in another realm..."

"Seems a bit tenuous," said Neve. "But I can follow up with them if you think it might help."

Athena shrugged. "It's worth trying anything."

"I'm sure whatever is happening is connected to our weird

shared dreams," said Rosemary. "Have any young girls gone missing lately?"

Neve shook her head. "Not that we have heard of. We can't really put much effort into investigating dreams. Even in the magical world, dreams are nebulous."

"What else did you find out?" said Rosemary, trying to get the topic back on track.

"Things have been particularly hairy around the cemetery," said Neve. "They're getting in experts to reveal the magic today. Something similar to what you and Tamsyn did, I think. I thought we might want to go and take a look after I've dropped Nesta home."

Nesta frowned. "Hey, I'm not made of porcelain, you know. I could come too."

"It's not just you," said Neve. "I want to protect the baby."

Nesta smiled, clearly pleased that Neve had adjusted well to their magical baby. "Alright, I'll go home then."

"Well, I'm coming to the cemetery," said Marjie. She threw on one of Granny Thorn's old felt hats and a billowing velvet cloak that made her look particularly witchy.

Rosemary grinned. "Okay, let's see what those creeps have been up to."

An hour later, they met Detective Neve on the outskirts of the cemetery. It had been cordoned off, but Neve raised the barrier and ushered them through.

"Up this way," she said, gesturing to the main path that led up the hill.

A grey mist hung in the air, obscuring some of the ground through which the tombstones protruded.

"Quite a big cemetery for a small town, isn't it?" Athena muttered.

"That was my thought at the funeral," said Rosemary quietly. "I suppose Myrtlewood has been here a long time."

"And a lot of these are very old graves," said Neve.

They wandered up through row upon row of tombstones, towards the structures at the back of the cemetery, which Rosemary assumed were mausoleums or crypts or whatever the term was.

As they continued walking, Neve pointed out some of the graves where a greeny-brown residue slime was splattered.

"Looks like the revealing spell worked," said Detective Neve as several spiders scuttled away – bright orange and black.

"Just like the shop," said Athena.

"Do you think they're connected with whatever is after us?" Rosemary asked.

"I wouldn't be surprised," said the detective. "I think the magic started here. And they brought some of it and deliberately plastered it around your shop. Didn't you notice the strange feeling when we were at the cemetery a few weeks ago, that we shouldn't be there?"

Rosemary nodded. "They must have a reason for trying to keep people away, right?"

Just a few steps ahead, the air felt thicker and Rosemary became a little woozy. "I don't like this."

"The clean-up crew will be here soon," said Detective Neve, "but I wanted a chance for us to get a good look before then."

"All right. Let's carry on," said Rosemary.

The slime seemed to cover the entire ground with a sticky layer under their feet.

"This is so gross," said Athena.

Rosemary grimaced. "Yes, it certainly is."

Marjie had been uncharacteristically silent the whole time, looking around, and perhaps keeping an eye out for Grace.

"Up there," said Detective Neve, pointing to the old gnarled yew tree that Rosemary had noticed on her first visit to the cemetery, which was covered in a thick layer of slime. Dark clouds of steam swirled around it.

"What's going on up there with that tree?" said Athena.

"Yew trees are traditional in cemeteries," said Neve. "They're believed to connect with the other side. Whatever magic they're drawing on, they're harnessing that old tree."

"That's where all this is coming from?" Rosemary asked, as she stared at the tree with its tall twisted branches and elaborate, old root systems. "Has it just lost all its leaves? Or is it dying?"

"I don't know," said Detective Neve, "but it doesn't look healthy."

"Wouldn't that be a good thing?" said Rosemary. "Maybe if the tree dies, all of this will go away."

"Oh no, dear," said Marjie. "Don't talk such ridiculous rubbish."

Rosemary felt a bit hurt, but Marjie carried on, apparently unfazed by how abrupt her words had been. "The tree's a guardian. If it dies, no good will come of it."

"So the tree is simultaneously letting in the underworld magic?" Athena asked, puzzled. "And also somehow protecting us?"

"Marjie is right," said Neve. "The tree isn't evil. None of this is exactly evil."

"It's just being manipulated somehow," said Athena. "They're using the magic of Samhain, aren't they, to draw the underworld into this realm?"

Neve nodded. "Something like that."

Rosemary looked at her very clever daughter, impressed.

Athena smirked.

"Okay, smarty-pants...now can we get out of here? I think I've seen enough," said Rosemary.

As they began to head back down the path, a whole hoard of people in hazmat-looking suits appeared with enormous hoses.

One team's hazmat suits were dark purple, and they seemed to be vacuuming up the sludge and spiders, while the other team, in white uniforms, was spraying some kind of substance to leave everything clean behind them.

At first, Rosemary thought it might be water, but on closer examination, it was definitely a kind of magic.

"Light energy," Neve remarked as they walked past, responding to her quizzical expression. "You know how they say sunlight is the best disinfectant – well, the fog is blocking the sunlight, so the clean-up team are improvising."

"I can make sunlight," said Rosemary, frowning. "But I didn't know it was good for cleaning. I suppose they do say sunlight is the best disinfectant, but I thought that was just a metaphor."

She still felt uncomfortable about the entire situation.

Marjie, however, looked thoughtful.

"Are you okay?" Athena asked her as they got back to the car.

"Me? I'm fine, dear. Don't you worry about me," said Marjie in a voice that only made Rosemary worry more.

Twenty-Eight

T hat evening, Thorn Manor was a hive of activity as friends
from around Myrtlewood descended on the house.

They hadn't been invited, exactly, though they all turned up
with more or less the same story.

Sherry had brought a pot of her famous beef and Guinness
stew over, looking uneasy.

"What is it?" Rosemary asked.

"I just had a bad feeling," said Sherry. "And I thought...well, I
thought maybe you had some kind of plan."

Rosemary shrugged and led her into the house.

"Should we have some kind of plan?" Athena asked.

"I don't know how to plan for this," said Rosemary.

Athena frowned. "What are we going to do tomorrow
night?"

Rosemary shook her head as she put the kettle on for tea.
"There's the Samhain ritual, and then there's the family reunion,

which you've already ordered thousands of candles for...so I'm already double-booked. Besides, if our enemies want to draw on the energy of Samhain, I'm sure they'll find us tomorrow."

"Umm, shouldn't we be prepared for that sort of thing?" said Athena.

"How do you prepare for the energy of death?" Rosemary asked, feeling a chill at her own words.

"Well, I created a small arsenal," said Athena dryly. She opened up the rather bulky coat she'd been wearing.

Rosemary laughed. It was lined with dozens of pockets, each labelled and containing various Athena specialties.

"You've got enough magic on your own," said Rosemary. "You don't need any of those things now."

"They might come in handy," said Athena. "Besides, I can give them to other people to use."

It was almost as if the doorbell didn't stop ringing the entire night. "What's the plan?" people kept asking. Una and Ashwyn showed up with the children. Neve and Nesta called around again. Even Papa Jack and his family made an appearance, and so did Athena's school friends – barring Elise, of course.

Marjie asked them all if they'd seen her. They shook their heads.

Marjie sighed, bowed her head, slumped over, and walked away.

"What's up with her?" Sam asked.

"She has been acting weird lately," said Athena. "Sort of energetic and also edgy. She sometimes snaps at us, but you know, grief is funny."

"It's not just grief," said Felix with a gleam in his eyes. "It's revenge."

"What are you talking about?" Ash asked.

"Marjie's been the most affected by all this rubbish," said Felix. "I bet she's out to get whoever did that to her friend and her bloody husband."

Athena shrugged. "You know, you might be right."

They had a pleasant impromptu potluck meal, with many Myrtlewood friends gathered around the fire at Thorn Manor, sipping hot chocolates and talking.

"This is a *real* family reunion," said Athena to her mother.

Rosemary smiled. "Friends are chosen family."

Athena nodded. "I'm not sure what Granny's got planned, but I bet it won't beat all of our friends coming together like this."

"Do you think we should prepare them for what might happen?" Athena asked.

It was a good question, but also a complicated one. There was far too much going on, and it all seemed dreadfully dangerous.

"To be honest," said Rosemary, "I'm hoping that they will stay home tomorrow. They'll be safer, hopefully, than if they're out and about."

"But we can't stop people from going to the Samhain ritual," said Athena.

Rosemary frowned. "That's true. And I bet whoever's after us is either going to attack there or later on that night."

"You think they'll go back to the cemetery, don't you?" Athena said.

Rosemary nodded.

It turned out not everyone was having cemetery family reunions for Samhain. But it was definitely a tradition among the older magical families, one that dated back for thousands of years.

Fortunately, many of their friends did not belong to such old magical families, as Rosemary and Athena's casual questions revealed. While some of them were planning to go to the ritual, many were planning on skipping the event, unless they were really needed.

"We'll be there if you think we can help," said Una, helping herself to a piece of Marjie's Allan-apple pie.

"But you'd rather not?" Rosemary said. "I think that would be wise. I don't know what's coming, but I would feel a lot safer if most of Myrtlewood stayed home tomorrow. We have to go to the cemetery because it's a family reunion, but..."

"But there'll be less to think about with all of us not there?" said Ashwyn.

Rosemary said apologetically, "Don't get me wrong, you've been really helpful in previous battles and things."

"But we're no Thorn witches," said Una. "This is serious business. Don't worry, we understand. And I don't envy you two," she added, giving Athena's shoulder a little squeeze.

"What about Dain?" Shelly asked. "Is he going to the reunion?"

Rosemary shook her head emphatically.

"He's not exactly part of the Thorn clan," said Athena. "Besides, Dad's still in the fae realm, helping Finnigan settle in and attending to whatever diplomatic treaty stuff he gets handed. He did send a message the other day checking in to see if we were okay, but other than that, I'm not expecting him."

"He'll come when he's called," said Una with a certainty in her voice that raised sceptical expressions from both Rosemary and Athena. Dain may have come a long way, but he wasn't the most reliable person.

"And Burk," said Ashwyn. "What about him?"

"Well, he's going to be at the cemetery anyway. He's got his own reunion to attend," said Rosemary. She was hoping Burk and his family might be able to help, although another worry stirred in her mind. If the Bloodstones were harnessing underworld magic, what if they managed to get the vampires under their control for their own sinister intentions?

Dora had implied she would team up with the Thorns, somewhat reluctantly, but they hadn't made any plans that Rosemary was aware of.

As if summoned by Rosemary's musings, Burk arrived with a bottle of wine, surprised to find so many Myrtlewood Village members at the Thorn residence. "Having a party without me?" he said jovially.

"Not an intentional one," Rosemary replied.

"Why does this feel sombre and morbid, like a last meal?" Athena asked.

She and Rosemary had gone back to the kitchen to help themselves to second helpings of Marjie's apple pudding.

"It's not exactly a festive time of year," said Rosemary.

Athena nodded. "Although it kind of does have its own magical charm, you know? It's nice that people set up candles and shrines and things. I've always thought it's better to celebrate death than just to avoid it."

Rosemary patted her daughter on the shoulder. "It does

seems like a more natural thing to do than pretend that we're immortal."

"Does it bother you?" Athena asked. She looked across at Burk, who was chatting with Liam in a rather friendly way, much more so than they would have in the past, at least.

"Does what bother me?" said Rosemary.

"Knowing that he's going to live basically forever," said Athena, her tone teasing. "And you're aging. You're getting really old, Mum."

"Thanks, darling," said Rosemary, with a chuckle. "You know...sometimes it does."

She felt a wave of emotion well up.

Athena narrowed her eyes. "You're not gonna go all Twilight on us and have yourself converted to a vampire, are you?"

Rosemary laughed. "It's not a religion. I'm not sure I could handle that, and besides, I don't think it works well with witch DNA." Rosemary shook her head. "No, I'm not foolish enough to go after immortality. And if Burk doesn't like me as I age, then that's on him. But I'm not going to try and freeze myself in time like some kind of Hollywood celebrity. Living and dying is natural. It's all part of the same process. I've done enough processing to not let my life be dictated by a pesky fear of missing out."

"You sound very wise," said Athena. "What's gotten into you?"

Rosemary shrugged. "Maybe I'll freak out about it some other time, but for now I feel strangely at peace. It's the season for reflecting on death, and that in itself brings its own kind of wisdom, I think. Death isn't evil. It's just part of the cycle."

"As much as I don't like that," said Athena, "I think you're right. And I'm glad you're not pursuing immortality because I hear it's a bit of a rabbit hole."

Rosemary laughed and hugged her daughter. "Maybe I'm not ambitious enough. My present goals are all centred around keeping my chocolate shop in business and surviving the Myrtlewood seasonal festivals. That's plenty for now."

Twenty-Nine

Just before sunset, Rosemary, Marjie, and Athena set off towards Myrtlewood Village.

They arrived in the centre of town to see preparations were well underway, not just for the Samhain ritual but also for the big Allantide market to be held afterwards.

So many people were crowded around the centre, some of them in costumes. Ferg handed out enormous glossy Allan apples to the young people.

"It's a tradition," Athena muttered. "Young people put the apples under their pillows at night to dream of who they're going to marry or something like that."

"I wish they'd take the apples and go home to sleep," said Rosemary. "The thought of all the people here, and the Travellers being involved in the market, makes feel uneasy."

"Stop being so paranoid about them, Mum," said Athena.

"You said it yourself," said Rosemary as she watched Travellers setting up their stalls and performance seats for the carnival. "They might all be in on it."

"Sure," said Athena. "I was worried about that. But the more I think about it, the more I realise that was probably just a few bad seeds. My instincts still say I can trust Hazel, Ursula, and Rowan. They've only been in the country for a few months. They hardly could have been embroiled in decades-long Bloodstone Society politics."

"But maybe they were trapped in a blood pact," said Rosemary.

Athena shivered, and it had nothing to do with the cold night air. "It's possible...but if so, they're victims too. And remember, Grace didn't try to attack them, just Gallium and that other woman."

"So far," Rosemary muttered.

"And Grace hasn't been back to the market since, as far as we know."

Rosemary shook her head. "I still don't like it. I wish Ferg would revoke their permit."

"Talking about me, Rosemary Thorn?"

Rosemary turned to glare at Ferg, who'd popped up right next to them, somehow. He was wearing an orange-and-black striped cape.

"I'm sure it's not the right day of the week for this outfit," said Rosemary, feeling grumpy. After all, Ferg had accused Marjie of murder, more or less. "I hope you've apologised."

"Apologised for what?" said Ferg. "Nobody forces me to wear things on different days. I merely find it convenient and somehow appropriate. But this is the season for mischief, after all! I *am* dressed appropriately."

Athena shook her head. "Mum means apologise for accusing Marjie."

"Oh, that," said Ferg. "Well, I was merely being cautious. Besides, she did confess to the crime."

"Only because she was confused," said Rosemary. "Don't expect us to be very happy with you for a while."

Ferg looked affronted. "But, Rosemary Thorn. You were my running partner for the mayoralty. You're a great witch of Myrtlewood. Have I possibly offended you?"

"Yes," said Rosemary and Athena simultaneously.

Marjie looked at the ground, staying unnervingly quiet.

Ferg stared at them, baffled, then he bowed low to the ground. "It seems I've let the incredible joys of bureaucracy go to my head. You're right to chastise me. Being the mayor has changed me. I'm no longer a mere pedestrian member of the town. I'm out of touch with my constituents. The people of Myrtlewood need me, not just to be a receptionist or a gardener or any of my other roles. I've forgotten to be a friend."

Rosemary sighed. "Ferg, I'm pleased that you're coming to this realisation, but we have other priorities right now."

"Very well. It's going to take some time to process this new information and see how it can be remedied."

Ferg melted back into the crowd, which had already started assembling around the town circle.

The sound of a bell rang – loud, deep, and resonant.

Everybody gathered around, including the Travellers who had

been busy moments before. Marjie stood silently next to Rosemary and Athena.

It was a much larger crowd than Rosemary had seen for the other seasonal rituals.

Some were dressed in costumes befitting the spooky season. There weren't many familiar faces, which Rosemary was glad about. She was concerned that a bunch of innocent people from out of town had come here for All Hallows', and they might somehow get trapped in the crossfire of whatever danger was afoot.

She was determined more than ever to keep them away from the cemetery and to keep whatever was brewing there away from all these people.

A familiar voice, creaky and scratchy, began to speak. Rosemary looked around to see a hooded figure at the periphery of the circle with white scraggly hair.

"Agatha," Athena whispered.

"That's a surprise. I've never known her to take such an interest in the rituals."

"Maybe Samhain's her thing," said Athena.

"Welcome, fellow villagers of Myrtlewood, and welcome to those who've come from near and far to celebrate this most sacred of ceremonies, as our sacred year officially comes to a close and we descend into the winter, to be reborn into a new year after the solstice."

Rosemary and Athena glanced at each other. This was the first they'd heard of it being a new year.

Agatha continued. "This is the time that we pay homage to those who have gone on from this world. We celebrate our families, our lineage, and we connect with our own past, releasing the old, clearing a space for new blessings to arise in our life, as the wheel turns ever onwards."

"She's quite poetic," said Rosemary.

"Shh." Athena elbowed her mother.

They remained quiet as the usual ceremonial parts of the ritual were carried out. The quarters were called, and the circle was cast, creating a sacred space.

The air almost prickled with the intensity of the magic. It felt thick and heavy, almost syrupy and palpable.

Unlike in previous rituals, Rosemary could actually see the boundary of the circle rising up and surrounding them like a great dome.

At least we're protected in here, she said telepathically to Athena.

Shhh.

But nobody can hear us when we talk like this.

I'm paying attention. Stop interrupting, scolded Athena.

After the initial formalities, Agatha suggested they all be seated. Rosemary wasn't sure how, exactly, but seating had appeared all around the circle, right behind them.

"This is going to take some time," said Agatha. "While we meditate, I want you to relax."

Meditation? said Athena telepathically. *I hope this doesn't take too long.*

I thought you said no telepathy, Rosemary grumbled. But she too was worried about the time, and what might happen in the graveyard.

Maybe we should have skipped the Samhain ritual, Rosemary thought to herself. *Though surely it's better to be here just in case the Bloodstones attack.*

We're all sealed in here. Rosemary surveyed the faces around. *If the Bloodstones are in here with us... It'll be hard for people to escape.*

It'll be hard for the Bloodstones to escape, too, said Athena, cracking her knuckles and clearly listening in to Rosemary's thoughts. *Either way, we're got them.*

But we're trapped here too, said Rosemary. *What if...while we're stuck inside the circle something even more awful is happening out there!*

Just relax, said Athena. *Maybe that's the kind of emotional stuff that you need to let go of, like Agatha said.*

"Take a deep breath," said Agatha. "And when you're ready, close your eyes."

She began to lead them through an otherworldly meditation.

Sink into the dark
  The dark of the deep earth mother
  Take a deep breath
  And release
  Letting go of the debris, of your mind
  Letting all errant thought slide to the forest floor

. . .

As you stand in the forest
    Autumn leaves falling around
    You notice an emotion
    Flaring inside
    You are drawn back to the last time a strong emotion was triggered in you
    Let it well up now
    Overflowing, pouring out
    Feel the root of that emotion, as you turn
    And begin to walk back along the forest path
    Back into your past
    Following the feeling
    Back through past events in your life
    Back to your childhood
    You reach a clearing
    Up ahead, is the way of the ancestors.
    Their different paths branching towards you in your family tree
    See the emotion flowing right back to its roots

As the leaves fall all around
    The light dims
    Walk slowly across the clearing
    A shadowy gateway has appeared
    On the other side is a guardian. A great powerful being of transformation who has a message for you
    Step through the gateway
    The guardian greets you

Listen as you receive the message

Now the guardian leaves
   You are alone in the darkness
   You feel it as roots grow from your feet into the earth
   Your limbs reach towards the sky
   You unfold into a glorious tree, glowing in the dark
   As life strikes you, branches and leaves fall to the floor, composting into rich nourishment for you and those around you.

Now thank the forest. The guardian. Your ancestors.

Take a deep breath and begin to return to this time and this place. Ever present.

Thirty

"Do you see her?" Marjie whispered as they emerged from the meditation.

"Who?" said Athena.

"Grace," said Marjie. "In the forest," she insisted, looking quite pale. "I saw her. In my mind – I saw Grace. She needs me."

Rosemary and Athena shot each other questioning glances.

"We're going to do what can we do to help Grace," said Rosemary.

Marjie sighed. "It's no use, I'm going to have to take it all on myself. I don't care what it costs me."

"We're here to help," said Athena.

Agatha gave them a stern glare, and they fell into silence as the closing of the ritual continued.

Rosemary felt the tension rising in the air, or perhaps it was just internally as the ceremony wound to a close.

She kept looking around, expecting enemies to emerge and attack.

It was almost worse when they didn't, and the tension continued to mount.

She slowed her breathing and told herself to calm down.

Finally, the circle was uncast, and the energy began to disperse.

"I was sure something bad was going to happen," said Athena.

"Look," said Rosemary, pointing to the side of the circle.

Standing back, near Rosemary's chocolate shop, was a girl with dark hair, dressed in black rags; her eyes glowed red.

"It's her," Athena whispered.

They both looked at Marjie, unsure whether they should tell her.

"I've got to go," said Athena quietly.

"But..." Rosemary started.

"We'll figure this out later," said Athena. "But I need to try again. I need to try to talk to her."

"Maybe Marjie can help," Rosemary suggested.

"Help with what, dear?" said Marjie. She looked over in the direction of the chocolate shop, and her mouth fell open. "Grace!"

Marjie began to run in that direction. But Grace took off.

"I've got to go," Athena said, running after her possessed friend.

"Not without us, you won't," said Felix, Sam, and Ash. They emerged from the side of the gathering crowd with bicycles.

Ash wheeled one over to Athena. "We're going after her."

"We're not going to catch up unless these are superpowered and electric," said Athena.

"They're enchanted," said Sam. "Another handy folk magic spell."

Athena locked eyes with her mother.

Rosemary had been kind of hoping that Athena would go with her to the cemetery, but now she knew her daughter had to make up her own mind.

"Go on then, if that's what you want to do."

"What about me?" Marjie cried as the team sped off on bikes. "I'm coming too!" She tried to run after them but was too slow. "Blast!" she yelled. "Rosemary, where are your car keys?"

Rosemary stood frozen on the spot. She wasn't sure if she trusted Marjie to go hooning off around town, especially not in her state.

She wasn't just worried about damage to Granny's old Rolls Royce. She was worried that Marjie wasn't stable enough to be left alone.

"Stick with me," said Rosemary. "We'll find them – something tells me they'll end up at the cemetery. That's where all the energy is congregating."

Marjie tried to argue, but Rosemary was distracted as something tapped her on the shoulder.

"Aren't you joining us for the feast?" It was Crystal Cassandra, with her floaty, slightly too high-pitched voice, and her blonde hair covered in a bright blue turban.

Marjie rolled her eyes. "We've got no time for feasting."

"You're worried about your friend, I can tell," said Crystal, her voice wavering dramatically.

Marjie narrowed her eyes, still clearly believing Crystal to be a fraud.

"What do you know about her?" Rosemary asked somewhat sceptically.

Crystal held her fingers up to her temple. "Grace, that's her name."

"Anyone could figure that out," said Marjie, crossing her arms.

"Oh, you two!" said Crystal, with a smile. "Don't you worry. I'll help. I can contact her right now and resolve all of this."

She held her hand up in the air and stared off into the distance. "Oh wait," she said, "Fire!"

"Fire?" said Marjie. "What's fire got to do with Grace?"

"No," said Crystal. "Look! Rosemary, isn't that your shop, on fire?"

Rosemary followed Crystal's pointing finger and saw that right where Grace had stood moments before, black smoke was now billowing out from the chocolate shop which was now engulfed in red and yellow flames.

"Oh no!" Rosemary cried, running towards the shop, watching all her hard work eaten up by flames. "Papa Jack was supposed to open tonight," she said urgently. "He said it would be good for business with the carnival in town."

She and Marjie exchanged worried looks.

"I'm so sorry, Rosemary," Marjie said with a sigh. "Do you think he's in there?"

They raced closer to the shop.

"It's all my fault," said Marjie as they tried to peer through the flames.

"Stand back," said Rosemary, pulling Marjie aside in case the window burst open. "It's not your fault at all."

"No...I should be more concerned with my living friends. Grace has already gone up. Yes, she needs to be laid to rest...But it's taken over my life. I haven't been there for you."

Rosemary gripped Marjie by the shoulders. "It's not your job to always be there for me; let me have a turn sometimes."

A fire engine pulled up and then Sid jumped out. "Ferg said there was a fire."

Rosemary pointed in the direction of the shop.

Neve looked at her quizzically as she approached. "Rosemary? I thought there was a fire. What's going on?"

"Can't you see?" Rosemary asked rather bluntly.

She turned back towards the chocolate shop to see that it was all perfectly in order; even her window display with the tiny pumpkins and bats and other cute Halloweeny things was untouched.

At first, Rosemary's mind raced in all kinds of directions. Surely all the chocolate would have melted from the flames. But the more she took in and processed of the situation, the more she realised the fire must have been an illusion. The interior of the chocolate shop was actually fine.

"What's really going on?" Rosemary said.

Not only was the shop completely fine, untouched by flames, but Papa Jack stood behind the counter, waving and smiling at them. A number of customers sat in the booths. It hadn't been this full in weeks.

"It seems like everything's alright here, false alarm," said Neve.

"I hope this wasn't some kind of hoax," said Sid.

"I'm afraid it's worse than that," Neve said.

"What do you mean?" asked Sid. "It's just some sort of Halloween prank."

"Do you think it's connected to the other stuff with the shop?" Rosemary asked. "Surely, I'm supposed to be the paranoid one here."

Neve laughed. "Sometimes your paranoia is dead on. I bet whoever drew your attention here was trying to distract you from something else."

The thought was unnerving. Rosemary looked around to see if there were any signs of further danger, but everything seemed to be in order. "It's not a very long distraction." Rosemary folded her arms. "Do you really think something else happened just now?"

Neve shrugged. "Nothing that I'm aware of. We have MIB officers stationed around the place. They refuse to bring in full forces because they're sure Myrtlewood isn't the powerhouse we make it out to be, but they did send some agents and they haven't reported any trouble. Everything seems fine."

"Maybe your magic ate through the illusion too quickly," said Marjie.

"I haven't even been using any magic," Rosemary protested.

"It's all around you," Sid said. "I can barely see you."

Rosemary frowned in confusion. She looked at her hands. Magical dust floated all around her, sparkling in the air.

"Oh, this is weird," she said.

Marjie grinned. "I suspect that's the Thorn defences kicking into gear, making you ultra-powerful. There is a danger here, we just don't know what it is."

"I have a pretty good idea of how to find out," said Rosemary, surveying the town square.

Despite the carnival and the fancy dresses, the fire juggling, and everything else, all still seemed to be in perfect order, but then again, this wasn't the centre of the Samhain energy.

"It's time we went back to the graveyard," Rosemary said, wishing Athena was with her but simultaneously hoping she would stay as far away as possible.

Thirty-One

A thena hadn't ridden a bike for a long time, but found it easier than she'd expected to pick it up again. Perhaps it was the magical enhancements that helped steady her as she rode with her friends.

"You were planning this?" she called out as they rode through the streets of Myrtlewood.

"Of course!" said Sam. "Did you think we were just going to let you do all the work in chasing Elise? We know you've been trying to go after her. And we knew she was going to turn up at some point. We figured the ritual was probably a good opportunity."

"And we knew you'd want to come with us," said Ash.

Athena smiled. She was wearing her bulky coat full of charms, as well as a backpack full of other odds and ends that she'd thrown together in preparation for Samhain night. It was a relief to have something extra to contribute to the whole operation for whatever was going to happen – magic she could give to her friends that might help protect them from harm.

"What do you think we're going to do if we actually manage to track her down?" Athena asked. Grace was powerful. Too powerful. Athena couldn't bear the thought of using her own magic against her – not with Elise at risk. "Though, I guess it's not that likely that we'll find her, is it?"

"Of course we're going to track her down," said Felix confidently. "I shot her with my slingshot."

Athena frowned. "That's why she took off in such a hurry. I don't think that helped."

"Or did it?" Felix raised his eyebrows and wiggled them around.

Athena couldn't help but laugh. "What did you do?"

"Magical tracker," he said. "It's one of my specialties, among other useful things for pranks."

Sam sighed. "I thought it was a terrible idea, but at least we now know where she's going."

There was almost too much for Athena to consider as they whizzed through the streets of Myrtlewood on the magically enhanced bikes, but Elise was out there. "Where is she?"

"Apparently in the woods," said Felix, looking down at the palm of his hand as he steadied his handlebar with the other.

Athena shivered. The dark mass of Myrtlewood forest was fast approaching them as they sped in that direction. It was an ominous sight.

Most of the trees were bare, making it somehow even more creepy.

"I don't know if this is suitable for bikes," said Athena.

"There's a track," said Deron.

Athena felt something wriggle in her backpack, and a morbid chill spread through her. Was it a curse? Had somebody dropped some kind of creepy-crawly magical spider in there when she wasn't looking? Was it about to bite her?

She flinched and then heard a familiar clicking sound.

"Hey, Athena!" said Ash. "It's your squirrel – he's peeking out of the bag."

Athena breathed a sigh of relief and then groaned. "Nugget! Why did you have to come with us?" The squirrel clicked again and then trilled and wrapped himself around Athena's neck so his golden tail brushed against her cheek. He sat there, gently nibbling her ear. "Don't try to distract me from being grumpy at you. It's not safe. Not for squirrels. Probably not for us either."

"Has somebody been neglecting their familiar?" said Deron.

"Probably," Athena admitted. "I've been so worried lately... and spooked. I haven't been paying much attention to the pets."

"He only wants to help," said Sam. "And who knows? Maybe he'll give us the upper hand."

"It's not just Elise," said Athena. "There's a whole lot of other stuff that I'm sure is going down tonight with the Bloodstone Society."

She could almost see the risks in her mind, spreading out in front of them like a great dark labyrinth.

"Well, whatever it is, we've got your back," said Ash.

Athena smiled grimly. "It's not me I'm worried about."

It was good to have support, but she didn't feel terribly optimistic about their prospects.

"So you think we're a bunch of weaklings?" asked Felix. "No wonder Elise got pissed at you."

"Shut up, Felix," said Sam.

"No, he's right," said Athena. "Maybe I've let the power go to my head a bit. And I haven't really been listening to any of you. And especially not Elise. She's been having a hard time, and I've just been telling her how she actually is really cool and powerful, but reassurance like that isn't really what helps is it?"

"Probably not," said Ash. "But I don't know what does..."

"Listening, I guess," said Sam, looking at Deron.

"Shh!" Felix held up his hand as he pulled his bike over to the side of the path.

"What?" Sam whispered.

There was a scratching sound.

They trudged through the dense forest, the skeletal trees towering above them like sentinels. The air was thick with the smell of damp earth and rotting leaves, and the only sound was the crunch of their footsteps on the forest floor.

"It's the house!" said Felix. "The one we went to for that horrible trip. It backs onto this forest."

Athena's heart began to race. Approaching from this side, the Brashville house was an even more imposing structure than it had seemed from the street. Its tall, peaked roofs and boarded up windows were menacing, and the whole place seemed to sag in on itself, as though it were barely holding together.

"She's gone home," Athena said softly. "This is the house where Grace grew up..."

Her friends nodded solemnly.

"This is it," Deron said, taking a deep breath as they approached the back door. "Are you all ready?"

Athena nodded and looked around at her friends. Their faces were set with determination.

The door creaked open and they hesitated.

"Just go in," said Felix, pushing ahead.

They entered the house, and it felt as if the darkness swallowed them up. The whole place smelled like mildew, and the floorboards groaned beneath their feet. Athena took in the familiar scene, the grey-brown peeling wallpaper, and there were old paintings hanging crookedly on the walls, but something was different.

"I don't think she's here," Sam said, their voice barely above a whisper. "Can we leave? This place is seriously creepy."

"She's here alright," said Felix. "Come on!"

They made their way through the house, but before they'd gotten to the hallway, the walls trembled. The chairs around the rickety dining table drew back, and old books flew off the bookcase nearby.

Writing appeared in dark red on the wall in front of them.

HELP

"She needs our help, see!" said Felix, rushing forward.

"Careful, dude," said Deron, pulling him back by the shoulder. "Take it easy. We don't know what's going on."

GET ME OUT!

The words scrawled themselves on the hallway as they slowly made their way through, and Athena's heart caught in her throat. Was Elise trying to call to her?

Athena's eyes scanned the rooms as they passed.

GET OUT!

They stopped in their tracks in front of a door.

There was a scream, and the whole house shuddered.

Suddenly, the air was filled with the sound of shattering glass. They spun around to see a vase, previously perched on a nearby shelf, now shattered into a million pieces on the floor.

"Grace is getting angry," Athena said. "We need to find her and put a stop to this."

The door flew open.

Grace stood in front of them, Elise no longer recognisable in her haunted visage.

Athena took a step back.

"Elise?" Felix said. "Elise, can you hear me?"

There was no response. The spirit had taken hold of her completely, and it was going to take everything they had to break its grip.

Athena closed her eyes. She could feel deep pain, trauma that wasn't her own. In the darkness of her own mind, old memories flashed through like a running film. *Grace's memories...*She was a little girl, playing in the garden with her tricycle, running around with her red-headed friend Marjoram. Her mother called them from the kitchen for afternoon tea. Laughter. It was a happy memory but weighed down by pain. She was older now and her mother was sad. Her father yelled. A vase smashed against the wall. She jumped out the window and ran to find her best friend. They giggled together. It was All Hallows and they dressed up as fairy tale witches. It was such mischievous fun, but then she had to go home. She didn't want to face her father, but something worse happened. She was chased. The older boy wouldn't stop following her. She ran faster and faster, through the woods. The sound of chanting. Everything went back. There was silence. Stillness. Until a tugging sensation pulled her back to her childhood home. It was the force of her mother's grief. Athena watched as Grace relived the years of memories in mere moments. Lady Brashville mourned for years upon years. Talking to Grace, who was bound never to answer back. Her mother passed away and Grace was still bound to the old house, stuck in the emotional residue, lonely and in agonising pain. Then they came, one night. A group of hooded figures. They lit candles and chanted around a picture, setting Grace free of the house, but compelling her to seek out the girl in the photo who would arrive the next day. Athena shuddered as she recognised her own face.

The Bloodstones had done this deliberately, they'd tried to compel Grace's spirit to possess Athena, but that had failed and she'd been absorbed into Elise, who was the next available victim...but they were all victims here.

"Grace," Athena said, reaching out through the anguish. "It's okay, Grace. Herb's gone. They're all gone. You can rest now."

Athena opened her eyes to see Grace's face trailed with red tears.

"It's okay," Athena repeated. "He can't hurt you anymore."

Grace screamed, blowing them back down the hall with the force.

She took off, smashing through the windows and out into the forest.

Athena and the others followed.

It wasn't hard, as the eerie scratching sound led them on.

They crept through the woods until they found Elise standing in a clearing.

"Stop following me," Elise said in a voice that was too low and resonant to be her own.

She hurled a wave of magic out, eviscerating the trees around her that crackled into ashes.

"Oh dear," said Deron.

"Elise...Grace..." said Athena. "We're friends. We care about you."

"Elise," said Felix, his voice croakier than usual. "Snap out of it. Stop running away like a weakling."

Grace glared at him.

"Shut up, Felix," said Sam.

"What? Everyone's been walking on eggshells around her, telling her silly platitudes. Maybe we need a different approach."

Grace's eyes glowed a brighter red.

Deron gritted his teeth. "I don't think insulting our possessed friend is going to work either."

They spread out around the circle. Elise was standing opposite Felix as he continued to give her a rather blunt pep talk. Her eyes glazed over.

"I think you're boring her," said Sam.

"What?" said Felix. "That's ridiculous. My speeches are inspiring! They're just the bucket of cold water she needs to come back to us."

"Maybe it's not Elise you're talking to at all, just Grace," said Athena, though the thought made her heart hurt.

"Well then, Grace," said Felix, with some inexplicable amount of swagger. "Get your spooky creepy butt out of our friend and go back to the underworld!"

"Felix!" said Sam.

"What?" he replied. "I'm not sure exactly how to insult a restless spirit."

"It looks like it's working," said Deron.

Grace's eyes burned with fire. She held out her hands and screamed.

The ground began to shake.

Felix ducked, just in time to avoid the blast of Grace's magic.

In that moment, the squirrel flew from Athena's backpack and latched itself onto Elise's back.

She screamed again and took off with the squirrel clinging firmly to her shoulders.

"That was a complete and utter failure," said Felix.

"Not to mention, you may have endangered not only us but Athena's familiar," said Sam.

Felix shrugged. "It was worth a try."

"No, it wasn't," said Athena, barely able to contain her rage. "But that doesn't matter now."

"You're angry, aren't you?" said Felix.

She was livid, but she knew Felix was trying his best to help, and that he was worried about Elise just like she was. "Not at you," Athena said. "It's just this whole situation...and I'm angry at myself."

Ash patted her on the shoulder, but it was cold comfort.

"What if she's gone? What if Elise never returns? What if she's not even there anymore?" Athena began to cry. Her friends crowded around for an impromptu and somewhat awkward group hug.

Athena leaned into Ash's shoulder and allowed herself a moment to relax. The situation might be dire, but it was so good to have friends she could trust.

At least I'm not alone in all this.

"We'll get her back," said Sam. "I'm sure of it."

Thirty-Two

The air seemed thicker as they approached the outskirts of the cemetery, and it was laced with traces of the putrid scent that Rosemary wished she'd never had the displeasure of recalling.

She checked her phone as she, Neve, and Marjie neared the gate, relieved to find a message from Athena.

We're all fine. See you soon.

Rosemary had a strong urge tell Athena to go home instead, and take her friends with her. She was sure the danger was imminent. And the cemetery was the worst place to be, but she couldn't very well exclude her daughter from a ghostly family reunion that she'd helped to organise.

Rosemary also figured that telling Athena what to do, at this point, was largely a waste of energy. So instead, she responded.

Just arrived. Got held up by an illusion. Tell you all about it later.

Marjie shivered next to Rosemary, who hadn't been able to persuade the older woman to stay home. Marjie had insisted on coming, along with Neve, even though they weren't invited to any particular family reunion.

"We're practically your family," Marjie had insisted.

"Sorry, you're stuck with us," said Neve.

Rosemary had sighed and relented. She didn't have time to argue.

As they made their way through the cemetery gates, the spooky feeling in the air increased. The chills that Rosemary felt were somewhat soothed by the various people milling about setting up shrines, lighting candles on graves, and various other places dotted around.

"Which one is the Thorn family mausoleum?" Detective Neve asked.

"I'm not actually sure," said Rosemary. "I don't tend to make it a habit to hang out in places like this."

"That one at the end, my dear," said Marjie.

A screeching sound rang through the air.

Rosemary looked around.

"Just a crow," said Neve, pointing to a nearby headstone.

"Whenever I see crows, I'm reminded of *her*," said Rosemary.

"Who?" said Marjie. "Galdie?"

"No, the Morrigan," said Rosemary. "You remember how I accidentally summoned her? She had a habit of turning into a murder of crows and ravens and swooping around in the air... quite stylish in a way, I suppose."

Neve smiled. "Least that's one thing you don't have to worry about this time."

"I've learned my lesson," said Rosemary. "Never again will I accidentally summon the Morrigan, although something tells me she might not be any less frightening than what we're about to encounter."

As they approached the mausoleum, Rosemary noticed that the graves, which had been washed to pristine cleanliness through magic only a day or so before, were now beginning to ooze with yellow-green slime again.

The stench of rot filled the air.

"This is gross," said Rosemary. "Can you call the clean-up crew back again?"

Neve shrugged. "Might be a little bit early, unfortunately. I'm afraid things are going to get more messy."

Rosemary grimaced. "At least when it was cloaked, I didn't have to smell it – or step in it!" She lifted her boot to see the slime stretching off of it.

"Oh, come on," said Marjie, pulling Rosemary on. "Stop stalling. We're already late."

The mausoleum didn't look exceptionally large from the outside.

A line of candles surrounded the entire building, and Rosemary smiled.

Athena had ordered thousands of candles and a bunch of other items from Granny's list.

The low stone building was lit up almost like Christmas, clad in wreaths. It was undoubtedly the most luxurious of all the mausoleums. She glanced at the row of them, wondering which one was the Flarguans' – Granny's biggest competition.

A few metres away, and she noticed a fairly elaborate setup. But it wasn't quite as spectacular as the Thorn mausoleum, and Rosemary couldn't help but feel smugly satisfied about it despite the eerie circumstances.

"Come on," said Marjie. "You better go in first. It's not like we were invited."

"All right," said Rosemary. "Should I knock?"

"Of course not. It's a tomb!"

Rosemary sighed and pushed the door open.

She gasped. It was a stunning sight.

The mausoleum was much, much larger on the inside, with high ceilings studded with fairy lights, and thousands more candles dripping wax all around the corners of the room, and great big bouquets of deep red flowers.

Not only that, the whole room was full of people.

"Uhhh...Maybe we got the wrong address," Rosemary muttered.

"There you are dear! Finally, finally!" Granny Thorn rushed forward, and Rosemary's heart stopped.

Tears burst from her eyes.

Her grandmother was solid, just as if she was still incarnate.

Galdie Thorn's hair was tied back in a red scarf, and she was wearing one of her blue lacy dance dresses with matching suede shoes.

"You're really here...not just a ghost," said Rosemary.

Granny Thorn wrapped her in a hug.

"That's the magic of Samhain," Granny said slowly, as if explaining to an infant. "The other side is closest to the realm of the living tonight, and this is a particularly potent one!"

"I never thought I'd be able to hug you again," said Rosemary, leaning into her grandmother and smelling that familiar musky herb scent of rose geranium, toffee, and cinnamon.

Granny Thorn chuckled. "Why did you think I was so interested in this reunion?"

"I had no idea," said Rosemary.

Granny tutted. "Now, I'll forgive you for being late because I'm just so happy to see you. But I simply must introduce you to some of your relatives."

Rosemary took a closer look around the room and realised that it was a full-scale party, complete with a band. A cellist, violinist, and viola player churned out old-fashioned music from the corner of the room. The party-goers were all dressed rather eccentrically in clothing from different eras – around a hundred Thorn ancestral ghosts returned back to physical form for the evening!

Rosemary was introduced to her great-uncle Ned, who had a very successful French horn business and also a knack for magical music.

"It's all vibration," he said after Granny Thorn had given her a flattering introduction. "You can do a lot with sonic waves through magic."

"We could have used you at the summer solstice," said Rosemary. "It would have been much easier to deal with those sirens."

Uncle Ned chortled before being whisked away by none other than Elamina's mother, Ada Bracewell-Thorn, who seemed oddly chipper. In fact, she smiled and waved at Rosemary as if she was a real human being for a change, rather than a snobby ice-sculpture as she usually came across. The effect was unnerving.

"And here," said Granny Thorn, "I simply must introduce you to your ancestor, Elzarie Thorn."

Rosemary felt a prickle of hairs on her forearms as she heard the familiar name.

She clutched her emerald pendant as her eyes fell on the woman seated in a green velvet chair.

Elzarie Thorn looked ancient, even for an ancestral ghost, with masses of white hair piled on her head and a great, beaming smile.

She was wearing the exact pendant that Rosemary could feel under her own fingers.

"How is this possible?" Rosemary asked.

"Sometimes the things that seem impossible are simply synchronicities in the realm of magic," said Granny. "Now, let me go and greet Marjie properly."

She tottered off and gave her old friend a hug while Rosemary took a step closer to Elzarie Thorn, as if drawn to her like a magnet.

"Take a seat, dear," said the old woman, who had a youthfulness about her expression.

"How long did you live?" Rosemary asked.

Elzarie chuckled.

"Sorry, is that rude?"

"Who knows these days," said Elzarie with a dismissive wave. "But I managed to get to the ripe old age of a hundred and seventy seven before I carked it." Elzarie cackled. "It was a good life, and it's been a most splendid afterlife."

Rosemary felt a synergy of sorts, a connection with this ancestor. "You're powerful," she said.

"And so are you, dear. The Thorn magic runs so strongly through your veins. I can feel it. It's giving me shivers."

It seemed a shame to waste this opportunity of meeting an ancient and wise ancestor. "Do you have any advice for me?" Rosemary asked.

Elzarie smiled. "You know, the world is full of good advice that nobody ever follows and bad advice that people always fall back on."

"Sure," said Rosemary, "like 'Follow Your Heart,' 'Reach for the Stars' platitudes. But I mean specifically, like what should I be doing? How do I get my life together? How can I be a better parent? What is in my future? Oooh, can you tell me that?"

Elzarie shook her head and cackled again. "Darling, you create your future. It's not my job. And as for your heart or the stars, those sorts of things only make sense in how you *hear* them. But I will say this: human beings, and I myself was equally culpable in this, we tend to always push forward as if we're striving for some external goal. When really, the magic always happens inside ourselves, in the present moment."

"What do you mean?" Rosemary asked.

"Instead of always focusing on the things we want to achieve, or want to stop, or want to protect – sometimes the real change needs to happen inside."

Rosemary frowned. "Are you going to tell me to meditate?"

Elzarie laughed. "That's not really a word from my time, dear. But it is true that within you lies a deep wisdom. And you know it. You've been there to our special ancestral place. You've seen me there when you restored the family magic."

"That was *you*?" said Rosemary. "But you looked...different."

"Younger, you mean?" Elzarie smiled. "That was a far different kind of magic from Samhain, I suppose. Besides, when I have my hair in plaits, it does give a more youthful appearance."

She winked.

"Maybe you're right," said Rosemary. "I'm always anxious and worried and trying to push for things and trying to protect Athena. I've got a lot of fire and air in me."

"As you should, too," said Elzarie. "Nothing wrong with a bit of hot air. In fact, one could say it powered the entire industrial revolution – that came after my time, though I did watch with interest."

Rosemary laughed.

"The lesson is one of nature," Elzarie continued. "If you really want to know."

"What do you mean?" said Rosemary.

"Nature is held together by tension, especially in this mortal life – especially in the earth realm. Everything that human science has revealed to us works through tension, and magic is no different."

"You're saying instead of fighting the tensions, I should...look within?"

"Indeed," said Elzarie. "Instead of resisting and projecting all of your emotions onto the outside world, there's a way to reach for those tensions internally. We know that the inner and the outer always reflect each other."

"You mean like when I'm having a bad week my bedroom gets really messy?"

Elzarie cackled again. "Exactly. There's a way to harness those tensions like reins, pull them towards you instead of pushing them away, energetically. And that's how you become the master of your own destiny."

"Mastery sounds nice," said Rosemary. "But I can't do everything myself."

"No. That's where friends and family come in. We're all here to help you, whether you can usually see us or not."

"Thank you," said Rosemary.

She turned towards the door to see Athena enter. "I should probably go...but before I do. I have a favour to ask."

"What is it, my dear?" Elzarie asked.

"Can I give you a hug?"

"Of course."

Elzarie rose from the chair and wrapped her dainty but strong arms around her great-great-great-great-great-great granddaughter.

Rosemary felt a wave of electrifying energy rushing through her, and her pendant tingled. "Ooh, that felt good," Rosemary said. "Remind me to hug more ghosts at Samhain in the future."

Elzarie laughed again and waved her away as Rosemary turned and headed towards her daughter.

Thirty-Three

"This is amazing," said Athena.

Rosemary smiled and hugged her daughter. "Well, you helped to organise it."

Athena stared at the room around them. "All I did was order some things for Granny and got them delivered to the mausoleum. She told me she didn't need any help to set up."

"I suppose she was right, then," said Rosemary. "Besides, she could get help from all these other deceased relatives who are totally solid for the evening."

"Strange, isn't it?" said Athena.

Granny Thorn appeared beside them and gave Athena a big hug before whisking her off for another round of introductions.

Rosemary sighed, wondering aloud if any of the refreshments were drinkable for mortals.

"They're all totally fine," said Elamina.

Rosemary almost jumped. Her very elegant cousin was

standing by the snack table, her back stiff, and her hair coiled up on her head, blonde and shiny to match her white-gold gown.

"You look really nice," Rosemary admitted.

"Thank you, cousin," Elamina replied, looking as though she was biting back her words.

"You're not even insulting me being dressed so casually," said Rosemary, beaming. "What's gotten into you?"

"I suppose there are some things that are more important than fashion," said Elamina.

Rosemary felt a chill. She wasn't used to Elamina being so friendly to her. Not unless she wanted something. But this seemed much more genuine and it was frightening.

"I've taken up my position in the Witching Parliament in Bermuda," said Elamina.

"Maybe the position of authority suits you," said Rosemary.

"And you look well, too, cousin."

"Is that a...compliment?" Rosemary asked awkwardly. Elamina didn't reply, so Rosemary searched for something else to say. "Err...Where's Derse?"

"Dancing." Elamina spat out the word as if it was in bad taste.

Rosemary turned to see that Derse was indeed dancing – enthusiastically, spinning around the room with none other than Elzarie Thorn.

"Incredible," said Rosemary.

"Isn't it?" said Elamina ironically. She took a sip of her punch and then passed a glass of it to Rosemary.

"It's not poisoned."

"How...kind?" said Rosemary, taking a sip despite her better judgment.

"I was surprised to be invited, actually," said Elamina. "The old woman and I...you must know, we never really got on. In fact, this whole side of the family..."

There was a shot of pain in her expression, and Rosemary almost felt empathy, though she struggled against it, considering how awful Elamina had been to her for most of her life.

Just then, Granny Thorn approached. "Now, now, Elamina," she said, taking Elamina's hands and pressing them to her lips. "I must apologise."

"For what?" Elamina asked cautiously.

"I was not the best grandmother to you, or to Derse." They looked over at Derse, who twirled Elzarie Thorn around in the middle of the dance floor to a jaunty cello tune.

"I suppose our side of the family is rather cold."

"Yes," said Granny. "That is probably what I was reacting to. Your parents were always so manipulative and calculating and snobby. And I just have an allergic reaction to that. It makes me come out in hives."

Rosemary muttered, "Maybe that's similar to my reaction to realtors."

Elamina glared at her.

Rosemary coughed. "Sorry, I'll stop ruining the moment. Maybe I'll leave..."

"No, you stay here," Granny Thorn said. "This is what family reunions are for. Neither of my children seem to like me very much, and it pained me so..."

Granny Thorn waved her hand, and two more people emerged dressed in polyester tracksuits.

Rosemary was startled to realise they were her parents. Gerald and Mariana Thorn looked absolutely mortified, and baffled as if they were waking up from a bad dream, only to find reality was even worse.

"How did you get here?" Rosemary spluttered.

"It would be rude not to invite them," said Granny. "I sent them a note and told them to be ready at seven."

"We didn't have much choice in the matter," said Gerald disapprovingly. "But we came prepared for the worst."

"We brought Holy Water," said Mariana.

"Save that for later," Gerald whispered.

So much for the brief moment when they thought our magic made us God-ordained superheroes, Rosemary thought, intending for her mental voice to be loud enough for her daughter to hear her.

Athena's mouth twitched.

Granny cleared her throat. "Now, now. Listen up, because I'm only going to say this once. I may be dead, but I still have my pride. And unfortunately, my pride stood in the way of us being closer. I wanted to invite you all here to this special family reunion—"

"We brought Bibles. Stand back, demon!" said Mariana.

"None of that!" said Granny Thorn. "I'm not evil. And I'm not a demon, either. I won't be here for long, so at least hear me out. My darling, Gawain..."

Rosemary's father furrowed his brows. "My name is Gerald."

Granny Thorn blew out a breath, then continued. "My son, I've always loved you. But you were born without an iota of magic, which left you feeling so bereft."

Gerald looked down at the ground. "I...I was?"

238

"I'm so sorry, my dear. I had to wipe your memory because you were in so much pain. I tried everything else, you see...and then, well, even that backfired on me."

Gerald looked up at Granny, and then made eye contact with Rosemary and Athena, before turning back to Mariana. His mouth and eyes crinkled in sadness.

"I should have learned my lesson by then – not to meddle too much. Not everything is a problem to be fixed," Granny continued. "You rejected me and filled your entire life with the church. It was an enormous betrayal. You broke my heart."

"I did?" Gerald asked.

Granny nodded slowly. "But, my dear, now I see more clearly – that even if we don't believe the same things, you're still family."

Rosemary's parents nodded nervously, looking very pale. They were on edge, as if they might be attacked at any moment, and both seemed to be muttering prayers under their breath.

"And Elamina," Granny Thorn said. "Wait—" She waved her hand again, and Elamina's parents emerged from the crowd and came to stand nearby, as did Derse.

Granny spoke again. "While I'm here, I might as well apologise to all of you. I was a terrible mother and an overly doting grandmother for only *one* of my grandchildren. I always felt that the world owed me children on my own terms. But now I have realised – and death perhaps has given me a better perspective – you need to live your own lives on your own terms, and whether that's through the Church or through trying to seize magical power, it really doesn't matter."

"Granny, I think you're only making this worse," Athena whispered.

"The Church matters!" Gerald stammered.

Granny sighed. "Maybe it was better before I tried talking to people. At least when I was dead and gone, you could try and make a fake memory of how wonderful and glorious I was. But I was selfish."

"It's okay to be selfish sometimes," said Athena.

Elamina nodded. "You lived your life, we are living our lives."

"We're different, that's all," said Rosemary.

Granny looked at her. "But, you and I are so the same."

"I was always envious," said Elamina, maintaining her cool composure despite the admission. "You were always this silly little thing with terrible taste, and yet you got all the attention. Granny was always more interested in her friends than her family until you came along. You two were close and did things together, as if I wasn't even worth her time."

It was all suddenly making so much more sense to Rosemary. "That's why you're always so horrible to me..?"

"Of course it was," said Elamina. "I'm sure even *you* could have worked that out."

Rosemary shrugged, unsure how to deal with the heartfelt family moment.

"People aren't perfect," said Athena sagely. "But, we are family. And even if we're polar opposites, it's good to let go of the past."

"You were always busy," said Ada, her tone cool, though her voice began to crack a little. "There was always someone *else* to help, some other magical catastrophe to solve. You never gave us what we needed when we were only children."

"That's right. I didn't know how to," said Granny. "I was never really cut out to be a parent. In fact, I felt kind of pressured into having you two, to continue on the Thorn family magic, and that's no way to bring a child into the world. I was busy doing my own thing, and I wasn't interested in a lot of what you had to say when you were children. I got so terribly bored."

"You never had any time for your own children," said Ada, her voice sounding almost childlike.

"I didn't, and I am sorry for that," said Granny Thorn. Tears were now streaming down both of their faces, and Elamina looked shocked and appalled, as did her father.

"Enough of this," Warkworth Bracewell-Thorn said. "We came here for a very important reason." He looked around at all of them. "To make sure that we upstage the Flarguans."

"That's right," said Granny Thorn decisively. "Let's go and spy on them!"

Rosemary laughed as Granny set off with the Bracewell-Thorns.

"Turns out they did have something in common after all," said Athena.

"Rosemary, Athena," said Gerald. They turned to look at him. "This will only hurt for a moment."

He pulled out a bottle and began to splash her with holy water.

"What are you doing?" Rosemary asked, squinting.

"Nothing's happening, dear," said Mariana.

Rosemary giggled. "Because I'm not evil, and your holy water doesn't really work."

"It's from our church." They shook their heads in confusion.

"Never mind that," said Rosemary as she and Athena backed away.

"It's time for you to go," said Granny, appearing again at their side. With a wave of her arm, a portal appeared. "This will take you two home, Gerald, Mariana. Again, I'm so sorry we couldn't have been closer, son."

She smiled sadly and gave them both a quick hug before scooting back towards Ada, Warkworth, and Elamina.

"Uhh, nice to see you," said Athena awkwardly.

Gerald nodded. "Please tell me this was all a dream?"

"I'm afraid not," said Rosemary. "It might all take a while to sink in, but maybe it will be...healing?"

"Lovely to see you, dear," said Mariana with a smile plastered to her face. "Shall we visit again soon?"

Rosemary gritted her teeth and shook her head. "Too dangerous."

"Right!" said Gerald. "Take care, then."

He pulled Mariana through the portal, which vanished a moment later.

"Families are complicated," said Athena.

Thirty-Four

The door to the mausoleum opened as Granny and the Bracewell-Thorns left.

Rosemary noticed a strange humming and a green glow shining through.

"We'd better go and check that out," said Athena. "I'll just grab my backpack." Her expression twisted as if she'd eaten a lemon.

"What is it?" Rosemary asked.

"I forgot to tell you," said Athena. "My familiar may have accidentally squirreled himself away. Pun intended."

"Where *is* Nugget, then?" Rosemary asked.

"Uhh...he also may have jumped on my possessed girlfriend and taken off wherever she went." Athena clenched her fists as if not quite knowing how to deal with the situation. "I really hope he's okay..."

Rosemary didn't know whether to laugh or cry. Instead, she patted Athena on the shoulder. "At least he's got company..."

"If Grace doesn't incinerate him!" said Athena.

"Let's just hope they're both all right."

They stood in silence for a moment. Rosemary tried to push worries about the rascal familiar out of her mind, because her anxiety wasn't going to help anyone.

"It seems strange to be at a party at a time like this where everything's going wrong," Athena said.

"Well, it *was* kind of enjoyable," said Rosemary.

Athena shrugged. "I suppose." She surveyed the various Thorn relatives and the historical outfits and sighed. "It would have been nice to spend more time with the extended ancestors."

"There's always next Samhain," said Rosemary. "Come on, let's go."

With their warm coats and their bags, they made their way out of the mausoleum.

It turned out the glow was coming from no specific source. Perhaps the entire cemetery itself was emitting some kind of low level of green light.

"This is so creepy," said Athena, looking out over the misty and slimy graves. "To the yew tree?" she suggested.

"That's right," said Rosemary. "Let's go."

Sam, Felix, Deron, and Ash had all been waiting outside, not wanting to intrude on the family occasion. They joined Athena as she and Rosemary made their way along the row of mausoleums.

"It's so creepy out here!" said Ash.

Rosemary wished the teenagers hadn't come, but she knew better than to try to convince them to leave when things were getting interesting. Fighting evil secret societies might be fine, but she knew better than to pick a battle with teenagers about what they were up to.

As the group walked along, they caught up with Bracewell-Thorns and Granny, who were laughing among themselves.

"We definitely upstaged them this year!" Granny crowed. "And I didn't wear my dancing shoes for nothing." She danced a little jig on the spot.

Athena and Rosemary glanced into the Flarguan mausoleum to see a rather sombre affair. Beryl and her sisters crowded around an altar of candles.

"It's a bit sad, isn't it?" said Athena.

"There you go, feeling sorry for her again," said Rosemary. "I'm proud of you. It takes a great deal of maturity to feel compassion and sympathy for one's sworn enemies. I haven't quite got there yet. Especially not with Perkins."

Athena smiled at her mother.

"Where are you guys off to?" Granny Thorn asked.

"Err..." Rosemary wasn't sure how much to tell her grandmother. Since passing over, Galderall Thorn had not taken a particular interest in the risks that befell the human world. She'd been more concerned with other matters. Perhaps this, though, would spark her interest. Only, Rosemary wasn't sure whether she'd be useful or just create trouble.

"Don't give me that look," said Granny.

Elamina rolled her eyes. "Something's going down, isn't it? You're always trouble, Rosemary."

Athena grinned. "And me, I'm trouble too."

The corner of Elamina's lip twitched. "How can we help?" she said quietly.

Her parents even looked mildly interested and so did Derse.

Rosemary and Athena did their best to fill them in on the recent strange occurrences.

"We think it's connected to the slime that's all over the cemetery and the old yew tree," Athena explained after Rosemary had given them a brief run-down of recent events.

"Well, that sounds ominous," said Granny, sounding rather smug.

"Why do you seem so happy about it?" Rosemary asked suspiciously.

"You may not have noticed," said Granny. "But we've just been at a gathering of many of the most powerful witches of the last several hundred years."

"Oh..." said Rosemary. "And you can use magic? That's excellent!"

"Do you think they'll want to help?" Athena asked. "It seems like they're having too good a time."

Granny Thorn whistled as if summoning a sheepdog. The Thorn ancestors emerged as quick as lightning from the mausoleum and crowded around.

"Listen up, you lot," said Galderall Thorn. "We've got ourselves a sordid Samhain situation here."

The Thorn ancestors rumbled their interest and encouragement as Granny explained the encroaching threats.

"Can we help?" Beryl asked.

Clearly, she and her sisters had overheard and come out of their mausoleum to join the crowd.

Athena raised an eyebrow.

"I'm not doing this for you," Beryl said bitterly. "I'm doing this for the town."

One of Beryl's sisters, a tall bony girl with the same shade of strawberry blonde hair, spoke. "That sounds like a nightmare and could seriously tarnish our whole reputation."

"That's Sissy," said Beryl. "And this is Petunia and Garnet."

"Hi," said Athena as the Flarguan girls scowled at her.

"You're the one who got our parents locked up, aren't you?" said Garnet. "Little thorn in our side."

Athena shrugged.

"Hey. I suppose they had that one coming," said Sissy. "All right. What can we do?"

A loud creaking noise interrupted them, followed by rummaging and a thud.

"I don't like the sound of that," said Rosemary. "Why don't we scope it out, see what's happening."

"We can break off into groups and check out the cemetery." Granny blew her whistle and quickly organised them into teams.

Rosemary, Athena, Galdie, Marjie, and Neve, along with Athena's school friends, made their way over towards the yew tree.

"I've been with the MIB agents," said Neve. "Making sure the cemetery is clear of civilians – except for you lot."

"Where are the agents?" Athena asked. "Are they going to help?"

Neve shrugged. "There's only a small handful of them and they've decided to guard the perimeter to make sure nothing nasty heads for the town."

"I suppose that's some consolation," said Rosemary.

There was a rumbling sound and the earth shook.

"Very bad news," said Rosemary, steadying herself on a tombstone.

The yew tree glowed bright green, but there was nobody in sight.

"There you are," said a vibrant voice. Azalea emerged from one of the underground crypts, clad in a silver and black spidery gown. "Charles, come quick. Oh, and Perseus, you too!"

The vampires began to emerge from the crypt, along with a bunch of other ghosts.

"Maybe this wasn't such a good idea," said Burk, eyeing his hungry family members.

They bared their teeth and some growled at the frail mortals who stood before them.

Azalea's eyes widened as she hastened to put herself in between the ancient vampires and tasty mortals. "You're right. I'll take care of the family," she said. "Perseus, Charles, and Dora can help Rosemary."

Rosemary shivered as Azalea skilfully rounded up her other family members. "Hopefully, she's strong enough to deal with them all."

"She'll be fine," said Burk. "At least she's aware of the dangers now."

Rosemary smiled. "Hello, you."

"I would kiss you, but I'm afraid we have more urgent matters to attend to," said Burk, looking out at the yew tree as the ground shuddered again beneath their feet.

"It's the Bloodstone Society," said Dora. "And I've been waiting for them." She was wearing a rather elegant fur coat, and underneath it, a combat outfit made entirely of leather and metal plating.

Rosemary and Athena gave each other a questioning look.

"But where are they?" Rosemary asked.

Azalea popped her head out of the crypt. "Before you go...and once you've dealt with whatever else you're doing," she called out, "make sure we all get a family photo together. The Thorns and the Burks together. Wouldn't that be nice?'"

"Uhh, sure," said Rosemary. "But in the meantime, we might want to save the town and/or the world from being overtaken by whatever this awful creepy magic is."

There was a scream from across the other side of the cemetery. Charles raised his binoculars.

"Why did you bring those? Bird watching?" Burk asked.

"Oh no. Haven't you heard the rumours?" Charles smiled.

"What rumours?" Rosemary asked nervously. She took a step backward and something cold, clammy, and slimy grabbed at her shins. She screamed, then looked down and screamed again even louder.

A rotting hand emerged from the grave next to her.

"And that's what he was looking for through the binoculars, I gather," said Granny.

"So it would seem," said Athena.

Burk gave Rosemary a hand as she extricated herself from the slimy limb protruding from the ground. "Thanks..."

She tried to blast the hand with magic, but that only seemed to make it stronger and faster. "This is not good."

"Mum, I think we've got bigger problems on our hands than just your ankle," said Athena.

They looked around; the ground all over the cemetery was moving, almost like an ominous bubbling pot, as various hands, heads, faces, legs, and torsos all emerged from graves.

"I knew it!" said Charles. "An army of the undead! I've been waiting so long for this."

He sounded so excited that Rosemary paused for a moment.

"Ignore him," said Burk, shaking his head. "He's never had the opportunity to see them outside of a few isolated incidents, but animated corpses are one of my father's special interests."

"I suppose that shouldn't surprise me," said Rosemary. "Do you think he might be...involved?" she whispered.

Burk shook his head. "Oh no. He's much more interested in how to stop a zombie apocalypse than how to create one. He's watched all the movies."

Rosemary sighed in relief. She and Athena ushered Marjie, Neve, Felix, Sam, Ash, and Deron into the Thorn mausoleum with the band, who still appeared to be playing a maudlin cello number, and instructed them to bar the door. At least the corpses in there were safely locked away, even if their spirits were clearly on the loose.

"What do we do now?" Athena asked. "Your magic didn't work against them, Mum."

"I'd say we've got about three minutes," said Granny, "before they all crowd around and attack us."

"Great," said Rosemary flatly. "How do we prepare in three minutes when our magic only makes them worse?"

There was a cackle of laughter coming from the yew tree.

Rosemary turned back.

The area was no longer deserted. Now, the space around the yew tree was crowded with the familiar robes and masks of the Bloodstone Society.

Up high in the yew tree was none other than Geneviève herself, her followers encircling the tree below.

"Rosemary, Athena, and friends!" She waved. "So glad you could make it to my party."

Thirty-Five

As Rosemary surveyed the scene in front of her, she momentarily forgot about the rising corpses struggling to free themselves from the graves.

Her attention was on the Bloodstone Society members gathered there. "You have a choice," she called out. "I know many of you have taken blood oaths, and you've been trapped for years, maybe decades, but you don't have to. You don't have to give your power to her anymore. You can break free!"

Geneviève laughed. "Nonsense. They'll all die!" she cried out.

"Oh well. Don't say I didn't warn you," said Rosemary. She could feel her power humming through her body to her hands.

"I knew it," said Dora, stepping forward, staring straight at Geneviève. "My old rival."

"Pity you don't have anywhere near the resources that I do." Geneviève giggled.

"Say that again, you bozo!" Dora shot right into the air, flying towards the tree, knocking Geneviève out from her perch. "You absolute dinglebat!"

The fight between them was so quick that it was impossible to see exactly what was going on, although it looked like there was a lot of kicking, screaming, punching, hair pulling, and the sheer force at which they threw each other around shattered graves. Perhaps the underworld energy was enhancing their vampire powers.

Rosemary pulled her attention away from the ancient child vampire fight. There were too many other compounding issues to deal with.

A low rhythmic thudding rang out, like the beat of a drum, as skeletal undead slowly marched towards them, forming an army of the dead.

Charles cackled. "Oh, there's one of mine!" he said as one of the newly emerged corpses fell face-first into the ground.

"What do you mean?" Athena asked.

"Didn't Perseus tell you I've been moonlighting as an undertaker?" Charles said with a dazzling smile.

"And?" Athena asked.

"I've been tying their shoelaces together!" said Charles triumphantly. "Just in case. I knew all my effort wasn't for nothing. Oh, there goes another one!" He laughed and skipped off with a camera. "Got to capture the photographic evidence of my brilliance!"

Burk shrugged. "That's my father for you."

"This is getting unbearable!" Rosemary cried as she frantically tried a few different variations of her magic against the approaching corpses. Fire seemed to be the most successful weapon she had, but it took so much energy to produce.

"Stop, Mum," said Athena, grabbing Rosemary's arm.

"I don't think this is the time to stop!"

"Seriously," said Athena. "Think about it. Death is sacred. These poor corpses have been desecrated by the awful Bloodstone magic."

"You're saying I'm only making it worse?"

"Wait a minute." Athena reached into her pocket and produced a small bottle. "Grandma Mariana gave me this before she left."

Rosemary rolled her eyes. "Holy water? Not you too! You saw how useless it was against the ghosts."

"The ghosts haven't been desecrated," said Athena, opening the bottle. She poured a little into the palm of the hand and sent it flying across to the nearest corpse, using magic. The being stopped in its tracks and slumped forward.

Rosemary shook her head. "Unbelievable. How is it that my parents were right about something for a change?"

"It's faith," said Athena. "Holy water is embedded with the power of belief in its sacredness. That, in itself, is a kind of magic."

"Remarkable girl!" Granny cried. "You might have just saved us."

"But there's only one bottle," said Rosemary. "Do you think we could get my parents back here with a bigger supply?"

"I've got something better than that," said Granny, taking a swig of the holy water as if it were a hipflask. "Focus on the energy of the sacredness and we can make more."

She held out her hands and a bright white ball of energy began to form between them. "This is not my usual flavour of magic, but it's not bad."

She hurled the ball outwards.

"No!" Rosemary cried, as it sped dangerously close to Burk, grazing his arm before hitting a corpse behind him, which slumped to the ground.

He reached up to clutch his arm. "No effect," he reported. "But I could have told you holy water doesn't hurt us. I suppose vampires aren't desecrated."

Rosemary breathed a sigh of relief as Granny Thorn crowed with laughter.

"You did that on purpose," said Rosemary, glaring.

"We have two minutes now," said Granny. "And I needed to know if the vampires could help or if they should get out of the way. Now we know they're not affected I'll figure out how they can help and you can get on with whatever you're here to do." Granny sent a wave of her sacred magic outwards. "That should buy you a few more minutes." Then she sped off to strategise with the other ghosts and the vampires, leaving Rosemary and Athena alone.

They practiced emulating the energy of the holy water, the spirit of faith and sanctity. It wasn't Rosemary's usual flavour either, but it felt pleasantly light and clean.

They hurled blasts of sanctified magic at the walking dead as they tried to approach. It had some effect, slowing their approach and stopping some in their tracks.

"It's working," said Athena. "But we're so outnumbered – a hundred to one. How long can we keep this up?"

Rosemary looked out towards Myrtlewood. "I wonder how those MIB agents are faring. I don't like the chances of the town below if the living dead escape that far."

Athena clearly had the same thought. "I've got to set up a barrier," she said.

"How?" Rosemary asked.

"Just give me a minute to concentrate. I think I can do it from here," Athena replied.

"Okay," said Rosemary, hurling more blasts of sacred magic outwards.

The problem was that even though they moved fairly slowly, and the holy-water inspired energy slowed them further, nothing seemed to completely stop them.

"Underworld magic...Underworld magic," Rosemary muttered to herself. She wasn't sure what she knew about it other than the bits and pieces Athena had told her. It was very, very old magic. The Bloodstone Society had been drawing on it. Something to do with Elise's possession as well...She looked out at the encroaching corpses. Perhaps they too were possessed, not with spirits, but with magic, as if they were being commanded and manipulated.

She looked towards the old yew tree again, hoping for a clue.

It seemed to be almost groaning, and a black sludge poured out from what Rosemary realised was some kind of wound in the trunk.

That was when she realised there was a gateway in the roots of the tree where the magic was pouring out from. It was dark green and hard to see as it turned into vapor and fog as it made its way among the tombstones.

"There must be a way to shut it," Rosemary muttered. "Close the gate...but first we'd have to get all the icky magic back inside."

Athena opened her eyes and coughed. "I think I put a barrier around the outside of the cemetery, at least."

"So that should keep us locked in with this enormous army of the undead..."

"Yep," said Athena meekly. "Not exactly my brightest idea."

"Perhaps it's perfect," said Rosemary.

"Why is that?" asked Athena.

"Because it's not just us. It's also dozens of our most powerful ancestors and some of the greatest witches who've ever lived," said Rosemary. "We can do this."

Thirty-Six

"Watch my back for a moment," Rosemary said, glancing over towards the old yew tree where the hooded Bloodstones seemed to be engaging in some kind of ominous chanting.

"Okay," Athena replied.

Rosemary put all her attention into creating another shield, similar to the one her daughter had just created, but smaller. Her idea was to keep out most of the zombies with the magical barrier, while keeping their allies around the yew tree and mausoleums protected inside.

"That's better!" she said, watching a satisfying shimmer of green light run over the sky, encasing them.

"Nice work, Mum."

Only, moments later the zombies began hammering against the shield, making holes.

"Why is your barrier staying up when mine is faltering?"

Rosemary asked.

"I think the main problem," said Athena, "is that the zombies don't actually want to leave the cemetery so they're not trying to attack my shield. They want to come after us!"

"Well, that means the town is safe," said Rosemary. "While we're around, anyway. And this is where the underworld magic is strongest." She could see it pulsating outward from the direction of the yew tree, covering the ground in a thick mist, spreading slime, and emitting a putrid stench.

Steam burst through the barrier, bubbling as if from a corrosive acid. "We can't fight them from within this ridiculous barrier," said Uncle Ned, who had somehow manifested a sword and staff and was clad in chainmail.

Rosemary was unsure exactly whether ghosts could die, even solid ones.

With a wave of her hand, Granny rounded up the entire Thorn family reunion crowd and began giving them orders.

"I'm going to do the same with our lot," said Charles.

Burk frowned. "I have a bad feeling about this."

"Don't worry," Charles said, as Rosemary made a door in the barrier to let him out. "The humans will be fine, and what vampire doesn't dream about a war with the walking dead?"

He saluted and disappeared away and down into his family crypt with Burk following close behind.

Rosemary shook her head, hoping that whatever the vampires were up to wouldn't sabotage their efforts.

"Help!" A sound interrupted them.

"What is it?" Athena asked.

Rosemary looked out. "Either the zombies have become rather human-like to trick us, or...some of your friends are here."

"Friends?" said Athena. She took a closer look to see Ursula, Hazel, and Rowan hammering against the barrier as the bony rotting limbs of zombies attacked from all sides.

"It's a trick," said Rosemary. "They're just trying to get us to break it down. They're not really friends."

"I'm afraid you might be right," said Athena. That's when she saw the look of anguish on Hazel's face that said otherwise. "What are you doing here?"

"Just let us through," said Rowan. "We promise we come in peace."

"Alright," said Athena, trusting her instinct. She cut through the barrier, allowing them in before Rosemary could stop her. "You have some explaining to do. How did you get into the cemetery in the first place?"

"We heard strange noises and thought we'd come to investigate," said Ursula.

"A likely story," said Rosemary, crossing her arms.

In the background, she could hear Granny rallying the troops and giving them clear instructions on tactics and strategy.

"Seriously," said Ursula. "Look. We came to the cemetery to help. And as soon as we got in, a barrier came up so we couldn't escape. And then we saw the zombies..."

"We're woefully unprepared for this kind of thing," said Hazel.

Their clothing was tattered.

Athena sighed.

"You really expect us to believe that?" said Rosemary.

"I don't know what you're supposed to believe," said Hazel. "I've never seen anything like this before. I knew that whatever was happening was dark magic, but this is something else."

"It's terrifying," said Rowan.

"And you know what?" said Rosemary. "I believe them."

"You do?" Athena asked, curious.

"Yes. I don't know why, but I just do."

"You're supposed to be this suspicious and paranoid one," said Athena crossing her arms.

"Well, we don't really have much time to waste on that kind of thing, now do we?" said Rosemary. "If they can fight, they can help us. If not, they can go shelter in a crypt somewhere. But either way, we've got bigger problems."

"Thank you," said Ursula, pulling herself up from the ground where she'd fallen in her attempt to get to safety.

"I don't know if we can help much," said Hazel. "But we'll see what we can do."

"I'll go look for weapons." Rowan dashed off.

Rosemary and Athena looked at each other and shrugged.

"I might regret that later," Rosemary said. "But like you said, they seem trustworthy, and we do have bigger problems."

The barrier began to quiver and crack as more of the slime made it through.

Rosemary coughed, trying to fan away the toxic stench of the steam. "I hope this doesn't have any long-term side effects."

"I think we can worry about the long-term a little later," said Athena. "What are we going to do?"

"We could drop the barrier and send out a huge pulse of magic. Hopefully, it will knock a bunch of these zombies over."

"Smart thinking," said Charles, who had emerged from the crypt with a straight row of vampires behind him. Some of them were muzzled, probably to prevent them from attacking nearby humans, but all their eyes gleamed as they stared out at the army of the living dead.

Rosemary raised an eyebrow. "Erm, why do you have a large supply of muzzles?"

There was a gleam in Azalea's eyes.

Burk shuddered. "Don't ask!"

Rosemary blushed and muttered something about Mary Shelley.

Athena shook her head. "Mum! Pay attention."

"Okay, ready?" said Granny, approaching them with the family ghosts in tow. "We'll focus on the north and east sides. You take the west and south," she said to Charles.

"What about us?" asked Rosemary. "Are we just gonna stand here?"

"You'll focus on the Bloodstones, and so will I," said Granny.

Just then, Dora and Geneviève crashed through the top of Rosemary's shield, sending sparks of energy cascading down in bursts.

"Now!" said Rosemary. She grabbed Athena's hands and they sent a huge pulse of magic rocking out across the cemetery from the edges of the shield.

"Let the battle begin!" Granny crowed, sending a beam of sanctified magic at a row of animated corpses with such velocity that it knocked them over like dominoes.

"Well, that's one strategy," said Athena.

"I'm pretty sure that the Bloodstone Society has just

commanded them to attack us," said Rosemary. "But we can use that to our advantage," she added. "They're headed straight for us in particular and not really after anyone else here. If there's ever a moment when our friends are in too much danger, we just need to move, and fast."

"We're outnumbered at least a hundred to one," said Athena. "I'm not sure moving around is going to be that much of an advantage."

"We could load them into a trap," said Rosemary. "Maybe create a chasm in the ground and send them back down to wherever they came from."

"Except where they came from is that tree," said Athena. "Or at least that's where the magic's been seeping out of. Could we send them back there?"

"We could try and funnel the magic out of them, but that's too complex to think about now," said Rosemary. She hurled a lightning bolt as a zombie began to clamber over a grave towards her. "Let's just fight, for now. See if we can knock them back."

There was a scream, and they looked towards the yew tree to see Dora tied to the bottom, restrained with what looked like ropes made out of the underworld slime itself.

The vampires advanced on the tree, but the Bloodstones gathered close around it, sending waves of underworld magic pulsating out.

Enormous spindly purple and orange legs emerged from the tree, followed by the bulbous bodies of spiders, at least four feet high.

"This just got a whole lot worse!" said Rosemary.

"Not to mention the bats!" Athena cried.

There was a screeching sound, and then huge purple bats burst through from the tree, claws and fangs bared, swooping down on the ghosts and vampires.

"What are we going to do?" Athena asked.

With a new wave of underworld magic, the zombies sprang forward with much quicker, more animated, movement. They jumped like frogs from grave to grave, stronger than many of the vampires who they began to wrestle with. The ghosts, despite their magic, struggled to keep them back. "This is going very badly," said Rosemary.

Rowan, Ursula, and Hazel emerged from the mausoleum along with Athena's school friends and the Flarguans.

"Let us help!" said Rowan.

"Go back!" Athena said. "It's too dangerous."

Sam and Barrow both gulped as they looked at the scene.

"Go back into the mausoleum," said Athena. "Hide there."

"We can't leave you here. Not like this," said Sam.

"Wait, look!" Felix pointed above them.

Floating in the air, twenty feet above, was Elise-Grace, her entire body glowing red. Her hair was long, now black with red streaks that coiled around her as if sentient.

Her eyes were glowing, an intelligent and menacing red.

She lowered herself down slightly and began to scream. The earth shook and laser beams shot from her eyes, hitting the tree where Geneviève was perched.

"Oh no, you don't!" said Geneviève. "I'm not going to let a stupid little possession stand in the way of everything we've worked for. Gallium, bring out the poppet."

A robed man pulled a dolly out of his bag. Something gleaming and blue was bound to it. "Elise's hair..." said Athena.

Before she could put all the puzzle pieces together herself, Rowan, who had been stealthily making his way through the rows of headstones, rushed Gallium with the great ornamental sword that he must have removed from one of the tombs.

The poppet fell to the ground, and Elise fell from the sky, far too quickly for Athena to react in time.

She and her friends ran over to find Elise's crumpled body, with Nugget sitting nearby, looking especially disgruntled but unharmed.

"Can you hear us?" Athena asked.

Elise's hair was still black and red. Grace was still clearly in control, but there was a pulse. She was alive at least.

"Take care of her," Athena said. "Take her to the nearest building and use whatever healing potions you can find in this." Athena thrust her bag at them. "Take Nugget too. At least that way he won't get into any more trouble."

The squirrel glared at her, and then whimpered.

Thirty-Seven

T he earth crumbled beneath them as more and more
creatures emerged from the yew tree, creepy crawlies and
slimy beasties.

"It's too much!" Athena cried. "We're done for!"

They surveyed the cemetery. By pulling themselves up to the
roof of the mausoleum, they could see the different teams that
had been formed, that Granny had coordinated. The Flarguans
were off battling zombies in one corner. They'd teamed up with
the Bracewell Thorns, and the vampires, and the family ghosts
were on other sides of the yew tree, battling the undead and
underworld beasties, trying to hold them back. Just then, one of
the bats caught sight of Rosemary and Athena. It squawked, and
as if in response, or perhaps like a hive mind, all the creatures
turned towards them. Despite the small armies of vampires and
ghosts trying to protect them, it was no use.

"How do we beat all these creatures?" Rosemary asked.

"With happy thoughts," said Athena. "I mean, what's the opposite of Halloween? Midsummer? No, that's not right, is it?"

"Beltane," said Rosemary. "Fight them with fire."

"It's worth a shot," said Athena, launching fireballs at the creatures. They sizzled, and some even fell to the ground. But despite their skin being singed and dripping off, oozing messes, the creatures didn't die or give up. In fact, they got riled up.

"I think we just brassed them off even more," said Athena. She screamed as a bat dived at her, knocking her almost to the edge of the mausoleum roof.

Rosemary grabbed for her, and Athena steadied herself, but another bat lunged, biting into Rosemary's arm. She screeched like a banshee as she blasted it away, taking out the bat that was biting Athena, and a spider that was crawling up onto the mausoleum roof.

It was too much.

The bats in the air were circling, gathering their forces, and dozens more enormous spiders were coming after them. Rosemary sent wave after wave of fire, but the singed creatures seemed to only find strength in it and battled on, more invigorated than before.

"That's not working. What about water?" Athena asked.

"I don't know," said Rosemary.

"It's too much. Do you think if we surrender, they might take pity on us?"

"Are you serious?" said Rosemary. "Surrender and face a world where the Bloodstone Society are not only at large, but could take charge completely. They could be in control of the town, and before you know it, in control of the whole magical world, and they wouldn't stop there..."

"You're right," said Athena. "But what choice do we have at this point? Maybe if we pretend to surrender..." Her voice trailed away.

"No," said Rosemary firmly. "What we need is to harness the power that they wield."

"You mean become dead zombies?" Athena shouted, shielding herself and blasting another bat as it flew at her.

"Not exactly," said Rosemary. "But I have an idea. You remember how I accidentally summoned the Morrigan that time?"

"Oh no," said Athena. "You're not thinking..."

"Well, she has dominion over the dead, doesn't she?"

"Isn't there some other god? Brigid maybe?"

"Maybe, but it's not really her forte," Rosemary said.

"You're right," said Athena. "But the Morrigan, she's scary."

"She's powerful," said Rosemary. "She's terrifying...But maybe that is what we need right now. And I don't care if I get put on trial, and locked up by the witching Parliament, if I have the chance to save the town. Maybe it's worth it."

"Sure about this?" said Athena.

"Cover me, I need a few minutes," she said to Athena.

She felt a shield go up around them.

Rosemary closed her eyes and reached into the dark, deep recesses of her soul.

Elzarie Thorn's words came back to her mind – about seizing the tensions and bringing them towards her. As a child, she had been terrified of the dark, and her imagination had run rampant.

The spooky events leading up to Samhain had stirred that dark fear in her again. But now, what would happen if she reached for that terror and took the reins? The meditation of the Samhain ritual came back to mind, and she found herself in the forest again.

From that forest and the peacefulness she connected, reaching out like tree roots towards that dark swampy energy that she associated with the Morrigan herself. It took Rosemary a moment to find the right words for how to summon – deliberately, for a change – the goddess associated with the battle and blood and death.

"Morrigan!" she called out. "It may have been an accident, but I was the one who freed you. And now, I need your help."

Rosemary listened, reaching with her mind into the darkness. Nothing stirred.

She thought back to the ritual that she had thrown together in the dead of night – the lightning that had struck – but all that she could feel was stillness.

Maybe now that the Morrigan was freed, she wasn't able to be summoned anymore. Maybe she was off still having her tryst with the Dagda, and didn't want to be disturbed. And Rosemary didn't particularly want to interrupt her in that case either.

Instead, she said anything that could come to mind, a plea for any god, any goddess, anyone who could help them.

It all felt so hopeless...then Rosemary realised she was de-centring herself. She was pushing too hard, trying too hard, leaning too hard into influencing the future instead of doing what she'd really intended to do all along, which was to take the reins like Elzarie Thorn had instructed.

She felt for that tension, that pushing, that reaching in her mind, and instead, she switched around and tugged it back towards her. Instead of reaching and pushing, she pulled it back, and centred herself.

"Come," she said, but now it was from a place of power. "I summon you."

Rosemary opened her eyes to the sound of thunder. Lightning crashed through the sky, and the Morrigan appeared, floating in the air before them.

"About blimin' time I was invited!" she cried out with a cackle. "Now, what do we have here?"

She sailed up into the air, reminding Rosemary of Grace, who had been floating up there not long before, only the Morrigan was so much more powerful.

"I can sort out this beautiful mess of beings...but the tree...it is dying," the Morrigan called out.

"Can't you save it?'" Rosemary asked.

"That is not my place, but I can take care of these others," the Morrigan replied, darting off towards the various corners of the cemetery.

Her hair stretched and hung down like tentacles, reaching out. A long coiling strand wrapped around a nearby corpse, struggling against a gravestone. Somehow, knowing where to go, it lifted the skeletal being up in the air and towards a specific grave, lowering down until it melted deep into the earth.

"This is going to take some time," the Morrigan muttered, as more and more strands of her hair began to work their magic, returning the dead to their rightful resting places.

Rosemary breathed a sigh of relief.

"What kind of bargain did you have to strike to bring her in?" Granny Thorn said, appearing next to them.

"No idea," said Rosemary. "I hope I don't regret it."

"Oh well." Granny Thorn winked, and then disappeared back into the battle.

Rosemary helped Athena up. They were both bleeding from bat wounds.

"Are you okay?" Rosemary asked.

"I'm fine, Mum. What about you?"

Rosemary looked at her arm where the wound was blackened and oozing. "I think we're going to need some medical attention, but at least it doesn't hurt."

"Yeah, let's hope they weren't venomous," said Athena, limping a little.

Rosemary helped her along. "Now, what?"

The Morrigan was still slowly working her way around the cemetery, removing the underworld creatures in her path, but there were still so many threats.

"What we need to do is save that tree," Athena said, "and I think I might know a way."

Thirty-Eight

Athena returned to the Thorn mausoleum.

Ash, Deron, and Marjie were gathered beside Elise, while Felix and Sam sat glumly in the corner, with Nugget curled up snuggly on a cushion between them.

"She's going to be okay," Marjie said. "Don't you worry, my dear."

Athena breathed a sigh of relief. She wanted nothing more than to stay with Elise and her friends, but she had to trust that her friends would do just as good a job without her. Healing wasn't her specialty, anyway, whereas Ash was quite good at it. Now that she knew they were safe, she had to find Ursula and figure out some kind of miracle plan.

Athena made her way back towards the yew. Rowan, Ursula, and Hazel had managed to tackle Gallium and restrain him. Rosemary wrapped some kind of magic around him to prevent him escaping.

Athena watched as her great grandmother's ghost fought with another of the Bloodstones. A mask came loose to reveal the familiar face of Crystal Cassandra.

"I should have bloody well guessed," said Marjie, who had clearly followed Athena out of the mausoleum.

"Where have you been?" Rosemary asked.

"I was just making tea, and then I helped with little Elise..." said Marjie. "I didn't realise things had gotten so out of control. But now, if you'd kindly step out of the way, Crystal is mine!" She grabbed a yellow bundle out of her bag and threw it at the gossipy medium. It exploded into butterflies in the air.

"A nice change from all the bats and spiders, at least," said Rosemary. "How's Elise?"

"Not great, but she's alive," said Athena. "I figured my best bet was to be out here trying to stop the bigger threat. Otherwise, we're all doomed."

"That's very sensible, love," said Rosemary.

"Wait, is that Granny fighting her own body?"

Rosemary turned to see that indeed, her grandmother was battling her own wicked and rotting corpse, cackling and howling in glee as she did so.

"Why wasn't she in the mausoleum with the other Thorns?" Athena asked.

Granny laughed. "Oh no! I needed some peace and quiet. I was very specific in my instructions – to be buried on the hill away from all the noise."

After restraining Crystal Cassandra, Marjie spotted another familiar face. Herb, still relatively fresh compared to others in the graveyard, came lumbering towards them.

"Time I showed Herb – or at least his corpse – how angry I am." She went after undead Herb with some magical assistance from Granny.

Rosemary and Athena didn't have time to watch justice being served.

"I need to get up there!" Ursula said. "The yew tree – I can feel it dying."

"We need to get closer," said Athena. "Come on, we'll form a protective barrier."

As they made their way closer to the tree, they caught sight of Dora, still trapped against the trunk. It looked like the coils around her were sapping the lifeforce out of her along with the tree itself. They both seemed to be shrivelling.

"Dora might be fading away, but Geneviève is practically glowing," said Athena, pointing up into the tree. They watched as the Bloodstone leader stabbed into it with a glowing Athame. "Isn't it a good thing if the tree dies?" said Rowan. "It's linked to all this evil."

"No," said Hazel. "The tree is the guardian. A yew tree in an old cemetery like this has an important role. If it dies, then all of this underworld energy will stay in our world where it doesn't belong. And plenty more could have rushed through besides."

"That's what we thought," said Rosemary. "Look, I'm going to knock Geneviève out of the tree." She turned to the Travellers. "Do you think there's anything you can do to save the tree?"

"I can try," said Ursula.

"That's how your magic works, isn't it?" said Athena. "You can make things grow."

"I can help them grow, but I'll need to get up high," Ursula said.

"I'll give you a boost," said Rowan.

As the various Thorn allies tackled the other bloodstones, Rosemary hurled a sharp ray of sunshine towards Geneviève.

The tiny vampire shrieked as her skin began to sizzle, and she fell to the ground.

Rosemary quickly built a case around Geneviève, weaving that same sunlight energy into a kind of cage. It wasn't something she'd done before and it was a little messy, but the little vampire cult leader continued to shriek and couldn't seem to break free, so Rosemary considered it a win.

Meanwhile, the vampires worked to free Dora with magical assistance from Elzarie Thorn.

Rosemary looked up to see Athena with Ursula and Rowan up in the tree, close to the wound that Dora had made in the trunk. "This is not looking good!" Ursula called out. "I can feel it. The life is ebbing away."

Thirty-Nine

Athena used her own magic to pull herself up into the yew tree while Rowan helped Ursula and Hazel up before climbing up himself.

Athena leaned against one of the large gnarled branches, while Ursula sat in the centre with Rowan standing behind her. Hazel found a convenient branch to perch in.

Ursula closed her eyes. "The tree is really suffering, I can feel it. It's so old and has been protecting the cemetery for centuries – now it's being drained of all its energy."

"Can you help?" Athena asked.

"I'm so tired," said Ursula quietly, her eyes still closed. "I was feeling exhausted before, but now that I've connected with the tree, it's even worse."

"We can lend you some energy," said Athena.

She looked out towards Rosemary, who was dusting off her clothes after adequately restraining the tiny evil vampire.

276

Mum, we need your help.

Rosemary looked towards the tree.

Are you sure you should be up there? she replied. *The yew is the epicentre of all this underworld power. If it dies, the whole thing could collapse, or worse.*

I know, said Athena. *Just trust me. Ursula needs energy. I'm going to give her some of mine. Can you help too?*

Of course, said Rosemary.

Athena reached down and put a hand on Ursula's shoulder and then closed her eyes. She began focusing on her own magic, both the fae side and witch powers coursing through her. She felt Rosemary's energy beaming through to her, warm, strong, and comforting, like sunlight on a cold day.

Athena took it in, absorbing it, and then focused on Ursula and the tree, merging the magic and sending it her way.

Even with her eyes closed, Athena could feel Ursula respond to the boost of energy. Her shoulder relaxed beneath Athena's hand, and a humming sensation rang through them.

"Your power," Ursula said. "It feels so good...and I can feed it through to the tree, but it's like pouring buckets of water into an endless void. It's not enough."

"I'll see what we can do about that."

Athena reached back to Rosemary in her mind. *We need more energy up here.*

I'll see if the other Thorn witches here can help, Rosemary replied.

Several moments passed and Athena held her concentration, then she began to feel it as, one by one, more magic joined in with hers, each with its own discernible signature. Her whole body was vibrating. It was almost too much, discordant, like a band playing out of tune.

There was a gasp and Athena opened her eyes to see Ursula had covered her ears.

"There's a lot of power going through you," said Hazel. "But it's not quite right."

"It's too much for Ursula," said Rowan. "We need more energy, but it needs to be harmonised with her magic. Is there a way you can do that?"

Athena's mind raced. Ursula's magic made things grow. It was a nourishing life force. The power coursing through her was all over the place. She reached back to Rosemary to ask for help to tune the energy into something they could use.

How do you mean? Rosemary asked.

Athena thought for a moment, and then replied:

Think of sunlight and spring
Think of safety and nurturing
Think of gentle rain...

Athena could see it now. All the energy pouring across the cemetery like beams of light, through Rosemary, and straight to her.

Ursula breathed a sigh of relief. "That's so much better," she said. "But I'm still not sure it's enough, and I don't know how much longer I can do this."

Hazel clambered down to her other side. "Let us help too."

Rowan shook his head. "I wish I could, but you know that all I ever get are random sparks of magic. I'm useless." He bent over and brushed Ursula's damp hair from her forehead. "I believe in you though."

"You can try," she replied, reaching up to caress his cheek. "Stop holding yourself back. I know you're scared that if you really try to use magic, it will only disappoint you."

Rowan shook his head. "I'm more afraid of disappointing you."

"Don't be," said Ursula. She took his hand. "Just trust."

Athena watched as the three of them joined hands and Athena noticed a triangle of light shooting all around them, even brighter than the energy coming to her from the other witches.

The yew tree groaned and trembled beneath them and Athena reached for a branch with her hand to steady herself while keeping the other resting gently on Ursula's shoulder.

Rowan began to shake. "I can feel all the magic," he said. "It's too much for me. I'm only getting in the way."

"No," said Hazel. "It's your magic too. Can't you feel it? It's opening up in you!"

Rowan shook his head. "You're just imagining things."

"She's not," said Athena. "I can feel it too. As soon as the three of you joined hands, it was like an electrical circuit closing."

Rowan took in a shaking breath. "It's intense, whatever it is."

The tree trembled again.

"Just relax," said Athena.

A moment later Rowan laughed. "I get it now!"

The three Travellers shared a giggle that Athena did not quite understand. She looked between them questioningly.

"I've been trying all this time to use my powers alone," Rowan explained. "But that's just not how they work."

"You're an amplifier," said Hazel, her voice buzzing in odd vibration. "This is incredibly ginchy!"

"That's great," said Ursula, smiling now. "Because this massive energy void needs a whole lot of healing power to fill it. Even now, it seems impossible."

"I've been stemming the flow because I didn't know how much Ursula could take," said Athena. "But I get the feeling we're running out of time. If we're going to save the tree, we have to give it all we have – all it needs – and we have to do it now. Ready?"

They all nodded at her. Athena closed her eyes and centred herself, then she sent out a silent signal to Rosemary.

Now.

The blast of energy was so powerful that for a moment Athena had no sense of self or time or space. Then, a radiance shone through that seemed to bring everything back together.

Athena opened her eyes again. It appeared almost as if they were in daylight. The vampires looked around, astonished and nervous about bursting into flames, but it wasn't exactly sunlight – just the energy of it – the sun, which feeds all life on earth. It was wonderous.

A darkness fell all around as the glowing ceased.

Forty

R osemary's heart caught in her throat. *Had the tree died? Had Ursula been unsuccessful?*

She could barely see anything at all. But then, stars began to appear through the blackness, and a bright light shone out from a nearby tree.

The ground shook again, and Rosemary grabbed Marjie, who was standing nearby. They steadied each other as they watched.

New leaves began to grow on the tree, despite the cold season. The earth shook again and more shoots began to appear in the ground around the tree, quickly growing tall and strong: more yew trees, young and vibrant.

"More guardians," Marjie whispered. "The old tree won't live forever. These young ones will take its place, one day, when the time comes."

Rosemary squeezed her friend's hand.

They watched as the base of the gnarled roots, the gateway

which had previously glowed green and let through so many beasties, shimmered in blackness.

Ursula, still sitting high up in the tree, collapsed forward and Rosemary worried she'd fall, but Rowan and Hazel caught her just in time.

They carried her carefully down with Athena trailing behind them.

"She's going to be alright," Rosemary asked as they approached.

"Hopefully," said Hazel. "Believe it or not, but I think we've been through worse."

Rosemary sighed. "Look, I'm sorry for not trusting you lot."

Hazel shrugged. "That's understandable, I guess."

Marjie pulled a large pink and yellow crocheted blanket out of her handbag, which she wrapped around Ursula to keep her warm.

"Marjie look!" said Athena, pointing towards the mausoleum.

Elise-Grace was walking towards them, Athena's friends trailing behind.

Her eyes faded from red to brown. Not the colour of Elise's eyes, but Grace's.

"Oh my goodness," said Marjie, rushing forwards to hug Grace tightly.

Athena hung back, looking anxious.

"I'm so sorry," Marjie said. "I should have gone...I should have been with you that night. It was my fault."

"No," said Grace. "No, Marjoram. It was not. I had trouble accepting that it was my fate all along – because I felt for so long that I was trapped in that house – that it was unjustified, that it was wrong."

"And it was," said Marjie. "You had your life was stripped away from you."

"Yes," said Grace. "But now all that anger that I had is gone. I've stolen someone else's body," she said. "And that's not right either. I must go."

"Please tell me you can visit," said Marjie.

Grace smiled slightly and said, "You know, I'll see if I can. And maybe we can catch up next Samhain. I hear the parties in Myrtlewood are the best." She winked.

"What's going on up there?" said Rosemary.

The Morrigan floated in the sky. She'd pulled together an enormous ball of black energy, swirled through with green and yellow.

"It's all of the underworld magic," said Granny, popping up again. "She's gathering it all together. I think she's going to push it back through."

"And that's where I need to go," said Grace. "It's time for me to leave."

Rosemary felt a tear squeeze loose as Marjie hugged her old friend, and then the outline of Grace's spirit floated out into the sky and then drifted towards the yew tree, disappearing into the gateway.

Elise fell to the ground. Athena stepped forward and caught her just in time.

"The danger hasn't passed," Rosemary muttered, but Athena didn't respond at all.

Forty-One

Elise lay crumpled in her arms. Athena's heartbeat echoed so loudly through her head that she could barely hear any other sound at all, until a subtle birdcall broke though.

Dawn was coming.

They lay on the soft grass that was thankfully no longer slimy.

"What happened?" Elise asked. "Did you save me?"

"I suppose...something like that," said Athena.

"At least we tried," said Sam. "Maybe Grace just needed to get her own kind of resolution. And now she's gone."

Elise looked almost anguished for a moment and Athena frowned in confusion.

"She's gone," Elise said.

Athena nodded. "It's okay, you're safe."

"But..."

"What is it?" said Ash, taking Elise's other hand.

"She was so upset," said Elise. "And I..."

"You were possessed," said Athena."

Elise shook her head. "No."

"Yes," said Felix. "We were in that haunted house, remember? That must have been when it happened."

"Were you asleep?" Sam asked.

"Sort of," said Elise. "But...she didn't steal my body."

"What are you talking about?" said Felix.

"I...let her in."

Felix looked ashen-faced. "Why would you do something so stupid?"

Athena shook her head, confused. "Why?"

"Why would you do that to yourself?" said Sam.

"We weren't so different," said Elise.

"How can you say that?" said Felix. "I mean, she was cool and everything. And I'm not saying you're not, but you're kind and she was mean. You couldn't be more *different*."

"Maybe on the outside," said Elise. "But underneath it all, we felt the same kind of powerlessness, and she..."

"She gave you powers," said Felix, scowling. "You're saying you put us through all of that just so you could have some nifty magic?"

"I'm sorry," said Elise. "I didn't know what would happen, but..."

"It doesn't matter now," said Athena. "You're back. It's okay. Everything's fine." But the tightness in her heart told a different story. She hugged Elise and repeated *everything's fine, everything's fine,* in her mind, willing it to be so.

She was too exhausted to think of anything else at that moment.

"Look!" said Deron.

They gazed up as lightning and thunder struck, illuminating the sky.

The Morrigan swept the last of the underworld magic into the enormous ball in the air. "That's hugely powerful," said Felix. "Do you think she's really going to send it back? What if she just changes her mind and blasts us all with it? It'd be like an atomic bomb."

"Shush," said Sam. "Watch."

The air thickened with anticipation as the Morrigan glided gracefully through the air, pushing the mass of black swirling energy without so much as lifting a finger.

"All right!" she cried. "Enough." She flicked the ball with her pinkie and sent it sailing towards the yew tree. It was sucked back into the hole in the trunk and beneath the ground, which bubbled like a geyser and then faded away.

"It's...gone," said Athena.

"It's really over," said Sam.

"What do you think she'll want in return?" Ash asked.

Athena got up and looked towards her mother. Rosemary was already walking towards the spot where the Morrigan had landed on the ground, several metres away, in front of some broken tombstones.

"I'd better go," said Athena. But she glanced back at Elise and noticed her sad expression. "What is it?"

Elise shook her head and smiled, but it didn't quite reach her eyes. "Nothing," she said. "We can talk about it later."

Athena gave her one final hug before getting up and approaching her mother.

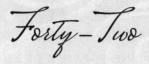

Forty-Two

Another bolt of lightning crashed through the air as Rosemary approached the Morrigan. There was a gleam in her eyes, which was quite unnerving.

"Errm...Thank you," said Rosemary, unsure of how to address an ancient goddess of war and death, a former Fae queen and uninvited houseguest, and maverick.

"Rosemary Thorn," said the Morrigan. "Why do you approach me?"

"I was the one who summoned you," said Rosemary. "And I expect there might be a price. So you might as well tell me now."

"A price," said the Morrigan, stroking her chin. "People these days are so instrumental."

"What do you mean?" Athena asked.

"So commodified," the Morrigan continued. "Everything is about money, costs to be paid, and it's a little bit boring, isn't it?"

"Maybe so," said Rosemary, not trusting the Morrigan one iota. "But you came and helped us."

"Well, it was a fun night," said the Morrigan. "And you should have invited me earlier."

Rosemary felt a shiver. It couldn't be that easy. She had read the lore around the Morrigan and knew that bargains made with her often ended in catastrophe. It was like accepting a gift from the Fae, where one had to be exceedingly careful with the terms. Only, there hadn't been time to negotiate. In the moment, she had been so desperate that she would have sacrificed herself if it would have saved the town, and Athena, and everyone else she cared about, but now...Rosemary was hoping for something a little bit less confusing.

"Well..."

"Oh, you're still waiting, are you?" said the Morrigan. "Very well. I want to be invited."

"Excuse me?" said Rosemary.

"Yes," said the Morrigan. "You have friends, and something here that's special. I want in."

"You want to come over for tea?" Rosemary spluttered.

Athena scrunched up her face in confusion. "You want to be invited to our social gatherings?"

"Cocktails," said the Morrigan. "I want cocktails."

Rosemary laughed. She couldn't help herself. "Is that really all?"

The Morrigan looked crestfallen. "It's been a long time since I've had friends. Being locked up in another dimension for a long time is isolating. So let me join your coven or whatever it is."

"We don't exactly have a coven," said Athena. "Although that might not be the worst idea."

"Very well. When you start your coven, you have to invite me. I want full membership," said the Morrigan.

Rosemary tensed. "You really want to come to our social gatherings?"

"I might not come," said the Morrigan. "I have other things to do, you know, but it's nice to be invited."

Rosemary and Athena looked uneasily at each other. Having a terrifying death goddess over for a casual dinner party might put a dampener on the mood, but it seemed like a relatively small price to pay for saving the town.

Rosemary shrugged and Athena nodded.

"Excellent," said the Morrigan. "I might not be around for a while though." She looked at her wrist, though there was no watch there. Rosemary wondered if she was just copying the gesture from people she'd seen.

"Things to do..." said the Morrigan.

She held up her arms. "Goodnight, Myrtlewood." She bowed and then, with an enormous lightning strike, she swirled up into the air, in a murder of crows and ravens, circling around and then disappearing off into the night.

"That was certainly something," said Athena. "I guess we've made a new friend."

A bell-like jingling sound came from above them, and something glowing appeared in the air.

"Oh no. What now?" said Rosemary.

A half-moon of light slit open, revealing Dain's face.

"Dad?" said Athena.

"Aha! I knew it," said Dain. "I heard a rumour there was trouble afoot. I'm coming to help!"

"Uhh, okay," said Rosemary.

Dain leapt from the sky, followed by an army of fae soldiers, clad in gold leafy uniforms and armed with weapons.

"It's okay, Dad," said Athena. "We've kind of sorted it – for now."

Dain looked crestfallen. "I've missed the action."

"I like your style," said Charles. "Very flamboyant."

Dain asked, "Who's this then?"

"Just more family, I guess," said Rosemary. "This is Burk's father, Charles."

"Doing well in your old age!" said Dain.

"Oh it's you!" said Granny Thorn, eyeing Dain with a stern gaze.

He visibly wilted.

Granny cracked a wry smile. "Just in time for the family reunion, take two."

The rest of their party gathered around, including Beryl and her sisters, and the vampires – most of whom were perfectly intact, though some were missing limbs.

"Err, I'm sorry about the arms and legs of your family members," said Rosemary.

"Don't worry, they'll grow back," Azalea said with a grin. "Time for that family picture, I think."

"I'll get my camera!" said Charles. In a jiffy, he was back for several rounds of group photos, once again dispelling the myth that vampires couldn't be captured on film. He demanded to capture various groups: the Thorn family reunion, the Burk family, both families together, and a big group one with everyone, including the Travellers and even the Flarguans, Detective Neve, and Athena's friends.

"Say 'boo', everyone," said Charles, before demanding they do several rounds of silly photos.

Athena wrapped her arm around Elise and gave her a squeeze. "This is definitely not how I expected my life to go," she said.

The rest of the evening descended into a wild and raucous party.

The band emerged from the Thorn mausoleum to play jaunty tunes.

There was a conga line, a limbo, and some very unusual dancing between ancient ghosts and vampires with a lot of agility that mere mortals could never hope to achieve.

Granny Thorn supplied endless quantities of punch that put everyone in a very good mood. Ash and Hazel tended to Rosemary and Athena's wounds and did quite a good job.

They had gone back to looking like normal giant bat bites, not slimy or blackened, and looked as if they would probably heal relatively easily.

As dawn arrived, the ghosts became more transparent. Burk said goodbye to Rosemary and the vampires vanished back underground.

"Thank you for the most wonderful evening full of adventure," said Granny Thorn, taking both Rosemary and Athena's hands.

"That's not exactly how I would describe it," said Rosemary, "but thank you, Granny. You we're amazing tonight."

"I'm not sure what we would have done without you and the rest of the Thorn ghosts," said Athena.

"I'm fading away now. Until next time, my dears," Granny Thorn said, pulling them into a hug.

Rosemary enjoyed the warmth of hugging her grandmother one more time before she faded into thin air.

The other ghosts disappeared too, as the sun rose.

Rosemary was prepared to drive some very tired teenagers home.

Elise said, "It's alright, my Mum's picking me up."

"I'll wait," said Athena.

"No, she's already here," said Elise. "She's been missing me. I've got to go." She gave Athena a quick hug before disappearing.

Detective Neve offered to take the others home, and all of a sudden, Rosemary and Athena were left standing in the middle of the cemetery.

"There'll be a big clean-up job. I hope the MIB crew is up for the task," said Rosemary.

"Come on, Mum. Let's go home," Athena said, putting her arm around her mother's shoulder as they walked out of the cemetery and headed back towards Thorn Manor where nice hot chocolate was definitely on the cards before a big, long sleep.

Epilogue

Elise peered out from behind the mausoleum. She'd hung back as her friends left because there was something she needed to do.

She took one more look towards Athena as she left the cemetery with her arm around her mother, then Elise crept towards the old yew tree.

She'd tried to explain to Athena earlier, but it was no use; none of her friends were going to understand, nobody she knew would.

She was different.

Everything had changed.

Grace may have left her, but Elise wasn't the same person she had been before the possession. Her hair was still black and still long. She, as Grace, had killed people, and though she hated to admit it, she'd enjoyed every moment.

She no longer belonged to this world.

She wasn't just Elise anymore.

She was so much more.

She'd tasted it – the blood, the fear, the power. And it made her wonder if she was evil.

But in the agonising crucible of pain that Grace had brought with her, there was something else – the echo of fate.

And now, even though Elise trembled with fear, an exhilaration ran through her in a way that she'd never experienced before.

She knew this was the moment where she had to leave everything behind. Grace had brought something new that wasn't there before, or perhaps she had unleashed an aspect that could no longer be contained within Elise – not in her former life.

This world didn't feel like home anymore, but neither did the fae realm. There was something else, a scent on the wind that she caught like a hunting dog. And she couldn't help but follow her instincts as she approached the tree.

The ground may have sealed over, but she knew exactly what to do.

She placed both hands at the base of the tree on the gnarled roots and shared the secret yearnings of her soul.

The earth trembled, but nobody else was around to feel it.

They'd all gone home.

A small, deep cavern opened up in the roots.

Elise took a deep breath and then allowed herself to slide down inside the earth, right through, towards the underworld.

She took a piece of paper that she had scrawled only minutes earlier, from her pocket, holding it as the tree and the earth reformed. Before completely letting go, she allowed it to be wedged there, for Athena to find.

Then, she slid away into the darkness with the echo of the words she'd written on her mind:

I know you don't understand, but this is something I have to do—to carve my own destiny.

I love you.
Goodbye.

Order Myrtlewood Mysteries book eight: Unspeakable Magic!
Want to read more fantasy based in the same world as Myrtlewood? You can also order The Witches of Holloway Road - set in magical New Zealand and providing the backstory Ursula, Rowan and Hazel who appear in this book and Myrtlewood Book eight: Unspeakable Magic

A NOTE FROM THE AUTHOR

Thank you so much for reading this book! It was so much fun writing it. I love Myrtlewood with all its quirky characters and cozy magical atmosphere.

If you have a moment, please leave a review or even just a star rating. This helps new readers to know what kind of book they're getting themselves into, and hopefully builds some trust that it's worth reading! You can also join the Myrtlewood coven - my reader list or follow me on social media. Links are on the next page.

About the Author

Iris Beaglehole

Iris Beaglehole is many peculiar things, a writer, researcher, analyst, druid, witch, parent, and would-be astrologer. She loves tea, cats, herbs, and writing quirky characters. Find out more at irisbeaglehole.com

facebook.com/IrisBeaglehole

twitter.com/IrisBeaglehole

instagram.com/irisbeaglehole

.

Made in United States
Troutdale, OR
09/20/2024

22996698R00184